The
Princess Plot

The Princess Plot

KIRSTEN BOIE

TRANSLATED BY DAVID HENRY WILSON

SCHOLASTIC INC.
NEW YORK

Published in Germany as *Skogland* by Verlag Friedrich Oetinger. Original text copyright © 2005 by Verlag Friedrich Oetinger. English translation copyright © 2008 by David Henry Wilson • All rights reserved. Published by Chicken House, an imprint of Scholastic Inc., *Publishers since 1920.* CHICKEN HOUSE, SCHOLASTIC, and associated logos are trademarks and/or registered trademarks of Scholastic Inc. • www.scholastic.com • First published in the United Kingdom by Chicken House, 2 Palmer Street, Frome, Somerset BA11 1DS. www.doublecluck.com

Library of Congress Cataloging-in-Publication Data
Boie, Kirsten, 1950– [Skogland. English.]   The princess plot / Kirsten Boie ; translated by David Henry Wilson. — 1st American ed. p. cm.
Summary: Believing that she is on a film set after auditioning and winning the role of a princess, fourteen-year-old Jenna becomes the unsuspecting pawn in a royal conspiracy.
ISBN-13: 978-0-545-03220-9 ISBN-10: 0-545-03220-2
[1. Princesses—Fiction. 2. Conspiracies—Fiction.] I. Wilson, David Henry, 1937– II. Title. PZ7.
B6358435Pr 2009   [Fic]—dc22   2008024403   10 9 8 7 6 5 4 3 2 1   09 10 11 12 13   Printed in the U.S.A. 23 First American edition, May 2009   The text type was set in Lino Letter. The display type was set in Marketing Script. Book design by Becky Terhune and Kristina Albertson

The Princess Plot

*S*candia was in mourning.

Above the palace the flag flew at half-mast, and thousands of umbrellas lined the boulevard. The gun carriage bearing the coffin proceeded at walking pace. It was covered with flowers in the national colors and drawn by six black horses that pulled it slowly up the hill to the cemetery.

The Little Princess walked behind the coffin — alone, upright, shedding no tears. Her shoulders were straight and her gaze was unseeing. She did not look at the crowds of people, who would have given anything for a glance so that they might encourage her with a nod or comfort her with a smile, and she did not look at the coffin in which her father was making his last journey.

She'd refused to let anyone shield her from the rain, which had been falling incessantly since morning out of a sky of unbroken gray, and her wet hair lay in rain-heavy, rain-darkened strands over her face.

"Poor child," whispered a woman in the second row, and pressed up close to her husband for shelter beneath an inappropriately bright and cheerful umbrella. "She may have her crown, her estates, her jewelry, gold, and silver, but they're not much use to her now, are they?"

"Nothing but bad luck," murmured her husband. He held the umbrella over her, so that the rain began to drip down the back of his neck. "The whole family. Nothing but bad luck."

Just a few steps behind the Little Princess, walking straight-backed and alone, came her only living relative: her uncle, Norlin. From now on he would be dealing with the business of government in her name. Norlin had instructed a black-clad court official to walk two paces behind him with an umbrella. His hair was immaculate, elegantly styled, its silver-blue sheen in contrast to his still-young face. But his mouth was twisted with sorrow, and everyone in the crowd could see how deeply he, too, was grieving.

"She's lucky to have him there, at any rate," the woman whispered, as the government ministers filed past them in the cortège. "The little girl won't be completely alone."

"Let's hope they'll get along," her husband whispered back.

The woman brushed aside his misgivings. "At least her guardian's a relative," she whispered, "and not a stranger. After all, it'll be more than four years till she comes of age, poor mite."

A young man in front of them turned and frowned. "Can you keep your voices down?" he demanded. "This is hardly the time for a chat. If you want to talk, go home and do it!"

Cameras whirred, and two helicopters circled high above the funeral procession. The princess was already well out of sight, and yet the crowd remained standing there, motionless, silent, and sad.

Only when the ten-gun salute rang out from Cemetery Hill, to tell the country that its king had been laid to rest alongside his wife in the royal tomb, did a collective sigh pass through the crowd of mourners, and they began to make their way home.

"If we hurry," said the woman as the crowd dispersed, "we can get the bus at quarter past. And I don't care what you say; with all the misery she's had to bear it's a blessing the little one still has her uncle. But if I was superstitious, I'd say there was a curse on this family."

"Never mind that now! There's our bus!" cried the man. He closed the umbrella and began to run. "Come on, we can still catch it!"

They pushed their way through to the back of the bus with a crowd of other mourners, and eventually managed to find seats.

"It's a good thing you're *not* superstitious," the man said, finally responding to his wife's comments. "A curse? We're not living in a fairy tale! If people encounter trouble and strife, my dear, they've generally brought it on themselves."

"Malena," said Norlin. He had insisted that he and the princess travel back to the palace together in the royal limousine. "Malena, what can I do to comfort you?"

The Little Princess sat there expressionless, as if she hadn't even heard him.

"The best thing is to get back into your routine, Malena." He was sitting a little apart from her, because her coat was so wet. "Today and tomorrow you'll stay in the palace so that both of us can sign the thank-you letters for people's condolences." He leaned forward. "Did you hear me, Malena? After that, you'll go back to school. Back to your friends. That'll help take your mind off all this. And in two months' time it'll be your fourteenth birthday."

Slowly, very slowly, Malena looked up. It still seemed as if she hadn't heard him. But then, without saying a word, she nodded her head.

PART ONE

1

The sun disappeared behind a cloud, and the two girls on the patio could feel the coolness as evening approached. The change of seasons had come at last, and the tender green of late spring was gradually turning into the rich colors of high summer. For the first time this year, they had done their homework in the garden, and now Bea gathered her pencils together in a single sweep.

"They shouldn't be allowed to assign us history homework like this," she said. She scowled at the large sheet of paper with its lines, and its lines coming out of lines. "History's so boring!"

Jenna sighed. "Everybody thinks that, and that's why she gives us such stupid homework," she said. "Miss Black wants to make herself seem important. I'll bet you that's the only reason why we're stuck here doing this now."

"Anyway, I'm getting cold," said Bea. "And that means good-bye to the family tree, and she can moan about it as much as she likes tomorrow. I'm going inside, and I'm not going to do any more."

Jenna looked thoughtfully at her sheet of paper, then she rolled it up and fastened it with a rubber band. "Maybe I'll ask my mother about it," she said. "There's hardly anything at all on mine."

"That's because of 'the foreigner,'" said Bea, but then, guiltily, she stopped herself and started over. "No, no, that came out wrong! You know what I mean. It's not fair for you to have to do this when your mother won't tell you who your father is. You can't put in any of that grandmother and great-grandmother stuff. You'll just have to hand in half a family tree."

Jenna shook her head. "My mother's side's not much better!" she said. "I don't know much about them, either!"

Bea's mother poked her head out of the French doors. "Girls!" she said. "It's getting too cold for you to be outside."

Bea twisted her lips. "No worries, Mom! We're OK out here," she said.

"Don't you 'no worries' me," said her mother, undeterred. "Dinner's ready. Aren't you girls hungry?"

Jenna shook her head. "I think I'd better be going home," she said. "You know what my mom's like. *She* gets worried even if I'm just a couple of minutes late."

Bea tapped her watch severely. "It's seven o'clock, sweetie," she said. "Time for a baby's bedtime story. Your mom's *such* a worrier. You really need to train her better."

Bea's mother put her hand on Jenna's arm. "Don't listen to her," she said. "Why don't you send your mom a text message? Tell her you're having dinner with us."

Jenna nodded and switched on her cell phone. She knew her mother would be annoyed. Daughters shouldn't just send their mothers text messages to say where they are and where they're staying. Daughters should call to *ask* if they can stay.

Still @ Bea's, she typed, hoping that her mother had actually switched on her cell. She was always forgetting to do that. **B back b4 dark. Love, Jenna**

Then she switched off her phone. She didn't want to get a message from her mother saying she must come home at once.

"Done!" she said, and plunked herself down on the fourth chair in the kitchen. *(Bad manners. Sit down slowly and sit up straight.)*

Jenna loved Bea's kitchen. It was always a bit of a mess, with a few dirty dishes, or washed ones still draining in the rack next to the sink, and on the wall behind the table there were so many notes pinned to a bulletin board that every so often one of them would come fluttering down onto the food: *The Flying Pizzaman — Telephone Orders 24 hours a day*, or *TV and Computer Repairs — Prompt, Reliable, and Reasonable*, or *District Drugstore Opening Hours 1997.* 1997 — wow! Jenna was convinced that Bea's mother had never taken a single one of those flyers off the board. She just kept pinning new ones on it. Jenna's mom would have died.

"Finished your homework?" asked Bea's father.

That was another reason why Jenna loved Bea's kitchen, Bea's house, and every meal in Bea's house. Because they were a real family. Father, mother, and child. Two children, when Jenna ate with them. And because Bea's father was always himself — friendly, a bit absentminded, never loud. Of course, she had no experience with fathers herself, but she was certain a good father must be just like that. Bea's always made her feel that he was happy to see her.

"No, you can't ever really finish the homework we had today," Bea was saying, while twisting a piece of salami in her fingers and then wrinkling up her nose before dropping it back onto the plate of cold cuts. "We had to do a family tree."

"Cool!" said her father. Jenna's mom would have passed out on the spot. (*Grown men should talk properly.*) "Well, did you get it all in?"

Bea tapped her forehead. "How could we?" she asked. "Do *you* know the names of Grandma Biggin's parents?"

Her father gave an earnest nod. "Ronald, Baron of Cowdung, and Betty, Baroness of Pigswill, née Chickenfeed," he said. "Do you want their dates of birth?"

Jenna giggled.

"Maybe making it up isn't such a bad idea. I'll think of something later," she said. "I've got nowhere near enough relatives. Otherwise our teacher will make my life miserable tomorrow."

"Do you need a few convincing names?" asked Bea's father, resting his knife on the bread.

Jenna shook her head and laughed. "Not like the ones you just said!" All the same, some help would have been useful. She found it especially hard to think of foreign names — Turkish might be the simplest, and would also better match her appearance. But Bea's father probably wouldn't be much good at those.

Bea's mother passed around the bread basket. "I wouldn't worry about it," she said. "You'll be out of school for the summer in a week's time. They must have finished grading the report cards ages ago, so it won't really matter what you come up with now. Though of course I shouldn't be telling you that."

At this moment the doorbell rang.

"Hello," said Bea's father, "are we expecting anybody?"

But Jenna knew exactly who was at the door.

"What do you mean, 'disappeared'?" cried Norlin. "Surely security must have had people there! The school was under surveillance twenty-four hours a day!"

The official hunched his shoulders as if he was expecting a beating — though of course there was no question of that in a civilized country like Scandia. "Apparently, Your Highness," he said, "just at that moment . . . apparently . . . there was a diversion . . ."

"So?" yelled Norlin. The curtains had not yet been drawn across the windows, and from the square in front of the palace the reddish-yellow streetlamps cast their light into the gloomy room. "What does the housemistress have to say? The headmaster? What do they think happened? Does it look like a kidnapping?"

The official took a cautious step backward, as if he really was about to bear the full brunt of the regent's fury.

"One can hardly imagine it being anything else, Your Highness," he said. "But the strange thing . . . the strange thing is . . ."

"Well?" demanded Norlin.

"The security men swear," said the official, "that there were no cars anywhere in the vicinity during the hours before she disappeared. And, as you know, you can see for miles across the countryside around the school."

"Only if you take the trouble to look!" growled Norlin. "And I hardly need to ask if anyone saw a helicopter, or a delivery van, or a horse and cart."

"Nothing, Your Highness!" said the official with complete conviction, and bowed. "The men are absolutely certain."

"Then whoever did it must have been very clever," murmured Norlin. He looked at the messenger and drummed his fingers on his desk. "Perhaps there's an underground passage. But I'm sure the whole area was thoroughly searched before my brother-in-law sent Malena to the school."

"An underground passage is unlikely, Your Highness," said the official, and bowed again. "The subsoil is too rocky. The leader of the search party —"

Norlin interrupted. "I want to talk to him!" he said. "Now!"

The messenger bowed his way backward to the door. "Of course, Your Highness," he said. "I'll get him to come straightaway."

"And not a word to the press!" said Norlin. "Do you hear? Do you hear? I need to know more first. Good grief, one word, one small blunder, anything — you hear? — anything could put my niece in terrible danger!" It seemed as if he had only now realized the implications of the news.

"I'll pass on your orders, Your Highness," said the official, reaching behind his back for the door handle. "And I'll tell the leader of the search party . . ."

"I want to see Bolström," said the regent, and sank back, exhausted, into his chair. "Send Bolström here, no matter where he is."

"Bolström, yes, of course," said the messenger, and now his voice sounded not only eager to serve but also relieved. "I'll send people to look for him."

And as he closed the door behind him, he thought what a good thing it was that, since the death of the king, Norlin had been working so closely with Bolström, the head of the Secret Service. Bolström would be better than the police.

"Won't you come in for a moment?" asked Bea's mother. "We're in the kitchen."

"Hello, Mom," said Jenna, without looking up.

Her mother stood in the kitchen doorway and smiled.

She's so beautiful, thought Jenna. *The exact opposite of me. Tall, blonde, and elegant. Of course she needs to be, for her work. But I can see that somehow she intimidates people, even just by standing in front of them.*

"I thought I'd come by and pick you up," said Jenna's mother, still smiling. "I got your text message, but it's getting a little late. I thought it would be safer."

Bea's father wolfed down his dinner. (*Don't take large bites. Don't talk with your mouth full.* Bea's father never obeyed the rules.)

"Won't you sit for a moment?" he asked, wiping his mouth with the back of his hand. *(Don't do that, either.)* "I'd have taken Jenna home myself. But I thought she'd be fine, since it's still light outside — now that it's summer . . ."

Jenna's mother smiled and Bea's father broke off. "Of course," she said. "Thank you very much. But I think we should be going now."

Jenna looked at the remains of the bread on her plate. She could hardly leave it there, but she couldn't just stuff it into her mouth, either — her mom definitely wouldn't approve of that.

Jenna stood and picked up the piece of bread. *(Rude behavior, too.)* "Thanks for everything," she said. "See you tomorrow, Bea. I'm really looking forward to history." She rolled her eyes.

"Stuff history!" said Bea.

"Bea!" cried her mother. (Even Bea's parents had their limits.)

There were shoes scattered around the hallway, and in the middle of these was a blue plastic bag with empty bottles sticking out of it. A dust bunny bobbed across the floor.

Jenna hadn't noticed any of it before her mom had arrived, but she did now.

"Later!" she called as her mother gently pushed her out the front entrance. "Byeeee!" Bea's mother waved and closed the door behind them.

"Mom," said Jenna, extracting her arm from her mother's as they walked down the driveway. "You always make me look stupid!"

"You're only fourteen," said her mother. "You don't know what terrible things can happen to a young girl in the city."

The sun was still shining brightly, even if it had sunk a little toward the horizon. Children were still playing out in the streets.

❧

"Bolström!" said Norlin. "What on earth are we going to do now?"

The servant quietly closed the door from the outside, leaving Norlin and Bolström alone.

"What did she take with her?" asked Bolström. The room was in almost complete darkness. Only the glow from the streetlights and the green shade of the reading lamp formed little islands of brightness, which made the areas around them seem all the darker. "Did she take anything at all?"

"What do you mean?" asked Norlin.

"Did she pack anything?" asked Bolström. "Did she take a bag with her? If so, my dear Norlin, then maybe she wasn't kidnapped after all."

"What do you mean?" Norlin asked again.

"Think about it," said Bolström. "If no one saw a car, she might simply have run away of her own accord."

Norlin stood up. "She didn't pack anything," he said. He went to the window and drew the curtains.

Bolström shook his head and switched on the light.

"All right, so she didn't pack anything," he said. "Well, her father just died, Norlin! Have you any idea what might be going through a child's head in that situation? She's desperate. She's confused. She's finding life unbearable. She . . ."

"You think she might have . . . done harm to herself?" cried Norlin, shocked by the very thought.

"Well, as far as I know, nobody has found her body," said Bolström, "though that doesn't mean a great deal. But she might just have gone off . . . wandering around the country-side. Didn't you say that after the funeral she seemed to be confused? Anything is possible."

"Good heavens!" cried Norlin, shocked anew.

"Well, confused wandering is still better than a kidnapping, you have to agree," said Bolström. "Now listen, Norlin. Let the Secret Service handle it. The important thing is that the public not know what's happened. It mustn't. Certainly not for now — otherwise we might . . . lose control of the situation. That's the real danger."

"Drats and darnation!" Norlin muttered. "And it's her birthday next week!"

"I know," said Bolström.

"We must . . ." whispered Norlin. "Bolström! How can we . . . ?"

Bolström put his arm around Norlin's shoulder. "You're worried sick," he said. "Perfectly understandable. But that's why I'm here."

Norlin stiffened.

"I'm depending on you, Bolström," he said. "You know how the people love their princess."

"Your parents' names, at least!" cried Jenna. "You must know the names of your own parents!"

Her mother had taken off her shoes and stowed them away in the closet. Now she was putting her jacket on a hanger, and pulling it straight.

"I do know the names of my parents," she said, looking in the mirror and brushing a blonde hair away from her face. "And I know the names of my grandparents, too. I even know the names of my great-grandparents, and my great-great-grandparents." She went into the living room and sat down in front of the television. "But I'm not thrilled at the thought of teachers nosing into family affairs. And that's exactly what this family tree business amounts to. Teachers should teach you, and they should help you, but your private life is none of their business."

"Please, Mom!" pleaded Jenna.

Mom shook her head. "Sit down and watch the news. End of discussion."

Jenna stared at her, then ran to her room and slammed the door. *(One must expect occasional fits of temper during adolescence. Good manners are no longer guaranteed, even from children who are extremely well brought up.)* Maybe her teacher didn't have the right to poke into a mother's private affairs, but surely that didn't apply to a daughter — to a student. Everybody wanted to know about their family. Why wouldn't her mother tell her what her father looked like? She had once let it slip that he was from another country and had a dark complexion like Jenna, but what did he do, and who were her grandparents?

Jenna flopped down on her bed. Whenever she asked about her father, Mom always changed the subject — ASAP. Of course, Jenna could sort of understand why. It just didn't fit with Mom's image: She should have had a smart husband who worked in a bank, wore Armani suits and handmade shirts — not some weird foreigner she was ashamed of.

Jenna rolled the rubber band off the family tree and sat down at her desk. The only time her mother had ever told her anything about her background was on her last birthday. They'd gone to a restaurant to celebrate. Jenna had had a glass of Coke, and Mom had had some wine, and then suddenly Mom had looked her up and down and said, "You're growing up. You're gradually growing up. When I was your age . . ."

Jenna had listened in silence, holding her breath.

"Not long after that, I met your father," Mom had said. "We were head over heels in love, Jenna — madly in love."

Still Jenna said nothing. She didn't want to spoil the moment.

"And one day, when it was my birthday, my eighteenth, we just ran away. We didn't bother with celebrations — we simply went to the seaside, near Saarstad. We sat on the beach, but it was still quite cold at that time of year, and as I had the key . . ."

"What key?" Jenna had blurted out, and straightaway she'd known she'd blown it.

"Never mind," her mother had said, startled, and she'd pushed away her wine glass to the center of the table. "Well, congratulations, Jenna. You're no longer a child, so I hope you'll have a wonderful time in your teens."

Back to reality. Jenna looked at the almost-empty sheet lying in front of her on the desk. Maybe it would be fun to invent a few names.

She stood up and switched on the light, even though it was only just beginning to get dark.

Outside, across the street, a man moved back into a doorway and waited.

She was clearly visible through the window: a small, slightly curvy figure with dark hair, standing in her room on the second floor and energetically pulling something from a shelf. Only when she sat back down at her desk was the brightly lit rectangle empty again.

2

During recess, Jenna saw two men handing out leaflets on the other side of the street from the school gates. They were there again when the final bell rang.

"You certainly did a lot last night!" said Bea, adjusting the strap of her schoolbag as it hung over her shoulder. It was Friday, school was over, and the weekend lay ahead. "Right back to your great-grandparents! Where did you get all those Turkish names from?"

Jenna laughed. The sun was shining, they didn't have too much homework, and . . . it was Friday! Same time next week, they'd be on summer break! "I called Imran, and he helped me. Want to go and get a latte?" she asked, gesturing toward the gate. "BTW, what are they handing out over there?"

Bea shrugged her shoulders. A crowd of kids had clustered around the two men with the leaflets. "It's certainly not coffee," said Bea. "And caffeine is what I want! Frappuccino pronto. Or do you think they're giving away swag?"

"Doubtful," said Jenna. "Anyway, it's your turn to buy! You'd better make it a double shot!"

They went around the corner without a single glance back at the school. Suddenly, they heard footsteps hurrying behind them.

"Excuse me!" cried a young man. "Aren't you interested?" He caught up with them.

"Hello! Aggressive much?" Bea said. "And what are you talking about?"

The young man smiled. He was good-looking, film-star good-looking. He was supercute.

"No one else can resist," he said, holding out a leaflet to Bea. "You're the only ones who didn't come over. I just had to find out what kind of girls aren't interested in becoming movie stars."

"Hello?" Bea said again, but now she sounded a lot more curious.

"Especially when they look like you two," said the young man. It was obvious to Jenna who he meant — Bea, of course, who had blue eyes and blonde hair and was tall and skinny. But he probably had to be polite; that would explain why he handed her a leaflet as well.

"We're looking for girls to act in a movie," he said. "It's all in the pamphlet. Ordinary girls like you. We're casting this afternoon. You'd have a pretty good chance." He winked at Bea, then turned and went back to his place opposite the school gates, where his friend was putting up a good fight against the hordes of girls freaking out over the leaflets.

"Roper's Inn!" said Bea with a snort. "Not a très cool place for an audition, I must say. Not exactly glamorous. They want girls between twelve and sixteen; he's right, that's us."

"That's *you*," said Jenna. "Didn't you see the way he was checking you out?"

"Shut up!" said Bea, with the indifference of someone well used to getting admiring looks. "He's way old — he could be my dad! But we *could* go and scope it out, couldn't we? Let's hit the coffee bar and dream about being movie stars, darling!"

In the garden at the café there were far too many folding chairs grouped around far too many tiny tables, and all of them were taken. From the counter to the middle of the lawn stretched a winding line of kids fresh out of school.

"You know my mother won't think it's a good idea," said Jenna. "She'd never let me do it."

"Then don't ask her!" said Bea. "Anyway, she'll be working. She won't even know about it."

"Still . . ." murmured Jenna. The line moved a few steps closer to the café door. Jenna couldn't bear to admit to Bea that she had never done anything behind her mother's back. There'd be trouble afterward.

Bea tried to look around the boy in front of her, so that she could see how much longer they'd have to wait.

"Caramel frappuccino," she said. "With soy milk. Mmmm! What about you?"

Jenna shrugged her shoulders. Of course, she shouldn't have been drinking double lattes at all. If she wanted to be as skinny as Bea, she should just be eating an apple, or baby carrots. She sighed.

"Let me tell you something, Jenna," said Bea, waving to a group of older boys who were walking past on their way to the bus stop. "Your mom's, like, majorly overprotective! Your own private bodyguard. You're fourteen already! And she always comes to pick you up, even before it's dark, and she won't let you go anywhere. My mom says it's often like that with single mothers — but that doesn't help your situation much, does it? I've got nothing against your mom, honest, but she should totally give you more freedom, that's what I think."

"She's not my bodyguard!" snapped Jenna. She could feel herself getting as angry with Bea as she was with her mother. What business was it of Bea's how Mom brought her up? And what business was it of Bea's parents'? The thought of them sitting in their messy kitchen and talking about her and her mother made her feel sick. She wouldn't eat there again anytime soon — not with people who said bad things about Mom when she wasn't there to defend herself. It was all right for *her* to be angry with Mom. She was her daughter, after all, and so she was the one it was all about. But nobody else had the right to criticize Mom. Absolutely nobody.

"I think movie stars are stupid, anyway," said Jenna. "You can go to Roper's on your own."

The farmer decided to take a break. For two days now he had been repairing the drystone walls around his upper fields, just as he did every few years, and as his father and grand-father had done before him. He had been picking up stones, cleaning them, and putting them back in the walls wherever they had been swept away by thunderstorms or knocked off by falling branches, and now, in the late afternoon, he was feeling satisfied with his work. There wasn't much left for him to do.

He sat down in the rich green grass, leaned back against the uneven, sun-warmed stones, and looked down over the valley. White fluffy clouds with ash-gray linings drifted across the sky and threw large, shapeless shadows over the landscape, momentarily plunging parts of it into menacing darkness.

The farmer pulled a packet of tobacco and some papers out of his shirt pocket and rolled himself a cigarette. Over on the other side of the valley, the towers of the school emerged from the shadow of a cloud, and its windows sparkled red in the afternoon sunlight. There was not a car to be seen on the mountain road, and it almost seemed as if the old buildings were deserted. But the farmer knew that when the wind blew in the right direction, even from this distance the voices of the girls laughing and shouting, and the occasional shrill blast of the teacher's whistle, could be heard.

He leaned back, drew a deep puff of smoke into his lungs, and closed his eyes. Things had been different yesterday, so this morning he'd decided to bring his binoculars with him. Yesterday there had been a constant coming and going along the road. Police cars, but no ambulances, if he was not mistaken. So it couldn't have been an accident that had brought the police to this remote spot. For a moment he'd wondered whether the area was in danger because it was so close to the northern coast. But if that had been the case, then they would have said something about it on TV. It could hardly be any sort of a crime, because the school had an excellent reputation — even the Little Princess was a pupil there.

"I just hope it has nothing to do with the Little Princess," he murmured, opening his eyes. "I just hope —" Then he stopped in midsentence. On the other side of the valley, a long way away from the school, something was moving behind a raspberry bush.

The farmer reached to one side, where his binoculars had lain unused all day.

He looked through them and tried to find the right spot. Trees and walls swam in and out of view at dizzying speed until finally he found what he was looking for.

Then he whistled through his teeth.

"Looks like a boy," he said.

The figure was wearing a beige-colored cap and a checkered jacket that was a bit too big. It looked as if there was some sort of camp among the raspberry bushes, because there was a brown blanket and various bits and pieces that the farmer couldn't quite make out even through his binoculars.

"Not a bad place to camp."

He recalled that many years ago, as a child, he had also spent a few days in that very spot, when he had run away from home. His father was a man of few words who was fond of thrashing him, and by the age of thirteen or fourteen he'd had enough and decided to go and see the world.

The farmer laughed quietly to himself. "You'll soon go back, my lad," he muttered, then stopped. There was a stream conveniently close to the undergrowth, and since it was now the start of the raspberry season, there was no need for a fugitive to go hungry. He took a last puff of his cigarette, stamped it out with his heel in the soft dirt, and put the dead stub in his pants pocket. Another hour or two of work, and then he could forget about the walls on this part of his land for a few more years.

It was only later, when he was on his way home to the farm, that a thought suddenly struck him, and once more he trained his binoculars on the raspberry bushes. Suppose all those police cars had something to do with the boy! Suppose he was a burglar, a thief, even a terrorist, who had attacked the school, or was planning to attack the school, or was planning to spy on the Little Princess . . .

He focused on the bushes, but the ground was now deserted.

The farmer took his cell phone out of his pocket, then put it back again. Just because he'd seen a boy who'd run away from home, or was simply having an adventure out there on his own, was really no reason to call the police.

At least, he wouldn't do anything before talking it over with his wife.

3

Jenna pushed open the hotel door and smiled at the woman who was sitting at the reception desk. She'd been glad to be done with her latte. She hadn't felt like sitting cozily in the sun with a friend whose family said nasty things about her mother.

But of course she couldn't say that to Bea.

"What do you mean?" Bea probably would have asked in surprise. "What did I do?"

And Jenna didn't know how to explain that she *always* thought it was bad when somebody talked about her mother behind her back. Unless they said something really nice.

"Ah, hello, Jenna," said the hotel receptionist. "Your mother's still in the back there. She's got another of those absolutely hopeless cases with her today."

"Thanks," said Jenna, and made her way through the lobby and the deserted restaurant toward the conference rooms.

It wasn't a particularly good hotel — that was obvious at first glance — but it was practical. It had conference rooms and a cocktail lounge, which was separated from the restaurant and kitchen by a sliding door. Whatever Mom needed for her tutoring sessions was easily accessible. She had dreamed for years of opening her own office, but just like so many things in life (said Mom), that meant money.

"And, sadly," she had said to Jenna the last time they'd discussed the subject, "we can't afford it. But anyway, the hotel isn't that bad."

But Jenna knew that Mom would have liked somewhere very different to conduct her courses in social etiquette. Somewhere more stylish, with the right furniture, the right tableware, the right food.

Jenna stopped and listened before carefully opening the door to the cocktail lounge just a crack.

"Good, wonderful, Mrs. Sampson!" Mom was saying encouragingly. "Just hold your chin a little higher! And now, imagine you're walking in a straight line — no, not like that! If you swing your hips too much, it looks a little vulgar, so you really must be careful. Yes, that's more like it! Tall and straight, without too much hip-swinging. That's precisely the impression we want to make! Perfect!"

Jenna took as deep and quiet a breath as possible. The plump little woman stretched her chin up toward the heavens and smiled majestically.

"I shall go and practice at home in the hall," she said, "and give my Reginald a nice surprise."

"I did mention last time that it would be a great help if you brought your husband along as well one day," said Mom. She noticed Jenna, and frowned for a second. "Now that he's chairman of the local council he must have quite a lot of public engagements. A little bit of practice would be very good for him."

"I keep telling him!" cried Mrs. Sampson, flopping down onto one of the threadbare hotel chairs. *(Bad manners. You must sit down slowly and you must sit up straight.)* "But my Reginald . . ."

"I understand, Mrs. Sampson. Let's just practice that once more, shall we?" said Mom, and in spite of her bossy tone she gave the woman another friendly smile. "How do we sit down when there's no gentleman there to help us?"

Jenna knocked timidly on the doorframe. "Excuse me, I'm sorry to disturb you . . ."

Mrs. Sampson turned around. "Oh, it's Jenna!" she said, and her voice softened with genuine affection. "Always so polite. So well brought up!" She held her hand out toward Jenna.

"Don't talk over your shoulder at the table, Mrs. Sampson, please!" said Mom. "What is it, Jenna? Is this interruption really necessary?"

Jenna lowered her eyes. "I only wanted to ask if, this afternoon . . . well, there were some movie people at our school . . ."

"Movie people?" asked Mom, looking shocked. "What do you mean, movie people?"

"They're going to be holding auditions," said Jenna, "for a movie! And I thought . . ."

"Auditions!" cried Mrs. Sampson. "How exciting."

"Certainly not!" said Mom, as if she hadn't heard her. "Jenna, I forbid you to go. Something so vulgar — you're not to get involved, is that clear?"

"Crystal!" cried Jenna. "But how do you know it'll be vulgar?" Until then the auditions hadn't really mattered to her — she'd just been curious because everyone else was going. And because of Bea, of course. But now, suddenly, she simply had to go, too.

"In ninety percent of cases, movies are vulgar," said Mom. "And that's all there is to it, Jenna, do you understand? Now then, Mrs. Sampson . . ."

Jenna could feel the anger rising inside her, but she didn't argue. *(One should never argue in front of others.)*

Mrs. Sampson sighed and smiled at her. "Your mother knows best," she said, and pointed to a plate that was sitting on the table in front of her. "Today we're practicing salads. Salads are so difficult! But I'm sure you know all about salads, don't you, Jenna?"

Jenna tried to smile, like Mom. "I practice with my mother," she said diplomatically.

Mrs. Sampson nodded. "I've recommended your mother to three more people," she said. "Ladies from my bowling league. I've told them how much I've learned from her about etiquette."

Mom looked at Jenna. "I'm going to be working a bit late again today," she said. "A client has just asked me to give her a quick refresher course. Warm up your food yourself, will you? And I'll be home around nine or half past."

Jenna nodded. "Good-bye, Mrs. Sampson," she said. "And for what it's worth, I have trouble with salads, too." Then she pulled the door shut behind her.

In the lobby, the receptionist was blowing on her freshly painted fingernails.

"I don't know how she stands it," she said, without looking at Jenna. "Your poor mother. Teaching all those common people . . ."

Jenna thought that was rather rude, but she knew what she had to say. Mom had drummed it into her often enough.

"She enjoys teaching good manners to people who've gotten somewhere in life," she said. "After all, in a democracy where everyone has equal opportunities, ordinary people can suddenly find themselves in the public gaze and need help with how to handle it."

The receptionist gave a cynical smile. "You know what I mean," she said. "But still, as long as she can earn a living, why not?"

"I've got to go. Bye," said Jenna, and waved.

"Have fun!" said the receptionist.

The policeman tapped thoughtfully at the typewriter keys. Here in the country, the police still used typewriters, and every time someone came in to report something, he felt embarrassed. He was still very young.

"Of course, this isn't a crime as such, you know," he said. "Not in the usual sense."

The farmer nodded. His wife had made him come. She, too, had thought that it was probably just a runaway who had set up camp among the raspberry bushes. But since her husband had told her yesterday evening about the police cars on the road leading to the school, she thought the police might be grateful for any piece of information.

"No one has reported any missing persons, and no one's looking for a boy like the one you've described. But since there was an incident *up there* yesterday . . ." The policeman hesitated, wondering how much he should reveal, then decided on discretion rather than risk getting into trouble later. "I'll put it on file, and pass it on."

"An incident?" echoed the farmer, and leaned across the desk. "Yes, I saw you'd sent someone up to the school yesterday. So what was the problem?"

The young policeman gave a final push to the carriage of the typewriter and took the paper out with a noisy flourish.

"No comment," he said. At moments like this, he enjoyed his job.

"It isn't . . . I mean, it doesn't have something to do with the Little Princess, does it?" asked the farmer. "Nothing's happened to her, has it?"

The young policeman shrugged his shoulders apologetically. "No comment," he said again, sympathetically. "Much as I'd like to."

The farmer nodded. "I understand," he said, with some disappointment. "But as soon as you . . . I mean, don't forget who brought you the information."

"We'll be in touch," said the young policeman, and pulled the telephone toward him. "Now, if you'll excuse me." All of a sudden, he had a feeling that a promotion might be just around the corner.

Out in the street, Jenna kicked a crumpled paper bag. It offered no resistance, and since she had kicked it too hard, she almost fell over.

There really hadn't been much point in her asking. Other daughters didn't need permission to go to auditions. Not if they were in the middle of the afternoon, in broad daylight. Not if thousands of other girls were also going (and maybe boys, too) and absolutely nothing bad could happen to them. The session wasn't in some dark back room, or some dingy dive, or somebody's backyard — it was simply, and almost disappointingly, in Roper's Inn, the oldest restaurant in town, where family parties were held and children played pin-the-tail-on-the-donkey in the basement on their birthdays.

And Mom hadn't been honest with her. Nobody could seriously claim that movies were always vulgar, not even someone who attached as much importance to style and manners as she did. When she got back from giving her refresher course, Jenna would tell her so. Because who was it who went to the library in the evening to borrow DVDs that Jenna found so boring that she often fell asleep while she was watching them?

"Overprotective," murmured Jenna. "Single mother and overprotective."

Of course Bea's parents shouldn't have said that. But it was the truth all the same.

"She doesn't even realize it," Jenna muttered furiously. "She's ruining my whole life — Bea's totally right."

When she looked up, she found herself outside Roper's Inn. She hadn't gone there deliberately; she was surprised herself. And Mom would never know, because Jenna wouldn't get a part in the movie, anyway. Not if the beauteous Bea was auditioning.

Hesitantly, Jenna opened the door to the restaurant. The other girls would all have had a chance to go home already, to shower and put on makeup. Only Jenna would be there in her school clothes, sweaty and tired. But it wasn't getting a part that really mattered. What really mattered was something quite different.

"Find him!" Bolström ordered. "Find this boy! He's the first clue we've had so far. The only clue! But keep it quiet, and by all means keep the media out of it. Discretion, that's the watchword."

Norlin nodded. "At least we've got somewhere to start now," he said. "A solid lead."

The Chief of Police bowed. He hadn't allowed anyone else to bring the information to the regent and his counselor, but now it seemed to him that maybe they were attaching a bit too much importance to this clue.

"Your Royal Highness," he said, "I'm not sure that this boy really has anything to do with the abduction. It's much more likely that he's simply a runaway who has probably gone back to his family by now. But of course we shall do whatever we can."

"You certainly will!" cried the regent. "And if you can't find the boy outdoors, then search all the houses! You don't seriously believe that this is just a coincidence? For months no one has seen any strange boys in the vicinity of the school, but now — by chance, by sheer chance — one turns up just at the moment when the princess is abducted. How on earth did you ever become Chief of Police?"

For a second the Chief of Police looked as if he was going to respond, but then he gave a slight bow. "Everything will be done as you have instructed, Your Royal Highness," he said stiffly. "The plainclothes unit is being briefed at this very moment."

He went to the door, but before he could open it, Bolström put a hand on his arm.

"Don't let the regent upset you," he said. He spoke so quietly that Norlin, who had now gone to the window and was looking out over the boulevard, could not possibly hear him. "He's worried sick about his niece. He hardly slept a wink last night. The thought that something bad has befallen the child is unbearable. I beg you, please do everything you can."

Somewhat mollified, the Chief of Police gripped the door handle.

"We always do, Bolström," he said. "But I would have thought that the regent already had ample opportunity to surveil our methods. Even if that was some time ago."

He left the room with a bow so slight it was barely noticeable.

Bolström let out a loud hiss. "Norlin," he stated through clenched teeth. "You must get a grip on yourself."

4

J̶he large hall at the back of the restaurant was crowded with about fifty girls between the ages of twelve and sixteen. On closer look, some who were not yet eleven and others who were seventeen or eighteen could also be found. None of them wanted to miss the chance of maybe becoming a movie star.

"Jenna!" cried Bea. She was sitting with three girls from their homeroom on the edge of the stage, in front of the worn red curtain, and was drumming her heels against the wooden paneling. "You made it — awesomeness!"

"Mom didn't mind at all," Jenna replied, a little coldly.

Bea looked a bit confused at first, but then she caught on. "Yeah, right. I'll believe you, thousands wouldn't. Want to borrow my mirror?"

Jenna shook her head. She knew that looking in the mirror would only make her miserable and depressed. Sans blowout and some lip gloss, she couldn't change much, anyway.

"How cool is this?" said Anna, one of the other three girls.

She was at least as blonde as Bea and at least as thin. And, even better, her face was almost heart-shaped.

"How many do they need, anyway?" asked Jenna, dropping her schoolbag on the floor. This wasn't exactly what she'd imagined an audition would be. It all seemed disappointingly unglamorous.

"We've been wondering that, too!" said Kate. "Maybe anyone who doesn't get a part can stand in as extras. If they're here, that is. With summer break starting next week, lots of girls will be gone on vacation."

Jenna didn't say that there was no way she would be anywhere but here. As usual. Mom couldn't take a break from her etiquette lessons because she needed the money, and she never let Jenna travel on her own. Not with any youth group, or even with Bea and her parents that one time when they'd invited her to go with them to a ski chalet they'd booked. *In fact,* thought Jenna, *considering my schedule, I'd be the perfect choice to act in this film* — and she could have burst out laughing. Skinny? No. Blonde? Nope. Sweaty? Oh, yeah. Plus no acting talent. But with time to spare over the next six weeks! The movie producers would be *super*psyched.

"What are you smiling about?" Bea asked suspiciously.

But before Jenna could reply, the door to the hall opened and in came the two guys who had been standing outside the school that morning. The one who had spoken to Bea and Jenna was carrying a heavy camera over his shoulder, while the other lugged a spotlight. Behind them stood an elegant woman in a dark blue suit that must have cost a fortune. Her gaze wandered over the crowd of girls.

"Fabulous!" said the young man with the camera. He gave a radiant smile. Earlier, he had spent some time looking carefully around the room, and had probably decided that there were enough pretty girls there. Even if the majority of them proved to have no acting skill whatsoever, there were bound to be some they could use. "Perhaps we should introduce ourselves first! My name is Tobias, the lady here is Mrs. Markas, and this gentleman is Raphael . . ."

"We'll start by registering you," said the lady, waving a pile of papers. "Now, this is how we're going to do it."

Jenna sat cross-legged on her schoolbag. Mom would have been happy to see how well organized the movie people were. And also how well dressed, and well behaved. Impeccable — not a faux pas in sight.

"Downstairs, in the bowling alley," the lady continued. "But first, please write your names on my list — as legibly as possible. When you get downstairs, just fill in a registration form — name, date of birth, address, and so on. I'll be using the list to call you up one by one to hear you speak, so bring your form with you then, please. OK, everyone?"

"I think I might as well leave," said Jenna, and stood up. After all, she'd done what she came to do. She slung her bag over her shoulder. "I'm not so into this, anyway . . ."

Bea looked at her sideways, seeing right through her.

"You're just afraid they won't choose you," she said. "Chicken! But you'd be way better at learning lines than me."

"Like that matters," said Jenna.

"Please take off your jackets or anything bulky and leave them downstairs during the audition," Mrs. Markas was saying. "It's not just your faces we want to see! You can entrust any valuables to my colleague here, and he'll give you a receipt. We don't want to hear afterward that something's gone missing — that's happened all too often in the past. And now would you please put your name on the list, check your valuables, take your receipt, and wait downstairs in the bowling alley."

"I really don't want to!" said Jenna. "I'm beat."

Ahead of her, Bea went to check her bracelet, but Tobias waved it aside.

"Only bags and any valuables in your pockets," he said. "Your cell phone, for example." He gave Bea her receipt.

Jenna turned toward the exit. "Good luck, Bea!" she said. And since the guy named Tobias was now staring expectantly at her, she quickly shook her head. "No, thanks. I'm having second thoughts. Guess I don't want to be a movie star after all."

Tobias looked taken aback. Then he smiled. "Come on, show some spark," he said, and looked deep into her eyes. *That's how they do it,* Mom would have said at this moment. *That's how men turn women's heads. And you're dumb enough to fall for it.*

"I think . . ." mumbled Jenna, turning red.

Tobias was still smiling. "Have some faith in yourself," he said. "A pretty girl like you."

Jenna thought she might faint on the spot. "I think . . ." she whispered again.

But Tobias had already stretched out his hand. "Any valuables?" he asked warmly. "Don't worry, you'll get them back. Schoolbag? Cell phone?"

Jenna nodded.

Bea was waiting for her on the stairs. "Yes!" she exclaimed, tapping Jenna lightly on the shoulder. "I thought you were going to sneak off. Even if we don't get a part, at least we'll have been to an audition. That's still pretty sweet, isn't it?"

Jenna nodded. But she shouldn't have given her schoolbag to the man. In it was her last sandwich, and all of a sudden she was feeling so weak that she was dying for something to eat.

"Sonya Richards?" Mrs. Markas called out, then checked the name off her list.

Sonya made her way past them up the stairs, and Jenna sat down on the polished floor near the bowling lanes. She hoped the whole thing would be over in a couple of hours: A girl couldn't starve to death that quickly.

"Mrs. Greenwood?" said the receptionist, sticking her head around the door of the hotel conference room. Jenna's mother was standing in front of a small man in a crumpled suit, teaching him to raise her right hand gallantly to his lips. "Phone call for you. At the reception desk."

Jenna's mother frowned. "Is it Jenna?" she asked. The little man swayed from one foot to the other in embarrassment, and since he didn't quite know what to do, he clasped her hand even more tightly. "She knows she's not supposed to call me here. And she's got my cell phone number."

"But you always keep it off during your lessons," said the receptionist, sounding uncomfortable. "And anyway, it's not Jenna. Would you please hurry?"

Jenna's mother could sense the anxiety in her voice. "Who is it, then?" she asked. She smiled at the man and gently took her hand out of his. "I'll be right back, Mr. Fraser. In the meantime, just practice a little on your own."

Only when the door had closed behind her did the receptionist answer her question.

"It's the police," she said.

Jenna sat on the floor and watched as one girl after another disappeared upstairs and came back down again, excited, sometimes nervous, but almost always hopeful.

"I've got a chance!" cried Kate, throwing herself down on the last vacant chair, next to Bea. "I've made it past the first round, I got a callback. Seriously!"

"Jessica, too," said Bea. "And Philippa. I wish it was my turn. Did you have to recite something?"

"Jenna Greenwood?" said Mrs. Markas. "Is that you? You're next."

She looked Jenna up and down in what seemed a very dismissive way. Had she stared at any of the other girls like that? Was she wondering how someone with looks like hers could possibly have the nerve to waste the judges' time, since she must already know that she didn't have a snowball's chance? Jenna felt herself turning red again.

"Go for it!" Bea called after her. "You'll do fine, Jenna. It's all good!"

But Jenna knew exactly what she was going to do next.

🌹

"Mrs. Greenwood speaking," said Jenna's mother, leaning over the reception desk to get to the phone. "Hello? Is there something — has something happened to my daughter?" She could hear her own voice trembling.

"Mrs. Greenwood?" said a deep voice at the other end. "It's the police here. Please try to stay calm, ma'am. Your daughter's going to be all right."

"She's . . . ?" whispered Jenna's mother. She felt her legs giving way under her. "She's going . . . ? But what . . . ?"

"I'm afraid your daughter's been in an accident, Mrs. Greenwood," the voice said slowly. "She was hit by a car."

"Oh, no!" Jenna's mother gasped.

The receptionist came and stood beside her, ready to catch her if she should suddenly collapse.

"There are a few broken bones, and at the moment she's still unconscious," said the voice. "Fortunately, there was a doctor at the scene of the accident who was able to attend to her on the spot, and it looks like she's going to pull through. She's at St. Katherine's Hospital in Longford."

"Longford?" Jenna's mother repeated. "But why is she in Longford?"

"The emergency helicopter brought her there," said the policeman. "St. Katherine's is some ways outside the town, on a street called Forest's Edge."

"Yes," whispered Jenna's mother. "I understand."

"Do you have a map of the town?" asked the policeman. "Will you be able to find the hospital? She's in intensive care. But you can go and see her. St. Katherine's Hospital, Longford. Forest's Edge."

"Yes," whispered Jenna's mother. She heard the man at the other end hang up.

The receptionist looked closely at her. "Shall I call a cab?" she asked. "You're in no condition to drive yourself . . ."

But Jenna's mother had already pulled herself together. "That would take too long," she said, already on her way back to the conference room to grab her bag. "Could you tell my client what's happened, please? I've got to go."

And then she started running.

5

Jenna didn't go straight to the stage. She stopped at the entrance to the hall, next to the table where all the backpacks, cell phones, and bags were being kept, and she looked for her receipt.

"I'm sorry I've wasted your time," she said. That was the correct thing to say. "But I've been thinking it over, and I don't want to do it." She held her receipt out to Raphael, who was in charge of all the valuables.

The movie people looked at one another. Maybe this was the first time such a thing had happened.

"I'm just no good at learning things by heart," Jenna said quickly. "And I'm no good at reciting. And I . . . I just don't want to do it."

Raphael took the receipt from her. "You don't want to do it?" he repeated, and looked to his two colleagues for help. "But . . . well, why not?"

I don't owe you an explanation! Jenna said to herself. After all, she was there of her own free will. But it would have been rude to say that to these friendly film people. She'd had plenty of practice at being polite, but hardly any at being rude.

She shrugged her shoulders. "Just because," she mumbled.

"What a shame!" said Tobias, and suddenly the charming smile was back on his face. "You, out of all the girls. Maybe you noticed this afternoon that I ran after you . . ." He consulted his list. "Jenna. It's Jenna, isn't it?"

Jenna nodded.

"Because it seemed to me right away that you . . . you're just the type we're looking for." He exchanged glances with Raphael and Mrs. Markas.

"All three of us had the same impression!" Raphael readily agreed. "Exactly the right type."

Jenna remembered the way the woman had looked at her.

"And now you're backing out," Tobias continued. "The fact that you can't recite lines by heart is no problem. Anybody can do that."

Jenna looked at him in amazement.

"Totally overrated," Raphael added, nodding.

"What matters is personality!" persisted Tobias. "If you know what I mean. It's all about presence, Jenna. And you've got it."

"Incredible presence," Raphael chimed in. "Real star quality. We all said so the moment we saw you. So wouldn't you like to just give it a try?"

Mrs. Markas said nothing.

What Jenna would have liked was to sit down. She felt slightly delirious. The young man had followed them because of her! Movie people thought she was more beautiful than Bea — or at least that she had greater "presence."

Presence, thought Jenna. It could be true. Mom was always talking about "presence" when she was giving her etiquette lessons to ugly old women. Maybe presence was the one thing that could make boring people interesting . . .

But of course it might also be that the part they wanted to cast wasn't some beautiful ingenue. Jenna thought of the movies she knew — especially movies for "young people." There was almost always someone who was fat and ugly and sweaty. Someone with acne, who was laughed at by everybody.

Maybe that was the sort of role they had in mind for her.

"I don't know," she murmured. Of course, she wasn't *that* fat. She just wasn't willowy-thin like Bea and Anna. And above all, she wasn't blonde.

"What sort of role is it?" she asked.

"Well, it's . . ." Tobias looked at the others again, as if he wanted reassurance that he wasn't revealing too much. "Look, Jenna, I'll have to ask you not to discuss this with anyone. We haven't told any of the other girls. If we tell you now, it's only because you're obviously on the brink of backing out."

"I won't say anything," said Jenna. "I promise."

Tobias nodded. "I'm sure you understand that keeping a secret is one of the most important things in the movie business," he said. "But I can tell you this much. It's about a princess. Yes! Don't look at me like that! It's a kind of . . . fairy tale. But for teenagers — not little kids. And it's set in the present."

"A princess!" Jenna cried in astonishment. She couldn't imagine that anyone could possibly conceive of a princess who looked like her.

"It's all very complicated," said Tobias. "Look, we've got to keep going. But like I said, when we first saw you, we thought straightaway that you were made for the part. So think it over. We've got more girls to audition."

"Yes," whispered Jenna.

"Yes you've understood, or yes you'd like to try?" asked Tobias. His voice suddenly sounded a little sharper, and Jenna felt ashamed that she'd been holding him up for so long.

"Yes, perhaps . . ." she whispered, ". . . perhaps I'll give it a try."

Tobias nodded. "Good," he said. He turned to Raphael, who fixed the spotlight on Jenna and studied her face on the camera monitor. Raphael nodded. "Now you can go back and wait with the others. We'll let you know when we're up to the second round of casting."

Jenna went back to the door. Her knees were shaking.

"And remember what you promised!" Tobias called after her. "Not a word to anybody!"

Jenna shook her head. She heard Mrs. Markas behind her on the stairs.

"Beatrice!" she called from the top of the staircase. "We'd like to see you next, please."

Jenna quickly squeezed Bea's hand as they passed each other. Little did either girl know that Bea didn't stand a chance now.

She'd raced along the fast lane of the highway at top speed, with her headlights flashing. She hadn't even looked at the speedometer. She hated fast drivers.

Why Longford? thought Jenna's mother. *Where exactly had the accident occurred?* She ought to have asked. And she ought to have asked exactly what had happened — had Jenna been thrown through the air? Or had she (the thought was unbearable) been run over? Would there be lasting damage, what sort of damage, what was wrong with her child?

As she forced every vehicle in front of her out of the fast lane, she felt her heartbeat slowing down, and yet, at the same time, the closer she came to the hospital, the more afraid she was. She had looked up the exit number on the map before she had set off, although everything had been a blur. But the route was easy to find. It couldn't be much farther. She would soon be there.

Jenna.

Perhaps she hadn't always made life easy for her daughter, but she had seen no other way. She'd been too afraid for her, right from the start. And now, despite all her rules and precautions, there'd been an accident. The irony of it was almost laughable.

Jenna's mother swung the car over into the far right lane to take the exit. She skidded around the bend, but immediately regained control of the car. Straight along the country road, and then to the right again.

The fields and meadows lay bathed in the warm light of late afternoon, and in the distance the towers of the city raised their heads above the horizon. Why had the helicopter brought Jenna here? To a hospital that was so remote? What sort of hospitals were built so far out of town? Rehabilitation centers, convalescent homes, accident clinics. Things must be bad if Jenna wasn't in a typical hospital.

"Jenna," she whispered. She would have to be strong, as she always was.

The road marked Forest's Edge was narrow, and had no center line. There were no buildings to the left or right, and it stretched for miles through the countryside, bumpy and full of potholes. What was it that had to be kept so far away from the public gaze? What was going on?

The road came to an end.

Jenna's mother braked at the last moment. A red-and-white chain barrier separated the road from the forest. No house in sight. No hospital in sight. Had she misread the road sign? Had she missed a turn? She put the car in reverse, and the tires squealed as she tried to turn the car around on the narrow strip of asphalt. The engine roared as she drove back, far too fast, along the road she had just taken.

Then she braked hard. Ahead, traveling almost as fast, a car was coming straight toward her. Instead of swinging over to the side, it screeched to a halt, its bumper almost touching hers.

She pushed open her door. "Thank God!" she cried. "I'm looking for —"

"—St. Katherine's Hospital," said the man in the driver's seat. He got out and approached her with a friendly look on his face. From the passenger side, his companion also got out, smiling broadly.

"And I was so stoked that I could still recite some of that silly poem!" said Bea. "You know, 'The Rime of the Ancient Mariner,' with the bird and the cursed ship. 'Water, water everywhere, / Nor any drop to drink.' Genius! At least you can make that sound really dramatic."

Jenna's stomach rumbled, and Bea giggled. "I hope you didn't do *that* upstairs!" she exclaimed. "What did you recite? 'The Ancient Mariner,' too?"

Jenna shook her head. "No, nothing," she said. She felt like she'd collapse from hunger any second now.

"Nothing?" asked Bea, and looked at her disbelievingly. "And they let you through to the second round?"

Jenna wondered how much she could say without breaking her promise. "It's because I looked right," she said cautiously. That could hardly be a breach of promise. "For some reason they thought I had the right . . . presence."

"Kate?" called Mrs. Markas from above. Kate gave them a little wave and then she, too, disappeared upstairs.

Now there were just the two of them left sitting in the bowling alley. After the second round, nobody had come back down again, and Jenna wondered whether that meant that they'd all been eliminated or whether it was simply so late that even the best candidates had been sent home for the time being.

"But that means they don't even know if you stutter, or have a lisp, or some sort of weird speech impediment or facial tic or something!" said Bea dubiously. "If you didn't actually *say* anything . . ."

"Anybody can recite," said Jenna, although even she thought that was a silly argument. Still, that's what Tobias and Raphael had said, and movie people had to have experience in these matters. "That's majorly overrated."

Bea threw her a look, but said nothing. "I want to go home," she said after a while. "We must have been here at least three hours by now."

"Bea?" Mrs. Markas called from the top of the stairs. "Take two."

Bea stood up. "Finally!" she whispered. "I'll call you later. To find out if you . . ."

"Byeee!" said Jenna, and waved.

She had never been alone in the bowling alley before. How many birthday parties had she been to here? Twice she'd knocked down all ten pins, but often she'd missed them all. She'd never gone bowling with Mom. Without them ever having talked about it, Jenna simply knew that bowling was not one of the leisure pursuits that were *comme il faut*.

Now that all the other girls had gone, the ceiling lights suddenly seemed to glare, and the polished floor was shabby and badly scratched. *You should never be alone in a place that's meant to be full of people enjoying themselves,* thought Jenna. Suddenly it seemed depressing. Like a carnival late at night in the rain, when the merry-go-rounds have stopped.

She looked at her watch. Mom wouldn't be home yet. Mom didn't need to know anything about all this. Even if Jenna got through the second round, she could still back out. Did she really want to act in a movie? Mom would never let her, anyway. And she'd be furious if she heard that Jenna had gone to the audition after she'd forbidden it.

"Jenna Greenwood!" Mrs. Markas called from the stairs. Jenna jumped up.

In the hall, the three movie people looked as tired as she was.

"Jenna!" said Tobias, beaming all the same. "I hope you're still feeling OK."

Jenna nodded.

"Because we've got some great news for you!" he said with a wink.

Jenna frowned. Shouldn't she at least have to recite something this time?

"You're in!" said Tobias. "You've done it, Jenna Greenwood, future star. Congratulations!"

"In?" asked Jenna uncertainly.

"You're through to the final round," said Raphael. He had lowered his camera and switched off the spotlight.

Tobias smiled. "And your prospects are good. You're the number one choice as far as we're concerned. But of course the final decision isn't up to us."

"Me?" asked Jenna, in a state of shock. "I've got the part? I'm better than . . . Bea? And Anna?" She should have been pleased, but instead she could feel herself beginning to panic.

The two guys looked at each other, then at Mrs. Markas, and seemed to hesitate. Then Tobias said, "Why do you find that so hard to believe? We told you before . . ."

"But I know my mother won't let me," said Jenna. "She didn't even want me to come to the audition."

Tobias made a dismissive gesture. "We know all about that sort of thing," he said. "It happens all the time, believe me. But when mothers hear that their child has made it — that they've been chosen out of a group of several hundred applicants . . ."

"These aren't the only auditions we've held for this film," said Raphael. Mrs. Markas gave him a disapproving look.

". . . then generally they're so proud that they forget all about their objections."

Jenna shook her head. "Not my mother," she whispered.

Suddenly she was overcome by a wave of despair. It wasn't because of the film, and it wasn't that she wanted to become famous. She didn't even know if fame was something she really wanted, anyway. It was because Mom never allowed her to do anything, because she would ruin everything — even if Jenna had been chosen out of hundreds of girls. Because it would always be the same, her whole life long.

"You know what?" said Tobias. "We'll just drive you home and have a talk with her. It would be absurd if she said no."

Jenna shook her head. "She's still at work," she said.

"Then let's go to her workplace," said Tobias. He sounded so sure of himself that for a moment Jenna almost believed everything might work out.

"She'll be angry," she murmured. "She hates being disturbed."

The movie people looked at one another.

"You know, it's just that . . ." Raphael began.

"We have to speak to her today," said Tobias. "Because the final decision has to be made this weekend, and we're not the ones who'll make it."

Jenna didn't understand.

"The director will want to have his say," explained Mrs. Markas. She looked as though she was hoping he would pick another girl. "And the producer. Obviously we can't make the final decision here. That's why we've got to fly to the film studio."

"Fly?" gasped Jenna. The hall began to spin before her eyes. With trembling fingers she opened her schoolbag. She took out her last sandwich and bit into it. The bread was curling up at the edges and tasted hard and dry, but gradually the food calmed her down.

Tobias laughed. "Whoa, you must be hungry!" he exclaimed. "Why do you think we held the auditions on a Friday? So that we can fly off straightaway to the studios with our candidate, and then hammer out the details over the weekend."

"I see," said Jenna.

This was the last nail in the coffin.

"Your mother can come with us, of course," said Mrs. Markas. Even when she said something nice, her voice sounded harsh. "We wouldn't expect you to come on your own!"

Jenna swallowed the last mouthful. "She teaches most of her etiquette classes over the weekend," she said miserably. "Nearly all her clients have jobs during the week. And she can't turn them away."

The movie people looked at one another again. "Had we known it would be so difficult . . ." Mrs. Markas began.

"Bea!" cried Jenna. "Bea's parents will definitely let her do it. And they'll fly with her. Give the role to Bea!" She suddenly felt quite light-headed. She had been chosen — of all the girls, she was the one they wanted, and that was the only thing that mattered. Everything that would follow after made her feel scared, anyway. What if the director found out that she had absolutely no acting talent? What if she got stage fright in front of the camera and totally froze?

The fact that she'd been chosen was wonderful. But she didn't want to be in the movie at all.

"Bea? You mean the girl we saw just before you?" asked Tobias. "No offense, Jenna, but she doesn't even come close."

"You're miles apart," said Raphael, ignoring Mrs. Markas's critical look. "No, I'm absolutely certain . . ."

Tobias sighed. "What number can I reach your mother at?" he asked. "Now, right this minute?"

"She'll be angry . . ." said Jenna, but all the same she took the pencil he gave her and wrote down the number of the hotel where her mother held her etiquette classes. "She doesn't like to be interrupted on the job."

Tobias looked annoyed. "I don't think you're quite getting this, Jenna," he said. "This is the chance of a lifetime. We're talking about a major motion picture here! And for that, I think we can disturb your mother for just a minute." He punched the numbers into his phone, then walked across to the far corner of the room. Obviously he didn't want Jenna to hear his conversation.

Jenna looked down at the floor. She was surprised at how soon he began to talk. Maybe Mom had already been at the reception desk.

The conversation lasted some time. Mom was probably reluctant to give permission. Now and then Tobias made expansive gestures, as if Mom could see him on the other end of the line. And then suddenly he laughed out loud. "Excellent!" he cried. "Thank you. You have a wonderful daughter." He flipped his cell closed.

"Phew!" said Tobias, and put his hand on Jenna's shoulder. "Well, that was a hard nut to crack. Good thing you warned me in advance."

Jenna looked at him uncertainly.

"She said yes," he said, and ruffled Jenna's hair. "She realizes what this could mean for you, and that she can't possibly stand in your way when you've got such an opportunity. She's a bit of a worrier, your mother, isn't she? But I managed to talk her into it."

Good thing I ate that sandwich, thought Jenna. *Otherwise I'd have fainted by now.*

"She said she'd send you a text message," said Tobias. "Aren't you happy? This is your big chance."

Jenna nodded. It all seemed completely unreal.

"It's beeping," she said, and took her cell phone out of her bag.

Mom's number glowed on the screen. There were three messages from her. Jenna opened the wrong one first. Then she opened them in the right order and read the whole text:

Dear Jenna, At first I found the whole idea frightening, but then the nice young man convinced me it would be all right. I agree that you should take this chance.

You know I have to work over the weekend, and I think it would be good if you could do something really special. Enjoy yourself, Jenna!

Perhaps I've sometimes been a bit too strict over the last few years. I'm keeping my fingers crossed for you! Stay in touch, though—text me. With love, Mom

Oh Mom, thought Jenna. *Dear, dear Mom.* And at long last she'd actually learned how to send text messages! She couldn't remember when she'd last felt so much affection for her mother.

6

*T*hey had stopped off at the apartment to pick up Jenna's toothbrush and pj's, plus enough clothes for two days. Tobias and Raphael had stayed in the car; only Mrs. Markas had gone upstairs with Jenna, and then she had waited in the hall. The woman obviously disliked her for some reason. Perhaps she was still wishing she could swap Jenna for one of the other girls.

It was only when the four of them were back in the car — the same one Jenna and Bea had seen parked outside the school that morning — that it really hit home that she was not imagining all this. Jenna knew she should have been jumping for joy, but all she felt was nervous and scared.

If only Bea was with me, she thought. *Or anyone else I know. I'm not a brave person, yet I'm headed to the airport with three complete strangers. Flying to a movie studio for a weekend — and I don't even know where it is.*

"Here we are!" said Tobias, turning to Jenna with a smile. "I'll get your bag from the trunk."

Jenna looked out the window and was shocked at what she saw. "That's the airport?" she spluttered.

She could see a runway, a building with a radar on the roof, cornfields, meadows, and a tiny parking lot. For sure the other kids in her class didn't jet off to their Mallorca or Canary Islands vacays from this dinky little airport!

"Oh, you didn't think we were flying coach on some commercial airline, did you?" asked Tobias cheerfully, holding the door open for her. "I'll bet that's the only way you've flown before, right? But now that you're in the movie business, you'll have to get used to this: our own private plane. Not scared, are you?"

Jenna shook her head no. And said "yes" as she did it.

She wished she could go back. It was bad enough to be flying to an unknown destination with three total strangers, but at least on an ordinary plane there would have been a lot of normal people sitting all around her, talking about their normal destination and having a normal fear of flying, just like her. Maybe then everything would have seemed like everyday normality.

Instead she was supposed to get into this little private plane, which only had six seats? And it didn't make her feel any better when Raphael, flashing her an encouraging smile, sat down in the pilot's seat.

"You'll love it, you'll see," he said. "It'll be a very smooth flight — no turbulence forecast — and you'll be able to watch the sun set over the sea. We'll be there in just two hours."

"If you say so," Jenna mumbled. The stern-faced Mrs. Markas helped her with her seat belt, and then, for the first time, she smiled. Only a little smile, but Jenna felt encouraged by it.

"I've never flown before, ever," she confided.

Mrs. Markas sat down on the other side of the narrow aisle and with two quick movements fastened her own seat belt. "There's a first time for everything," she said.

"I don't know what . . ." Jenna started to respond. But the propellers began to spin, the engine roared, and she stopped in midsentence. She would have had to lean across the aisle and shout into the lady's ear, the noise was so loud.

Mrs. Markas said something, but Jenna could only see her lips moving. Then the plane jerked into motion and went faster and faster until suddenly Jenna felt the nose lift and they were off the ground.

So this is flying! she thought in amazement. *It's so simple, and you soar up so quickly into the sky, up and up, so easily and so naturally.*

Mrs. Markas unfastened her seat belt and leaned across to Jenna. "That wasn't so bad, was it?" she asked. Her smile was still as thin as before, but all the same Jenna felt immensely relieved.

"No, not at all," she answered.

The plane shuddered a little, kind of like a car on a road pocked with potholes, and then they were above the clouds.

For a moment Jenna closed her eyes — the brightness of the light was blinding.

And suddenly she felt happy. *They chose me, me, me!* she thought, and looked down at the shining white clouds. *I'm flying above the clouds on a private plane, because I've got the right "presence" — me, me, me! Not Bea, not Anna, not Kate — me! And when I go to school on Monday, I can tell them all about it. As long as it doesn't sound like I'm bragging, of course.*

The only annoying thing was that she hadn't brought a camera, and her cell was too old to have one. Otherwise she could have taken photos — of the little plane, of the clouds outside the window, of the two cute guys sitting at the controls. And she could also have taken pictures of the final audition over the next two days. Without photos — without proof! — the others back home might not even believe her.

"Chewing gum?" Mrs. Markas offered. Maybe Jenna had been mistaken about her. Maybe the woman didn't think she was unsuitable after all. Maybe she always had that unfriendly look on her face — some people did; you could even feel sorry for them.

"No, thank you," said Jenna politely, and shook her head. The clouds beneath disappeared, and a great expanse of sapphire blue water stretched out below as far as the eye could see. "What's that?" she asked.

"The North Sea," said Mrs. Markas. "First we're flying directly north, and then we'll turn."

"Really?" said Jenna, shocked. "Where are we actually going?" She was surprised at herself. Why hadn't she asked them earlier?

"To Scandia, of course," said Tobias, turning to her with a smile. "But when we start our descent, you should chew some gum — it helps relieve the pressure in your ears."

Find Liron as quickly as possible — that would be the best thing to do. Sitting up brooding all night long hadn't helped a bit.

But how to travel? Not by rail or bus, obviously. Too many people watching. What other alternative was there? Perhaps it would be possible to stop a car. It would be way too far on foot. And everyone would stare at a small stranger in an extra-large checkered jacket . . .

There was no choice but to hitch a ride — the sleepless hours had made that clear. But what would Liron say when this stranger suddenly turned up on his doorstep?

(Even if everything could be explained.)

Regardless, reaching Liron was the answer. With luck, Liron meant safety.

And if possible, find another coat! Checks were too conspicuous, and a skinny kid in an extra-large checkered jacket would make anybody turn and look. Still, it was impossible to go without a coat altogether. It was too cold in the mornings, even though it was summer, and it was even worse at night — especially here in the north, with its bright clear skies.

At least the cap was plain enough not to attract attention.

The last half hour had probably been the best of the whole flight. The sun had shifted to the edge of the sky — really the edge, as if the earth was not a sphere and the universe was not infinite. Its light had changed from a clear radiance to a gentle pinkish gold; up here, the blue hour between daylight and darkness was a reddish hour, warm and friendly, saying good-bye to the day.

Below them, after they had swung around in a wide curve, land had suddenly appeared, and they had flown lower and lower, the indistinguishable dark surface turning into forests, lakes, then little settlements, farms in clearings, even individual trees.

After that, it went dark. Jenna wondered if maybe her companions had deliberately timed the flight so that she could experience all this: the dazzling light above the clouds, the red glow of evening, and then, right at the end, the carpet of countless lights, frayed at the edges, over which they circled until the pilot took the plane down and the houses of the city emerged through the dusk. The jet glided above the roofs before finally, almost imperceptibly, touching down on the runway between rows of red, green, and white lights. And here was the kind of airport that Jenna had expected to have taken off from — huge, noisy, with small and large planes in their various stationary positions, and a brightly lit terminal.

"Touchdown!" Tobias said proudly, turning to Jenna, while Raphael carefully steered the plane, with its ever more slowly revolving propellers, away from the main landing area. "Welcome to the capital."

Jenna pressed her face against the window. This was the way to arrive after a flight, exactly like this: lights, people, bustle and buzz. She took her cell out of her bag. In a moment, she'd be able to switch it on. She'd text Mom and tell her how fab the flight had been. And how they'd had a fantastic landing. And that she wasn't scared anymore — not scared at all.

"Yes, welcome to Scandia!" said Mrs. Markas, taking her bag down from the overhead compartment. There was a touch of pride in her voice. "I hope you'll enjoy your stay with us."

The plane came to a halt in front of a hangar. Mrs. Markas opened the door and pushed down the steps. A man in a suit came toward them, his hands thrust deep in his pants pockets. If the suit was expensive enough, Mom always said, then hands in pockets could look stylish. Otherwise it was simply bad form.

And who could tell at first glance whether a suit was expensive?

Raphael climbed out from behind the controls and disappeared into the hangar.

"Hello, Bolström," said Tobias cheerfully, jumping out of the cockpit. "Here we are now, entertain us."

He must be the director, thought Jenna. *Or the producer.* He looked just the way she'd always imagined movie people to look: tall and fair-haired, with broad shoulders and a tanned face lit up by a warm smile.

"Well?" Tobias asked.

"Is that her?" Bolström replied, nodding toward Jenna. "First impression — yes, it could work."

He took a step toward her and held out his hand. "Jenna?" he said. "That's correct, right? Your name is Jenna?"

Jenna nodded. It *was* an expensive suit.

"Welcome to Scandia," said the man.

Jenna's cell phone gave a beep.

"Are you the director?" she asked timidly. "I haven't recited any lines yet . . . I might not be any good at it . . ."

The man laughed. "Yes, the director! That's me," he said, and shook her hand firmly. "I'm the director here. And as far as acting is concerned — we'll talk about that later. For now, Tobias and Mrs. Markas will take you to Osterlin for the night. Tomorrow morning we'll see what you can do."

"Osterlin?" asked Jenna. "Is that where the studios are?"

Mrs. Markas came to join them. "Osterlin is a country house just outside the city," she said. "It's beautiful, with every conceivable comfort. Tonight you can relax there after all the excitement of the day. I should think it *was* quite exciting for you, wasn't it?"

Jenna nodded. "Are the others spending the night there, too?" she asked.

The director casually waved a hand. "I'm off now," he said to Mrs. Markas and Tobias. He nodded to Jenna. "I'll see you tomorrow morning." Then, without a backward glance, he disappeared beyond the edge of the runway.

For a moment, Mrs. Markas watched him go, and then she sighed. "What others?" she asked. "Who do you mean?"

"The girls from the other auditions," said Jenna. A black limousine drew up, with Raphael at the wheel. "The ones who are here for the final screen test."

Tobias laughed as he opened the car door. "You're our favorite," he said. "I thought you'd realized that by now. You're our number one. So as long as you don't let us down, my dear, the part is yours."

"You mean there aren't any others — I'm the only one?" Jenna asked in surprise. Slowly the limousine crossed the runway toward a large gate. A young guy in coveralls, also tall and blond — who himself looked like he was acting his part in a movie — opened the gate, and they drove out onto a wide main road. Smoothly and silently the car merged into the flow of traffic.

"I thought you'd understood," Tobias continued. "The director has to have the final word. Tomorrow and the day after, he'll be testing you, and that could be quite stressful. But he has a brilliant idea — you'll be blown away."

"It won't be anything . . . anything difficult, will it?" asked Jenna, feeling her fear return.

Mrs. Markas, who was sitting beside her in the car, laughed.

She almost sounded happy. "Nothing difficult at all," she said. "In fact, the opposite. You'll be surprised. You'll like it. Any girl would like it, believe me."

Jenna watched through the car window as the houses sped by, grand white houses with columns and sculptures and stucco carvings above the windows. Beneath the streetlamps, along the sidewalks, people wandered to and fro, with shopping bags or snacks in their hands — groups of young people laughing, and older men and women, usually on their own, their heavy footsteps showing how tired they were at the end of the workweek, and how eager to get home.

Just like evenings at home, thought Jenna, and leaned back in her seat. A bit brighter, perhaps. Everything looked so . . . posh. But otherwise, pretty normal.

Then she remembered her cell.

Dear Jenna, Mom had written. **You must have arrived by now. Please write soon and tell me how you are. (Don't phone! I've got a group class!) I love you. — Mom**

Jenna called up the menu on her phone and pressed REPLY. A less anxious mother would certainly not have sent so many text messages. Perhaps her overprotectiveness did have an upside, after all. It was comforting to read her messages. Especially because she sounded so affectionate — she was never like that in person, when Jenna was at home.

Flight was awesome. I'm looking 4ward 2 2moro. Jenna hesitated for a moment, then typed: **Luv u 2. — Jenna**

7

*O*nce they had left the airport and the city, there wasn't much for Jenna to see out the window. The countryside slipped past them in the darkness — mainly forest, occasionally meadows, and once Jenna caught sight of a herd of deer in a field, silhouetted against the charcoal sky and taking no notice of the car at all.

After a short drive, they swung onto an avenue of trees. At the end stood an old brick gatehouse lit by two coach lamps, one to the left and one to the right. The driver slowed down, and the car crawled up a long cobbled driveway toward the main building, which shone dull white through the dim twilight.

"That's Osterlin?" Jenna asked in a whisper, barely breathing. Standing there in the moonlight, it looked almost like a castle, and was infinitely more beautiful than any of the houses Jenna had ever been in. "Is it . . . a hotel?"

There were country hotels and even castle hotels, where people with lots of money could spend their vacations. Bea's parents once considered going on a tour over spring break, taking the two girls and traveling from one country hotel to another. Bea's mom had shown Jenna the brochure, and one of the houses in it looked almost identical to the one now before her. But back then, of course, the trip had turned out to be too expensive, and they never did take it.

Mrs. Markas laughed. Ever since they'd sat next to each other on the plane, she had been a lot friendlier.

"It's an old estate that belongs to the royal family," she said. "In earlier days, when journeys took a lot longer, they used to come out here in the summer, to get away from the city and the business of government. Today, of course, it takes no time at all to travel back and forth. The Little Princess liked coming here. The family have their summer residence on the north coast now, though, and they've got another one on an island in the Mediterranean."

"Oh," said Jenna, a little disoriented. She tried to recall what she'd read about Scandia, but she didn't even know exactly where it was. "And why are we . . . why am I . . . ?"

The car stopped, and Rafael got out. The gravel crunched under his feet as he walked back to the trunk to get her bag.

But Jenna was waiting for an answer before she would open her door.

"It's the ideal place for you to relax and prepare for the next part of your audition," said Mrs. Markas. "Don't you like it? We're really lucky to be able to stay here." She ducked her head and got out of the limousine.

I'm very lucky, too, thought Jenna. *At least I think I am. I've flown for the first time in my life, and now I'm staying in what's practically a palace! I have to write and tell Mom. And Bea!*

She looked up at the welcoming white façade, and then she looked back again at the old trees along the avenue. The day had been unreal. Like a fairy tale — no, like a film! She wished more than ever that she hadn't left her camera at home. Not just to prove all this to Mom and her friends, but also to prove it to herself.

Tobias pointed invitingly to the impressive entrance. "Let's go in," he said, and opened the tall door onto a huge empty hallway.

All that was missing from the scene was a butler in white gloves and a tailcoat.

The man had set out early in the morning from the mountains in the north so that he'd reach the capital in time for his Saturday meeting. Of course, South Island wasn't very big, and for years now the roads had been so good that you could travel at top speed; but all the same, he liked to leave himself plenty of time for the drive, and to take a good look at the surrounding countryside every now and then. He loved his country, as all Scandians did, and he knew how well-off he was. They all were. *Even the farmers,* he thought, *our free Scandian farmers — they work hard, but they have a good life.*

The dew was still shining on the grass alongside the road. He turned on the heat, though only to a low setting. In the mornings, when he was driving through the forest regions and the sun still hadn't penetrated through the trees to warm the earth below, he always felt cold, even in the car.

Not far ahead, two deer crossed the road. The fields lay still in the morning light — fertile land, a light green expanse of wheat. The canola seed had just finished blooming.

He saw the figure long before he reached it, for at this point in the journey the road climbed straight up a hill, as if it had been drawn with a ruler. Someone was huddled by the roadside, brown and gray like the dirt, and for a fraction of a second he was afraid there might have been an accident, that an injured person was lying there. But then the figure sprang up, and he saw the typical gesture. Someone wanted a ride.

The man hesitated. In the past he'd always stop, especially out in the country; it was often children wanting a ride from one farm to another, because the distances were long and there weren't always enough buses. He'd also picked up young people who were touring their beloved Scandia and wanted to be dropped off at the nearest train station or youth hostel, tired after a day's walk through the dark forests. He'd been happy to take them, and had talked to them and been pleased to help them, at no cost to himself.

He slowed down. In recent years he'd become more cautious about hitchhikers. You had to get a good look at whomever it was you were picking up, and even once you did, you still couldn't be certain all was safe. There had been trouble among the people in the north, and now there was unrest everywhere; everyone in the south was afraid.

He turned off the car heater. The person by the side of the road appeared to be a boy no older than twelve or maybe thirteen. And he looked frozen, as if he'd spent the night in the forest. Just a boy in a checkered jacket that was much too big for him and — now that the man could get a closer look — with a strand of fair hair poking out from under his cap.

The driver breathed a sigh of relief. He opened the window on the passenger side and leaned across the seat. "Morning!" he called cheerfully. "Where do you want to go?"

The man couldn't see much of the kid. He had tucked his head down low between his shoulders and hugged his arms around his body. The morning sun was still not strong enough to give any warmth.

"Are you heading to the capital?" The youngster's voice trembled with the cold.

The man nodded. "We're going the same way," he said. "Get in, lad."

The young hitchhiker opened the door, dropped down into the seat, then, almost as a reflex action, pulled the cap down low.

"Thank you."

The man put his foot on the accelerator and turned the heat all the way up. "You'll soon feel warmer," he said. "Have you been waiting there long? You look frozen."

His new passenger didn't look at him, but stared straight ahead at the road, with a face so dirty that it might have been camouflage. *Shy kid,* the driver thought, *but that's how they are at this age.* He'd been the same himself.

"There aren't many people around this early," the hitch-hiker said quietly. "And whoever is, is in a hurry."

Despite the shabby clothes and the dirty face, it was an educated voice, without a trace of the North Scandian dialect. The driver relaxed.

❧

When Jenna woke up, a sunbeam was shining between the heavy curtains and onto the floor beside her bed. Half past six. Way too early.

She sat up and swung her legs over the side of the bed. It was high — much higher than her own at home — and old-fashioned. A kind of canopy arched up above her head.

Last night she had hardly been able to sleep, she was so excited. The house had been empty when they'd arrived, and was only dimly lit by the night-lights in all the hallways. They'd gone up to the second floor, and Mrs. Markas had escorted her to the corner room, then laughed when Jenna had asked if such a big bed really was for her. Mrs. Markas told her to go straight to sleep because the next day was going to be strenuous, and she'd shown Jenna a hidden door that led to a large, brightly lit bathroom. She'd then left the room, but returned soon after with two bottles of fizzy lemonade and a little tray of bread, cheese, and pieces of roast chicken.

"In case you're too hungry to go to sleep," she'd said.

Jenna had rarely spent a night away from home. Sometimes she slept over at Bea's, but that was it. She'd never been allowed to go on school trips, and she'd definitely never stayed in a country house before — never mind a swank mansion! Intrigued, she had wandered through the bedroom, pulling out the (empty) drawers of the dresser, looking out the window over the dark courtyard in the front, and sitting down on one of the tapestry-covered chairs. When she had at last gone to bed, she had left the bedside lamp on.

Now, she was glad the night was over. As she climbed out of bed, the wooden floor felt almost warm beneath her feet. There were dark wooden inlays in the light-colored parquet, forming patterns that, in a few places, were covered by heavy carpeting. Jenna drew back the curtains and looked out through the side windows.

The radiant light of morning flooded the garden. Lawns were strewn with carefully tended flowerbeds, and shrubs trimmed into the shape of balls or goblets formed symmetrical borders. A bird was singing somewhere, and another was answering. Otherwise, everything was still.

How many gardeners would it take to tend a garden like that? Jenna wondered. And how many cleaners were needed to maintain the house? Who could afford to live here? *Perhaps they don't live here all the time, and that's why it's so empty,* Jenna thought. *Or maybe it's always as empty as it is now — abandoned because the king has a new summer residence or two. Or ten . . .*

Did the king and queen and all their royal children ever come here? Did they even actually have any children? *I wish I knew more about Scandia,* thought Jenna. *I'm completely clueless when it comes to who's who in the royal family.* Not that she knew much about the royal families in other countries, either. Whenever shows came on TV about the royal houses of Europe, Mom always seemed to get annoyed and change the channel.

"What a bunch of baloney!" she'd say, with an intensity that startled Jenna. "Total and utter nonsense! Who do they think they're fooling? It's all a great big lie."

And Jenna hadn't really been interested, anyway. She was more into pop stars and celebutards. Now, though, she thought that she might have been better off if she had at least learned a *little* something about the Scandian royals — since she was currently sleeping in one of their beds!

Jenna giggled. She pulled the rest of the curtains open so wide that the light poured all across the room, and then she flopped back on the bed. Maybe it belonged to the Princess of Scandia — if there *was* a Princess of Scandia. Imagine if she had slept in a princess's bed last night!

She sat up, took the last chicken leg from the plate, and bit into it. The fat under the skin tasted cold and greasy this morning, and she put it back.

"I'm the Princess of Scandia!" she stated in a deep voice, walking across the room with her arms outstretched. In the mirror above the vanity she saw a girl with a dark, tousled bedhead, wearing a tank top and pj bottoms that had long since grown too short, striding earnestly across the room, proclaiming, "I'm Jenna, Princess of Scandia!" Maybe the movie people had chosen her yesterday just for exactly this. Maybe *this* was what they had meant by her "presence." After having slept in this room and awoken in this bed, she could suddenly imagine herself as a princess.

"Me, and not Bea!" she cried, and hopped back onto the bed. "Me, and not Anna! I'm the Princess of Scandia!"

Then she shocked herself into silence. If she made too much noise, she might wake someone in the neighboring rooms. It would be *soooo* embarrassing if someone had heard what she'd just been shouting. Totally. Mortifying.

Jenna listened, but there wasn't even the creak of a bedspring from the other rooms. She let out a deep breath. She'd be more careful from now on.

On the table by the head of the bed sat an old-fashioned white telephone, like something you'd see in a classic movie. She could call Mom! She picked up the receiver and held it to her ear, surprised at how heavy it was.

No, hold up! She put it down again. She couldn't just make a long-distance phone call at the expense of a stranger, even if that stranger was the king of the country and would certainly have the money to pay for the call.

That was not the point, she reminded herself. The point was that a phone call at someone else's expense was theft — that's what Mom would say. So Mom definitely wouldn't want to be on the receiving end of a stolen phone call.

On tiptoe, Jenna ran to the chair where she had laid her clothes and took her cell phone out of her pocket. Maybe she shouldn't call anybody so early on a Saturday morning, but she could still send a good morning text message.

She wrote to Mom that she had slept well. That the sun was shining. That the whole place seemed dead and that in her next text she would tell her who else was staying here. **CU, Jenna**

Bea was next. **Hi, Bea,** Jenna wrote. **U R not going 2 believe me, but I'm in a mansion in a 4-poster bed! Txt back! xoxo Jenna**

She pressed SEND and waited for confirmation. She waited and waited, and then, just as she was about to flip her cell closed, a message appeared: CONNECTION FAILED. RETRY?

Jenna frowned. It couldn't be her phone, since the message had just gone through to her mother. What was up with Bea's cell? Bea could be pretty ditzy, but she always had her phone on.

It really was very strange.

Well, the main thing is that Mom's getting my messages, thought Jenna. *I can tell Bea about all this day after tomorrow.*

At that moment, the white telephone rang.

"Jenna?" Tobias said in a friendly voice. "I hope I haven't woken you. But we'd like to have breakfast with you now. You've got a very busy schedule ahead of you. Would it be all right if Mrs. Markas came to get you in a quarter of an hour?"

"Yes, of course," said Jenna.

The fear and excitement were back again.

They'd driven the whole way in silence, and soon they would be arriving in the capital. Most of the time, the boy had kept his eyes closed, as if he was asleep. But every now and then he'd grasped his cap with an almost startled movement and pulled it down lower over his eyes.

The man smiled. He would have liked a more sociable companion, but he didn't even dare turn on the radio in case it might disturb his passenger. Nevertheless, he felt relaxed and happy. It was nice to be able to help a kid who obviously couldn't afford to travel by train, however well educated he was.

About an hour outside the city, they were overtaken by a sports car just as a truck was coming from the opposite direction, and the man braked sharply.

"Maniac!" he yelled. "Some people just can't get where they're going fast enough."

The hitchhiker was flung forward, eyes wide open in shock, then slowly sank back into the seat again and asked, "Are we nearly there?"

The man nodded. "Do you mind if I turn off the heat? You should be warm enough by now."

In response the passenger unbuckled his seat belt and took off his oversize jacket. "Yes, thank you," he said. And again the cap came down.

"Don't you want to take your hat off, too?" the man asked, trying to lighten the mood. "Aren't you a bit hot under that?"

There was no reply — only a silent shake of the head.

"Oh, come on, you don't need to wear it inside!" said the driver, and jokingly reached over to pull the cap off the kid's head.

Everything happened quickly after that. The hitchhiker seized the man's hand and bit down hard, then snatched back the cap, opened the door, and tumbled out. For a second the man almost lost control of the steering wheel and the car nearly plunged off the road.

The man let out a cry, blew on his injured hand, braked sharply, and screeched to a stop. He backed up the road a bit, but there was no one to be seen. The boy had disappeared into the forest.

The man looked at the tiny tooth marks on the back of his hand and the ball of his thumb, and groaned. He considered calling the boy back, but then thought better of it. He wouldn't return — he was probably frightened now. And anyway, the man's hand was turning purple, and he felt a resentful anger rising inside him. He decided to drive on. His conscience was clear. It wasn't as if he was abandoning the boy, since he'd been all alone when he'd picked him up. And it wasn't all that far to the city from here.

He leaned over to the passenger seat, picked up the checkered jacket, got out, and laid it down at the side of the road.

No doubt the boy would come out of the forest and find it as soon as he heard the car drive away.

It was only just before he reached the city, when the pain in his hand had begun to ease, that the man remembered something strange: For the fraction of a second that the boy had been without his cap, the driver could have sworn that waist-long fair hair had fallen down over his shoulders.

8

Jenna held her breath. The banquet hall was so huge it could easily have seated a hundred guests. But now the only people sitting at a long table at the far end of the room were Tobias and, next to him, the man who had met them last night at the airport — the director.

"Good morning, Jenna!" said Tobias. His voice echoed around the great hall. Here, too, the parquet floor was inlaid and shone in the light that fell through tall French doors. Behind these Jenna could see the balustrade of a narrow balcony and, beyond that, the park at the back of the building.

"Good morning," said Jenna, and she and Mrs. Markas sat down opposite Tobias at the two vacant places where the table had been set for breakfast. The dishware was rose-colored porcelain with gold edges, but on the polished tabletop between the place settings were just a basket of toast, butter, and a selection of jams, just like at home. Jenna felt a bit more at ease.

"I hope you slept well," said Tobias, and held out the basket of toast. *All that's missing are servants*, thought Jenna. *Serious-looking gentlemen in black jackets and white shirts, with cloths over their arms, or young women wearing white bonnets on their heads and little triangular aprons over their black dresses.* "You'd better have a good breakfast to keep up your strength through the morning," Tobias continued, breaking into her thoughts.

"Thank you," Jenna said quietly. As she spread butter on her toast, the director watched her closely. Although a place was set for him, he didn't eat anything. Jenna couldn't understand whatever he was discussing with Tobias and Mrs. Markas; something about a certain district in the city, but she was having trouble concentrating. Once, when she asked Mrs. Markas to pass the raspberry jam, she caught the director looking at her — and it was an approving look. Still, she felt uncomfortable. *How rude,* she thought as she carefully bit into her toast, and hoped that no one could read her mind from the expression on her face. It wasn't polite to stare at someone, especially when they were eating. And you'd think that people in a luxe house like this would know how to behave.

"More toast?" asked Tobias as Jenna dabbed her mouth with her napkin.

Jenna shook her head. "No, thank you."

The director smiled at her. "Excellent!" he said. "Any girl we'd have to teach good manners to would have been out of the question right from the start. But obviously that's not a problem! You must have been very well brought up."

Jenna nodded. For a moment she wondered if she should tell him that her mother taught manners for a living. But what interest would that be to him?

"Jenna," said the director, leaning across the table toward her. "You must be *bursting* to know what we have in store for you on this beautiful sunny day."

Jenna nodded again. She felt very alone.

"Well, Tobias and Mrs. Markas have already told you what it's all about. This weekend we want to see whether you can act the part of a princess convincingly. And I'm sure they've mentioned that, for us, the way you look is more important than whether you can learn lines by heart or recite them properly. Of course, we could simply ask you to audition for us again, but what would we learn from that? Auditions are too artificial."

"Yes," Jenna mumbled, though she didn't know what he was talking about. Wasn't the whole purpose of her coming here to audition again?

"Now, Jenna, you're in luck," said the director — and his smile was so radiant that Jenna wondered whether he practiced it in front of the mirror every morning — "because I happen to know the royal family here in Scandia. I'm a personal friend of theirs, Jenna." He smiled on. "That's why we've been allowed to spend the night in this magnificent place. And that's why you, Jenna, this weekend" — he paused for a second — "will be allowed to act as if you were the Princess of Scandia."

He stopped.

Jenna stared at him. "What?" she asked, taken aback. Had they overheard her earlier when she'd been shouting so childishly that she *was* the Princess of Scandia? Were there hidden cameras in the rooms, or microphones? Duh! How dumb of her not to think of that! This was a palace, or at least something *like* a palace.

"It's true," said the director. His megawatt smile made Jenna feel uncomfortable all over again. "You have the chance, Jenna, the unique chance, to stand in for the princess tomorrow at a party. You will act as if you were Princess of Scandia — all day long. There couldn't be a better audition. If you succeed in convincing the people of Scandia that you are indeed their princess, then we shall know for certain that you have all the qualities to play the role."

Jenna shook her head fervently. "But that's not right!" she said hoarsely. "That's like identity theft, isn't it? I can't do that!"

The director laughed. "Whether you *can* do it is exactly what we've got to find out, my dear Jenna. And it is certainly *not* like 'identity theft.' You're going to play the part with permission from the royal family and from the princess herself, who is pleased and grateful for the chance to be relieved of one of her public duties."

"But the people," Jenna protested. "They'll believe that I really am the princess. And that's a lie."

Mrs. Markas intervened. "But they won't be getting anything different or anything less than what they'd get if you were the real princess," she said. "So what's so wrong about that? You are a very honest girl, Jenna: We've noticed that and we respect you for it. But a trick that doesn't hurt anyone and helps us to see if you can act the part — can you really call that a crime?"

Jenna unfolded her napkin, folded it, and unfolded it again. "I don't know," she murmured. She remembered Mom's anger: *It's all a great big lie!* Was that why she always got so furious whenever the royals were on TV? Because she thought they were all a bunch of poseurs and phonies?

"You'll see, it'll be fun," said the director. "And just think what you'll be able to tell your friends afterward!"

True that! Jenna thought wryly. *The only question is whether they'll actually believe me!*

"But first we have to make a few small tweaks to your appearance," said the director. "Though you'll be surprised how little there is to do. Then His Royal Highness the regent is going to pay us a short visit to see if he can give us the go-ahead."

"His Royal Highness?" whispered Jenna.

The director nodded. "That will be special, won't it?" he said.

Jenna sat back. *Well, why not try it?* she thought. *Now that I'm here. They'd be pretty angry with me if I refused now. After all, it is why they brought me here in their little private plane. I can still say no at any time if I want to.*

"OK," she consented.

The director put his hand on her shoulder. "Good!"

The kid with the cap and the checkered jacket opened the door to the telephone booth. It had not been easy to find a phone that took coins — most of those had been done away with long ago. Not to mention the problem of scrounging up enough money to make the call. But using the cell was not an option — there was no easier way for a call to be traced to its source.

The line rang for a long time. Had Jonas shut down his cell?

"Hello?" said a boy's voice at last, thankfully. "Jonas speaking. Hello?"

"Jonas?" Traffic roared past the booth, and with all the noise it was almost impossible to hear what he was saying. "It's me. Can you hear? Can you hear me?"

"Of course I can hear you. Why wouldn't I?" asked Jonas. "What's wrong?"

"Jonas, listen! Tell Liron! I'm on my way. He's got to hide me! I . . . I can't . . ."

There was a quiet click, then the flatline of the dial tone. The money had run out.

The simplest thing would be to skirt around the edge of the city to get to the housing projects. You couldn't miss the high-rises — their windows shone out in the lingering darkness over the whole area, like a mosaic of light. And behind one of them lived Liron.

"Ready!" said the makeup artist. "There was hardly anything for me to do." She turned to Mrs. Markas, who was leaning against the wall by the window and watching. "It's incredible! You'd almost think —"

"Thank you, excellent work!" Mrs. Markas replied. Her words sounded like a good-bye.

The makeup artist bent over Jenna's shoulder once more and straightened a strand in the wig. "But . . ." she asked, ". . . what's all this for?"

"We told you before, it's a birthday surprise for the princess," said Mrs. Markas, and Jenna was chilled by the almost threatening tone of her voice. "We've sworn you to absolute secrecy, and you know that breaking a promise to the royal family is regarded as high treason, to be punished accordingly."

The makeup artist recoiled. "But I've no intention of saying anything!" she protested. She sounded more insulted than afraid.

When she had left, Jenna carefully stood up. The wig felt tight and uncomfortable, and she couldn't imagine spending a whole day walking around with it on. Her head already felt hot and itchy.

"May I look now?" she asked.

Mrs. Markas nodded, and Jenna went to the vanity, which had a large, three-winged mirror. She could feel her heart thumping with excitement.

The makeup artist hadn't done much. She'd plucked Jenna's eyebrows, helped her place blue contact lenses in her brown eyes, and put on the wig, all the while shaking her head in disbelief.

"Incredible!" she'd murmured, dusting pale-colored powder over Jenna's face. "Incredible! If your hair and eyes weren't such a dark brown, you could be her twin!"

She'd also given her a pair of shoes with such high heels that Mom would certainly have forbidden her to wear them. High heels were bad for the back, especially when you were still growing.

"You're shorter than her, you know," the makeup artist had said. "By about two inches, according to the figures I've got. And if you wear high heels you'll also seem slimmer. The princess's build is not quite as . . . athletic . . . as yours." She had smiled. "But, blonde wig, blue contacts, high heels, and voilà! You could be her twin!"

And that was precisely what Jenna now saw in the mirror. To guide the makeup artist, Mrs. Markas had propped a large photo of the princess on the vanity. She was a slender girl, about fourteen years old, with waist-length blonde hair and sad eyes. Jenna would never have thought she could look that beautiful and sophisticated herself. And yet, gazing out of the mirror at her now was the face of the princess — still with a darker complexion, of course, despite the dusting of pale powder, and still a little rounder, regardless of the high heels, and without the sad eyes, and yet . . . definitely the princess.

"I look . . . just like her!" whispered Jenna, and turned to Mrs. Markas with an expression of disbelief.

Mrs. Markas levered herself away from the niche by the window and came to join her at the vanity.

"Of course, you don't *really* look like her," she said quickly. "But now you see what a good makeup artist can do." She put her hand on Jenna's shoulder. "The regent's waiting in the library. I'm dying to hear what he'll have to say."

Jenna stood up and followed her through the hallways of the great house to a wing she hadn't been in before. Mrs. Markas opened a tall white-and-gold double door.

"Your Royal Highness, and Mr. Bolström," she said. "Here is the girl."

Jenna stepped forward. The director was leaning behind a massive chair, close to a wall that was covered with bookshelves right up to the ceiling; in the chair sat a man whom she had not met before. He was tan, and his youthful face contrasted strangely with his shining white hair. When he stood up, she saw that he was significantly shorter than the director.

"Good morning," Jenna said in a subdued voice. Her mom had taught her all she could, and Jenna knew how to behave in almost any situation, but she hadn't learned how to talk to kings or regents.

The regent took a step toward her and held out his arms as if to embrace her. "Malena!" he exclaimed quietly. "No — Jenna!"

Then, as if he had suddenly realized that the gesture was out of place, he lowered his arms again.

Jenna stood still. There was something so weird about all of this.

"Yes, this is Jenna, Norlin," said the director, and went and stood beside him. "Now, tell me, isn't she just the spitting image of Malena?"

The regent didn't seem to hear. "Jenna," he whispered, and then hurried toward her. "Jenna."

"Your Royal Highness," said Mrs. Markas, and Jenna detected a hint of unease in her voice. "As you yourself say . . ."

"Jenna," the regent repeated. He raised his right arm and tenderly caressed her cheek with the back of his hand. "Jenna."

Jenna stood frozen.

"Sir, she is *not* your niece!" Mrs. Markas cried in alarm. "She is not Malena, Your Royal Highness. She's a complete stranger."

The regent continued to stare at Jenna as if he was searching for something in her face. "No, not Malena," he whispered. "Not Malena."

"Norlin!" the director interjected sharply, taking a firm grip of his arm. "Pull yourself together, man! You knew she was coming. This is Jenna, and you've granted permission for her to play the role of the princess tomorrow, just for a day. What's the matter with you?"

The regent looked as if he had just awoken from a dream. For a second he seemed to sag, but then he straightened his shoulders and gave a little bow.

"Yes, quite remarkable," he said in a firm voice. "So, you're young Jenna, and tomorrow you shall take the place of my niece, Malena, on her birthday, so that she can enjoy the day without all the hassle."

"*And* so that we can see whether Jenna will be able to play the role of a princess in my film, Norlin," the director prompted. "But of course you already know all that."

Norlin gave another little bow. Jenna wondered if kings were supposed to bow to commoners. Or if regents were, for that matter.

"Then we shall see how well you can play the part," he said. His eyes were a deep blue, and now he looked Jenna up and down. "I think it will work. We'll meet again tomorrow morning, and Mrs. Markas and Tobias will tell you all you need to know."

Then he turned and went out through the double doors without even saying good-bye.

❧

The man stopped his car. He loved the view from the hilltop just outside the city: the redbrick towers of the centuries-old churches; the town hall with its great clock; the royal palace shining white amid the green of its parks, with the broad boulevard stretching out in front of it; the bustling streets and narrow alleys of the old town; and, behind it all, gleaming in the sunlight, the sea and its islands. If he turned his gaze a little to the right, he could shut out the high-rises on the extreme edge of the city, that dark district that was dangerous by day and by night, strewn with litter and flaked with plaster from crumbling walls.

Mistakes had been made.

The man drove on. The pain in his hand had eased, and it wasn't too badly swollen. He shouldn't have tried to snatch the cap off the boy — no wonder he'd been so scared.

As the car slowly descended the slope, he turned on the radio, just in time to catch the news. If the traffic report was bad, he would take a different route; he knew some shortcuts.

". . . the police are asking for information," the announcer was saying. "Twelve-year-old Hugo Haldur has been missing from a hospital in the north of South Island since yesterday morning. Hugo is wearing a checkered jacket that is several sizes too big and a beige-colored cap. He suffers from a rare disease and is urgently in need of medical attention. He is mentally confused and, as such, unable to give any indication of his identity or origin. Hugo is also probably very frightened, so the police are asking that no attempt be made to communicate with him. Anyone with any information concerning Hugo's whereabouts in the last twenty-four hours is asked to contact the police at the following number . . ."

The man braked. "Hugo Haldur!" he said out loud. He took his hand off the steering wheel and looked at the blue marks where the boy's teeth had sunk into the ball of his thumb. "It all adds up. And there's stupid old me, scaring him even more!"

He pulled over onto the side of the road and took his cell phone out of the glove compartment. Then he called his boss to tell him that he would be an hour late for the meeting, and explained why.

After that, he phoned the police.

Throughout the afternoon, Jenna had been practicing with Mrs. Markas and Tobias. Stepping out onto the balcony, smiling, waving, walking past a crowd as it cheered and offered her flowers (Raphael played the part of the crowd).

"It's as if you've done it your whole life!" Tobias exclaimed at the end of three hours of rehearsal. "Keep your wig on, and I don't see how you can fail."

"So you think I'm right for the part?" asked Jenna. "I mean, I haven't had to say a word yet."

"No, whatever happens, you must stay as quiet as a mouse," said Tobias. "Is that clear? Tomorrow you're *not* to *say* a *single* word, not even when they mob you. A smile is enough."

Then Jenna was allowed to take off her wig and her heels and carefully remove her contact lenses. Tobias and Mrs. Markas left her.

She took out her cell, switched it on, and found that she'd received one message while she'd been practicing.

Darling Jenna, Mom had written. **It's all so exciting! I hope you're really enjoying your time as a princess! I'm looking forward to hearing all about it when you come home. All my love, Mom**

Jenna checked her watch, then dialed her house. No answer. It was Saturday. Mom was probably teaching late.

Jenna knew that Mom didn't like being disturbed when she was working, but she just couldn't wait. And Mom would certainly be very proud of her.

She dialed and held the phone up to her ear. *"The person you are calling is not available at the moment,"* said the recorded message. Jenna pressed END. Stupid her — of course Mom's cell was always switched off when she was with a client.

She'd send her a text message, too, and Mom would read it after work.

Now look xactly like princess! wrote Jenna. **Everyone says I'm her double. Regent = strange. Looking 4wrd 2 2moro, not 2 scared. Will txt again tom nite! Jenna xoxo**

It would soon be suppertime. Just one more day in Scandia — and not even a full one.

Bizarre: She was actually beginning to feel sorry she was going home.

The headmistress bent over her desk. For hours she had been trying to concentrate on her work, and for hours her thoughts had been wandering elsewhere.

It never should have happened. How had the Little Princess managed to escape from the school? There were guards everywhere — not too conspicuous, because they mustn't disturb the girls when they were in class or at play, but still sufficiently well positioned to notice if any of them tried to leave the grounds.

The police assumed that the princess had been abducted, but there were no signs of that. The only vehicles that had entered the grounds that day had been the laundry van and the vicar's ancient car. The princess could have been smuggled through the gate in either of them (though the headmistress thought it highly unlikely), and so both had been seized and thoroughly examined, the laundry man sighing and the vicar raising his eyes to the heavens all the while.

The headmistress had been sworn to absolute secrecy. She couldn't even tell the vicar what he was suspected of. She had asked the housemistress to tell the girls that, as had often been the case before, Princess Malena was traveling abroad.

There had been no ransom demands, but of course there could be all kinds of reasons for a princess to be kid-napped — political, maybe; insurgents wanting to use her as a bargaining tool. The headmistress groaned, but not because she feared for her job: She just couldn't stand the thought that she would be held responsible if anything had happened to the princess.

When the telephone rang, she picked up the receiver even before the end of the first ring. Every minute now she was on tenterhooks, waiting for news.

"Hello?" The voice at the other end made her jump. "It's the regent here. I thought I'd call you personally to give you the news. Malena is back."

"Back?" exclaimed the headmistress. "Oh, thank goodness!"

"It was just a childish prank," said the regent. "Not a kidnapping or anything like that. She simply slipped out of the school. So now you can relax."

"Oh, thank goodness!" said the headmistress again. "But how . . . where did you . . . ?"

"We'll be in touch again in the next few days," said the regent. "But till then, please, complete secrecy, as before. Not a word to anyone. It wouldn't be good, as I'm sure you'll understand, if people began to learn that the princess had run away."

"No, no, of course not!" cried the headmistress. "I'm so relieved."

"Then I'll say good-bye," said the regent.

There was a click on the line. The conversation was over.

9

This time the makeup artist finished the job even more quickly. Mrs. Markas had made just a few adjustments to the wig and helped Jenna get dressed. Jenna thought the outfit itself was hideous, but it looked just like the ones young princesses wore on TV: a bit stiff, a bit dull, a bit too long, and a lot expensive. It would have been much more fun to put on a fairy-tale princess's dress, as she had done once for the school play when she was in grade school. Now she didn't even have a crown.

"A crown? Where do you think you are?" Mrs. Markas had cried. "Scandia is a modern country. The princess only wears her crown on formal occasions — when foreign heads of state come to visit, for instance. Today is just her birthday." Then she took Jenna into the bathroom to look in the full-length mirror.

Jenna gasped. Seeing herself in this unfamiliar, formal dress, she could almost have performed an old-fashioned curtsy to the girl in the mirror.

"It feels really strange," she whispered.

But at the same time she felt a tingle of pleasure — the kind of excitement she usually only experienced when she woke up on her own birthday, or when she was about to open her presents on Christmas, or when, like last winter, she'd been totally crushing on the new boy at school. Could anyone at home ever have believed that she could look so beautiful, and so royal? Could she have believed it herself?

But from now on, things would be different. She blew a kiss at the beautiful princess in the mirror, then turned to Mrs. Markas.

"I'm ready," she said.

Once again the four of them got into the limousine that had brought them to Osterlin. For a moment, Jenna was surprised there was no escort, no convoy of police and bodyguards, but then she realized that she wasn't on princess duty yet. Once they were in the capital, they would try to sneak her into the palace as discreetly as possible so that no one would notice the deception, and at the same time they'd smuggle the real princess out another door. Only when she was inside the palace would Jenna really "become" the princess; only then would she need bodyguards; and only then would the charade begin.

Through the tinted windows she tried to see as much as possible of "her" country. Jenna giggled. *My country*, she thought. Well, she should know what it looked like, at least!

Densely wooded hills extended almost to the outskirts of the city, and between them appeared the occasional flash of water — lakes or sheltered coves. The villages they passed through were small and cozy, and everything seemed clean and well cared for, as was only right and proper when the princess was celebrating her birthday.

It isn't just the cleanliness, thought Jenna as they drove down into the city. As she had noticed when she arrived, the tree-lined streets with their elegant white houses gave off an air of comfortable prosperity. The people were tall, fair-skinned, straight-teethed, and well dressed, and this Sunday they were all heading in the same direction. (The stream of pedestrians grew denser the farther they drove, and with a little shock Jenna realized where they were all going — to the palace.) There was no sign of poverty anywhere: no boarded-up store windows like there were on some of the streets at home; no litter on the sidewalks or in the gutters; no empty bottles in the bushes; no plastic bags in the tree branches; no peeling plaster. Instead, there were just beautiful flowerbeds, freshly painted buildings, and large, well-polished cars parked in front of them.

"Is it like this everywhere?" asked Jenna.

Mrs. Markas was in the middle of talking to Tobias. "What?" she asked, frowning.

"Everything here is so . . . beautiful," said Jenna. "So rich! Is it like this everywhere?"

Mrs. Markas smiled. "This is Scandia, Jenna," she said. "Ours is a prosperous country. On North Island there are mineral deposits that won't run out for many generations, and farther out at sea there are oil rigs. We have factories and the most up-to-date technology. Every Scandian has a healthy income, and every Scandian is financially secure." She nodded to Jenna. "And *all* Scandians love their princess."

Jenna leaned back. *My country*, she thought again.

They drove slowly down a narrow street, past a long, high wall, until the driver suddenly swung the steering wheel around sharply. An inconspicuous door in the wall had opened at precisely the moment they'd reached it, and the car had hardly passed through when it locked itself behind them.

"The palace!" said Mrs. Markas, and again Jenna could hear the pride in her voice.

But Jenna didn't need a news flash: It was pretty obvious what the immense turreted building was. Enclosed by the wall was a huge park that, Jenna could tell, had been there for hundreds of years. There were tall trees with massive crowns, broad expanses of lawn, and big beds of roses. As they approached the rear of the palace, they came to a formal garden with gravel paths, manicured hedges, and cascading fountains.

"It's beautiful!" gasped Jenna.

The car came to a halt right in front of a narrow side door.

"We'll go through the kitchen," Tobias said from the passenger seat. "Then no one will see us — and if anyone does, they won't ask questions. Now remember, Jenna, you're *not* to *say* a *word*. You can smile — smile as much as you like. But stay quiet. Quiet as a mouse!"

Jenna nodded. She would at least have liked to know how the princess's voice sounded, but to speak would be risky, the biggest risk of all — Tobias, with all his "quiet as a mouse" commands, had made that perfectly clear! And if she was to cross paths with the cook or the gardener, how could she possibly come up with the right words to make her sound like a princess? She didn't even know which of the palace servants the princess knew, and whether she spoke to them formally or informally.

To show Tobias and Mrs. Markas how seriously she took the warning, she pressed her finger against her lips.

The low passage behind the door looked surprisingly normal, even a little shabby, with its worn tiles, and when Tobias opened the door at the end, Jenna was met with the smell of roasting meat and all sorts of spices.

"Excuse us, everyone. Don't let us disturb you," Tobias said politely, and maneuvered their little procession between cavernous ovens, vast pots, and huge steel worktops. "Our birthday girl wanted to have a breath of fresh air before getting down to the serious business."

For the first time, Jenna experienced what it was like to have people bowing to her. The women made a deep curtsy, and right next to her a girl who was certainly no older than Jenna banged her knee on the hard stone floor. "Oh, I'm sorry, I'm sorry, Your Highness," she gasped, without looking at Jenna. Jenna could hear the fear in her voice.

Embarrassed, she held out her hand to help her up, but the girl's dark eyes filled with panic and she shook her head violently.

Jenna flushed red. *A princess mustn't do such things*, she thought. *If a princess tries to help someone up, they'll be scared. But at last there's someone here who looks like me — someone with dark hair and honeyed skin, too.*

"Your Royal Highness," said a stout woman wearing a cook's hat with a few reddish curls peeping out from underneath. "Kaira hasn't been with us for very long. The silly girl is fresh from the North Scandian forests, and I beg your forgiveness on her behalf. All of us here in the kitchen wish you a wonderful, wonderful day, and for the coming year we hope that it . . . that it . . ." She hesitated. Then she went on talking so quickly that her tongue almost tripped over itself: ". . . that it will be much, much happier than the last one, Your Royal Highness. You'll get over it, Your Highness. My sister-in-law died when my nephew was just eleven . . ."

Jenna stared at her. She had no idea what the woman was talking about, but it didn't seem the right moment to react with a smile.

"Goodness me, cook, we haven't got time for your life story," Tobias intervened. "The princess thanks you from the bottom of her heart for your good wishes. All of you. But now we really do have to go upstairs — the regent awaits."

Jenna smiled on cue. *This* was definitely the right moment for smiling! And the dark-eyed girl who had knocked her knee while curtsying received a special twinkle.

꧁

It was not until she entered the large salon and heard the shouts and the hum of the crowd down below in the square that Jenna realized no one they'd met on their way through the palace had noticed anything out of the ordinary. Even though the servants and staff must see the princess almost every day, all of them had bowed or curtsied to her (most of them more skillfully than the little kitchen maid), and had called out their birthday wishes. *Now I really am Princess of Scandia,* thought Jenna, brimming with happiness. *I've got to call Mom as soon as all this is over, before I fly back tonight. I am Princess Malena of Scandia, and I feel like a superstar! It's almost as if I'd never been anyone else. With fake hair and a fake face and a fake figure, I definitely don't feel like the old, shy Jenna. I don't even care what happens with the movie. It's this, this moment, right now, that counts. Nobody I know has ever experienced anything like it, and it's the most wonderful thing. Ever!*

"Jenna," said the regent, breaking into her thoughts. He was standing with the director behind a large desk, holding a glass of cognac in his hand. "My word, you look wonderful!"

Jenna felt a little thrill. She waited to see if he would come across to her again, stroke her cheek, and stammer her name. But this time he stayed on the other side of the room and just smiled at her.

"You know what's next," he said. "The two of us will go out together onto the balcony, with Mrs. Markas, Tobias, and Bolström behind us, and the bodyguards as well, of course. There's nothing to worry about, we have snipers at almost every window, and there are enough security men down below — the first rows behind the police barricades consist almost entirely of our people. We've allocated extra space to the North Scandians quite far back, because of course we can't stop them from coming. Perhaps we shouldn't even try. Those who have come to cheer you on your birthday — who want to cheer Malena — are loyal to the crown, we can be sure of that."

"Let's hope so," Tobias muttered through clenched teeth.

Jenna looked at the regent. Once again, she found herself clueless as to what was being referred to, but it couldn't have been important for her role, could it? Otherwise Mrs. Markas and Tobias would have told her about it before.

"Don't start worrying the girl about all that as well!" said Bolström, the director, with a forced smile. Jenna now realized why it looked so insincere. It reminded her of the fake smiles she'd seen in TV commercials and magazine ads. "Jenna, when you're on the balcony with the regent, first of all you'll simply wave to the crowd. They'll cheer and shout 'Hooray, hooray for Malena!' or something like that. You'll listen to them for a while, smile, smile, smile, and keep waving. Do you understand?"

"I've been practicing with Tobias and Mrs. Markas," Jenna answered.

The director nodded. "Then you'll have to do your first stint of acting, and it'll be something that I know will be quite difficult for a girl of your age," he said. "But there will be several scenes like this in the script, and so I'm sure you understand it's of vital importance that you act it out convincingly today. When you've been waving for a while — smiling and waving — Norlin here, the regent, will suddenly come to you and take you in his arms! This is completely against protocol, but the regent and his niece are very close, and the people know that, so they'll be waiting for this gesture. We need you to lay your head on his chest and snuggle up to him as if you needed protection — that's what the princess would do. Just imagine that Norlin is the only person you have left in this whole world, the only one and the dearest one. That's the look we're after. Can you do that, Jenna? We'll all be watching you."

Jenna nodded. Now all the tension returned. If only it had been another man! She knew it was just pretend and not real, and that actresses did it every day. But why, of all people, did it have to be the regent, the man who had already behaved like such a weirdo toward her?

But he isn't being weird now, she reprimanded herself. *Today he seems almost normal. I'm sure I can "snuggle up" to him OK for a few moments, even with a thousand people watching. Piece of cake. I'm just being silly.*

"No problem," said Jenna.

The director smiled. "Then let the battle commence!" he said and, with a dramatic flourish, flung open the French doors.

The night had been terrible. Even now, in the summer, the nights on South Island were generally still cool, and the conspicuous checkered jacket, though warm, had had to be abandoned on a bench. Obviously it would provide the police with a clue, but it was still far enough away from Liron's home, and from the bench the trail could lead in any direction.

The child pulled the cap down low. It was best to be careful here; blonde hair was not universally liked, and some people were all too quick with their baseball bats.

Between the high-rise buildings, a few people dressed in their Sunday best were heading toward the center of town for the birthday celebrations of the Little Princess. Their route took them past dumpsters, overflowing or upended; past concrete walls smeared with graffiti; past shattered windows.

It was an appalling place to live, and considered to be proof of the inferiority of the North Scandians that they felt most at home amid such filth, that they couldn't control their children, that even after years spent in the south they hadn't managed to adapt to the southern way of life. After the situation had been ignored for many years, the king himself had pointed out in interviews how difficult conditions were for the northerners when they came to the south, with nothing except their willingness to work and their desire to build a new life for themselves. Recently, however, there had been a number of television exposés in which the camera focused on the mountains of trash and zoomed in on dark-skinned youths wearing gangster gear, making rude gestures, and uttering obscenities in their distinctive North Scandian dialect. The simple fact was that northerners were seen as a problem by the people of the south, and that the king — however much his people loved him — had not always handled the situation wisely. Now that the situation had made the news, viewers breathed a sigh of relief. If only these dark-haired migrants had just stayed in the north — everyone knew there was enough work for them in the mines and on the oil rigs — and if they'd stayed in their own areas of the city and been content to do what work was generously offered to them, it could have been bearable. But, as the TV reports and newspaper stories proved, the northerners just could not behave properly, and the limit of the southerners' patience had been reached.

The kid in the cap looked cautiously in all directions before slipping through a half-open door, the glass of which had obviously disappeared a long time ago, and entering one of the apartment buildings. A pile of vomit pooled in the hallway, the elevator was out of order, and raw wires stuck out of the wall where the illuminated apartment numbers should have been.

The stairs were the only way up. Not until the ninth floor did a number at the end of a long, dark corridor — in which the bulbs in the ceiling lights had burned out months ago — reveal that the traveler was safe at last.

After the doorbell had been buzzed, it was some time before the door opened.

"Yes! I knew it!" Liron laughed. "Hugo Haldur!" With a swift movement he pulled his visitor into the apartment and closed the door. The dark corridor was empty once more.

10

*T*he crowd cheered.

The moment the regent thrust open the glass door, the noise mounted, and when Jenna finally stepped out onto the balcony, her ears buzzed with the tumult.

It was no mere thousand people gathered in the palace square and along the broad boulevard — how could she have been so naïve? *Tens* of thousands had come to congratulate their princess on her birthday. As far as the eye could see stretched an ocean of blond heads and waving flags, half white and half blue with a pine tree in the middle — Scandia's national emblem.

Jenna gasped for air. If Mrs. Markas had not been standing behind her and given her a nudge in the back to keep her moving forward, she would have turned around and fled.

"Smile!" hissed Mrs. Markas. "Keep smiling, Jenna! Wave! Just like we practiced!"

Jenna forced herself to look over the balustrade at the crowd. *They're all down there*, she said boldly to herself, *and*

I'm up here. No one can do any harm to me, and no one wants to do any harm to me, and even if they do, they don't mean it for me personally. The cheers aren't for me, or the waving or the flags, so why am I freaking out? It's not half as bad as trying to walk the balance beam in gym class. For that, you need courage. For this, not so much! Get a grip, Jenna.

She stepped up to the balustrade and raised her right arm to wave. The cheers redoubled.

"Ma-le-na! Ma-le-na!" roared the crowd. "Hooray! Hurrah! Hurrah!"

It's just like being a rock goddess, thought Jenna, and smiled and waved and smiled. *No one at home is ever going to believe me when I tell them about this. But there are bound to be photos and newspaper articles and videos I can use as proof. Though maybe no one will believe that the blonde girl at the royal palace is me.*

She began to look more closely at the scene in front of her.

Among the flags streamed the occasional banner, cobbled together from bedsheets tied to broomsticks and held up on both sides by cheering people. On one that was fluttering high above the heads she could see *Malena for Queen* (um, wasn't that self-evident since she was now princess?), and another urged her to *Be Brave, Malena.* But why did she need to be brave?

And on the edges of the crowd there were also banners for sale, professionally printed and all with the same slogan: *Malena and Norlin — A Strong Team!*

Jenna turned to look at the regent, who stood waving beside her. He had the advertising smile on his face, just like the director earlier, and Jenna realized that at this moment her own face must have looked exactly the same. She turned back to the balustrade and went on waving.

Some distance away from the palace she could make out a group of people in the crowd whose heads shone dark amid the sea of fair hair. Their flags looked different, too, and were considerably more DIY than the professional banners in the nearer groups but, since they were so far away, Jenna couldn't read what was written on them.

"Now!" Bolström suddenly hissed behind her. "Now! Norlin! Now!"

The regent turned away from the crowd and took a step toward Jenna.

"Malena," he said, and gazed tenderly into her eyes. "My little Malena." He held out his arms and pulled her to him. Jenna remembered the weird way he'd acted the day before, and felt herself turning red. She started to sweat. "May your next year be happier than the last one! Whatever I can do to make it so, I will do."

For a second, Jenna's body stiffened, but then she recalled what the director had told her and tried to relax. She let her head sink down onto the regent's chest and breathed in the scent of his expensive aftershave. It was a pleasant smell, but all the same, the whole scene was making her nauseous.

"Enough!" hissed Bolström behind them. "Enough! Let go!"

Gently Norlin loosened his grip, then bowed to Jenna and kissed her on the forehead.

"Wave!" Bolström stage-whispered. "You, too, Jenna! Wave!"

Jenna took a deep breath. It was silly to be so sensitive. Down below, "her subjects" were waving and cheering. Jenna waved and smiled back at them.

"She looks better than she did at the funeral," said the man who had hurried with his wife to catch the bus. "Not so desperately unhappy. She's even got a tan. And she's fatter. Put on some weight — that's a good sign. Though I'd never have thought she would get over it so quickly."

"Oh, you men!" said his wife, nudging him playfully on the arm with her flag. "You see how well she gets along with her uncle? You didn't believe me, did you?"

Then she waved her flag high above her head again.

"Long live Malena!" she cried. "Long live the Princess of Scandia!"

Later, Jenna and the regent were driven along the main boulevard at walking pace. They sat in the open backseat of a glossy black limousine, with cheering crowds on either side and an escort of policemen on motorbikes and mounted cavalry officers in old-fashioned uniforms. Jenna could still feel her knees trembling. She didn't think she could have stayed out on the balcony much longer, but in the car she was beginning to recover.

She was waving and smiling, like the regent beside her, when he leaned his head close to hers.

"It's more tiring than one thinks, little Jenna, eh?" he said. "Especially at the beginning, when it's all so new."

Jenna nodded. She knew she must remain as "quiet as a mouse," but surely here in the car no one could hear her.

"Why did you call me Malena up there on the balcony?" she asked, still waving to the crowd. "Why did you do that when no one could hear you?"

Norlin laughed. "There are lip-readers in Scandia!" he said. "And there may even have been hidden microphones, though of course we had the area thoroughly searched in advance. But you can be sure that there were those down in the square deciphering every word I said to you."

As they rounded a bend, they suddenly came to a group of dark-haired people standing along the right side of the road. Policemen tried to force them away from the car and confiscate their banners before Jenna could see them, but there were too many. She was able to read a few before the police took them. *Long Live Malena!* said one. *Down with Discrimination Against the North!* said another. Jenna tried to remember what "discrimination" meant, but she wasn't sure. *Malena, Protector of North Island!* proclaimed the next banner, and *Down with the Traytor!* yet another. Malena had no idea what traitor they were referring to, though she did immediately notice that the word had been misspelled.

"Wave all the same," whispered Norlin, and then Jenna wondered what *that* meant. "Most of them are harmless. Good, we're out of it now."

The regent leaned back and breathed deeply in and out. "We have to be careful," he said, as if an explanation was necessary. "You never know if one of them might . . ."

At this moment, about a hundred feet ahead of them, a lone figure ducked under the arms of a policeman and dashed out of the crowd at lightning speed. "Malena!" the boy cried, waving his arms wildly. "Hey, Mali! It's me! Mali! Yesterday, what was up with that?"

Two policemen seized him roughly by the shoulders and dragged him back behind the barricades.

"Mali!" screamed the boy. He was small and dark, and about the same age as Jenna. "Call me!"

Then, as if he'd done it a hundred times before, he stabbed his elbows into the stomachs of his two stupefied guards and disappeared into the crowd.

Jenna stiffened.

"Who was that?" she asked, startled. "What did he want?"

"Smile!" hissed the regent beside her. "Wave! That's exactly what I was talking about — you always have to expect some unpleasant incident like that. There are always the crazies who think you love them, and who are in love with you.

Every king has to put up with it, and every princess. People who follow you around and never leave you in peace. Now you've seen it for yourself. Fortunately our security usually works pretty well." He smiled at the crowd. "But what happened there," he said, in a tone that didn't fit his facial expression at all, "will have its consequences. Security guards who can't stop a single boy . . ."

Jenna waved. She was beginning to think that it might not always be so nice to be a princess.

1 1

They had driven around in a wide circle to return to the front of the palace, where the large crowd was gradually dispersing. They switched cars behind the wall in the park, and the regent clumsily stroked Jenna's hair.

"Good-bye, little Jenna," he said, and his voice sounded hoarse. "You acted your part very well."

"Thank you for letting me do it in the first place," Jenna responded politely. "And please give my best wishes to the princess." She was glad that she wouldn't have to deal with him anymore. The man was strange.

Her stay in Scandia was over. Just one more hour, maybe two, and she would be sitting on the plane, flying over forests, lakes, and the North Sea on her way back home — back to normal, everyday life.

Only on the way to Osterlin, sitting next to Mrs. Markas in the rear of the car, did she realize how absentminded she'd been. "We could have brought my bag with us from Osterlin this morning," she said, slapping her forehead. "Then we could have gone straight to the airport."

"It's not very far to the mansion," Mrs. Markas said coolly. "You've still got to change your dress, and Bolström will certainly want to have a tête-à-tête with you."

"Oh, right, of course," said Jenna. The movie had completely slipped her mind; she'd totally forgotten that everything she'd seen and done these past two days — those minutes on the balcony, the drive through the city, the smiling and waving and the crowds — had only been a test, nothing but an unusual way of casting.

She leaned back. Some of the streets were still barricaded because of the crowds. The driver grumbled, and had to change his route.

Here, too, the houses were white and well kept, nestled in tree-lined streets, and with large, expensive cars parked beneath them. What Mrs. Markas had told her was true: Scandia was a wealthy country, and no one was excluded from its prosperity.

"And here, on the right-hand side," said Mrs. Markas, pointing to a long building on the water's edge that looked at least a hundred years old, "is the parliament building. The kingdom of Scandia has had a parliament for a very long time."

"Oh, really?" said Jenna. Although she was not particularly interested in politics, the building itself was magnificent — sandstone with intricate carvings, ledges, friezes, and gargoyles that reminded her of cathedrals she had seen on the History Channel.

The driver swung the car around to the left. Behind the parliament building, just a few steps away, was a huge crater — much the same size as the building next to it — in a scorched grassy area, sealed off from the road by red-and-white plastic tape. The trees and shrubs around the edges of the area were blackened, and stretched their singed branches like dark, bare arms up toward the sky. In some places, they had been felled, sawn into foot-long pieces, and stacked on the ground.

"What happened there?" asked Jenna. The car crossed a bridge over a narrow inlet, and the parliament building receded into the distance. The crater could no longer be seen. "It looked like . . . a meteorite crashed there."

People could be killed by meteorites; it was said that the dinosaurs had been wiped out when a gigantic one struck earth millions of years ago, where the Gulf of Mexico was now. Jenna remembered how, when she was a little girl who loved dinosaurs, she had heard about this and had been so scared that for weeks she couldn't sleep because she was afraid a huge rock might fall out of the blue, right on top of her house.

"No, no, nothing to worry about," said Mrs. Markas, and looked out her window, as if that was an adequate reply to Jenna's question.

Jenna waited. "But what did happen there?" she asked eventually.

Mrs. Markas didn't answer, but instead Tobias turned around from the front seat.

"You're right, Jenna," he said. "It does look like the sort of hole a meteorite would make. It's a huge crater. We didn't actually want you to see it, because we didn't want you to worry, though to be honest there's really nothing for you to worry about. Nothing at all." He smiled at her, then stated, "Rebels made it. People who aren't satisfied with anything in our wonderful country and are trying to spread fear and terror everywhere. But, thankfully, there are only a few of them at present. And they'll be duly punished."

Jenna nodded. She wasn't worried. Scandia's problems weren't hers, and anyway, she was practically already home.

"What do you mean there's no trace of him?" asked the regent. He swallowed his cognac in a single gulp. He had not offered any to the Chief of Police.

"I mean there's no trace of him," said the chief, and gave a small bow — a little too small, perhaps; it could have given the impression that his respect for the head of state was not very great.

"Weren't his clothes conspicuous enough?" asked the regent. "And weren't we informed yesterday that he'd hitched a ride here from the north, and that he must be somewhere very close to the city by now? Surely it can't be so difficult to track down a twelve-year-old boy. What are your officers doing about it?"

The Chief of Police looked him straight in the eye. "Today, nearly all of our officers were on duty to provide security for the princess on her birthday," he said. "And yesterday it was for all the preparations. We've brought men here from all over the country. At least we were able to redeploy those who'd been hunting for the princess, now that she's turned up again of her own accord, thank goodness. With hindsight, it's just as well that, in accordance with your wishes, Your Royal Highness, we didn't carry out a nationwide search and worry the people unnecessarily over her disappearance. In any case, when it came to searching for the boy, we simply didn't have very many men to spare. Especially since there's obviously no kidnapper involved, but just a . . ." The chief paused to glance at Norlin. ". . . a perfectly normal boy who's run away from a hospital. Your interest in him, Your Highness, is therefore somewhat . . . surprising."

"Nevertheless!" snapped the regent, helping himself to another glass of cognac. "We must have some idea where he was heading."

"We did find his jacket, Your Highness," the Chief of Police reported. "You'll be interested to learn that there were some hairs on it, which we're processing for DNA. We'll have the results soon."

"Hair," murmured the regent.

"According to the driver, it was long and blond," said the Chief of Police, straining to read the regent's expression, but he looked away quickly. "Of course, it might have come from a wig; that's to be determined. And we will also search the area where it was found, now that we've got enough manpower available, Your Highness."

But by now the regent was no longer listening to him.

They reached Osterlin in the light of late afternoon, and Jenna marveled at the sheer beauty of the countryside surrounding the estate — the hills and fields, still shining green, the sun's reflections in the lakes, the forests. She and Mom had never had a real vacation. They couldn't afford to take the time off, no matter where Mom was working — and sometimes, of course, she had been out of work. Only since she had launched her modest business of etiquette lessons had they been relatively comfortable.

Jenna didn't know much about the world outside her own home, and she had certainly never seen anything as breathtaking as this. "It really is a beautiful country," she said, and Mrs. Markas nodded contentedly.

Jenna was surprised at how confident she was that she would be acting in the movie. Was there anyone who could play the part of the princess better than her? Doubtful! *They were right that I didn't need to recite anything first*, thought Jenna. *Other things are way more important.*

She got out of the car and stretched. Then she turned to Mrs. Markas. "Should I go and pack . . . ?"

"Jenna dear!" Bolström exclaimed. He had left ahead of them, and now came striding across the courtyard toward her. "I must congratulate you on your star-is-born performance! We always thought you were right for the part, but we never would have dreamed that you'd do it so perfectly the first time out, right off the bat. I can only congratulate you."

"Why, thank you," Jenna said, blushing. One should look people in the eye when talking to them, but now she was much too embarrassed. She stared down at the ground.

"And so, Jenna dearest," said Bolström, affectionately putting his arm around her shoulder and steering her to a bench. "I'd now like to be so bold as to make a request. Well, in actual fact, it's the regent who's making the request. I've been on the phone to him the entire drive back from the city, and we are both in agreement. Now the only question is whether you will say yes."

His arm lay loosely on her shoulder, and Jenna turned to him. "What is it?" she asked.

Bolström smiled. "Please, sit down," he said. "Now then, we flew you here so we could go through this unusual casting process, and that's why we didn't tell you very much about Scandia and the princess. But now, because you've proved yourself to be such a good actress, it could be that it might lead to a greater role — provided, of course, that you agree — and so we need to tell you a bit more about her."

"Lead to a greater role?" Jenna repeated, puzzled.

"You see, Jenna," Bolström continued, "the princess has been going through a terribly difficult time." He sounded more serious now. "Her mother died when she was born, but her father the king took such loving care of her that there was never any major problem. She got older, carried out more and more of the duties that are expected of a princess, and the country loved her."

Jenna nodded.

"But then," said Bolström, "just two months ago, a tragedy occurred. One night, quite unexpectedly, her father died, too."

"Her father, too?" Jenna echoed. She realized that it was a good thing they hadn't told her any of this. She would never have known how to act the part of a princess who has just lost her father.

"He always worked very hard," Bolström explained. "He was an exemplary king. His heart simply couldn't keep up with it, even though he wasn't an old man. He just took on too much. We laid him to rest just a few weeks ago."

"The poor princess," whispered Jenna.

Bolström gave a tired smile. "Yes, she took it very badly," he said. "She hasn't been the same since. She's withdrawn, and cries often. Her uncle, the regent, felt that at such a difficult time one shouldn't ask too much of her, and so he took over all her official duties himself. And the princess was grateful."

He sighed. "So neither he nor the princess had any objections when I suggested that we use the birthday as a test for my potential star actress. They were both convinced that the stress and strain of the day, and especially driving through the very same streets where only two months ago Malena followed her father's coffin, would be too much for the princess herself."

"Poor princess," Jenna whispered again.

"Well, she's starting to recover," Bolström went on. "Thanks to your help, Jenna, she was able to celebrate her birthday in a secret location far away from the city, and Norlin, who's been on the phone to her several times — of course he'd have loved to be at her little private party, but you can understand why that wasn't possible — he says that she sounded more relaxed and happy than she has since her father died."

"Yes, I understand," murmured Jenna, thinking to herself that no, she didn't really understand at all.

"But now," said Bolström, "you're flying home, and in just a week's time the same thing will be required of the princess all over again: She will have to stand on the balcony and smile, give interviews, face the cameras, and drive through the streets. An important new law is to be signed by the head of state, and even though it's the regent's signature that's required to make it valid, not Malena's — because she's underage — the people will still want to know that she's agreed to it, and they'll want to see her and cheer her.

You've seen for yourself how the people love the princess."

"Yes," Jenna whispered again. She knew what he was going to ask her even before he said it.

"But how can she fully recover in a week?" asked Bolström. "I'm sure you will agree that it is very unlikely the princess will have regained her strength enough in such a short amount of time . . ."

"You want me to do it again?" asked Jenna. "The whole thing, again?"

"A repeat performance. An encore. It was the princess's own idea," said Bolström. "Malena, our unhappy Little Princess, begs you with all her heart to do it. She needs to be spared for a while more, to rest, and you are such a marvelous understudy, Jenna," he explained with a smile, "that you would make her very happy if you would agree to do it."

"So you want me to come back next weekend?" asked Jenna. In a week's time it would be the end of the school year. If she accepted the offer, she would be going away for a summer vacation for the first time in her life! "Will you come and get me again?"

"Not *come back*, Jenna," Bolström replied, and now he gently placed his hand on her forearm. "If you like — but only if you like — we would be very happy if you would *stay*."

1 2

The problem was Mom.

Jenna was sitting on the four-poster bed in her room, minus the wig and contact lenses, in her own clothes. She was herself again, and she was gazing at her cell phone, which she had taken out of her jeans pocket a while ago.

She had no doubt that she wanted to do it, now that she had calmed down, now that she had proved to herself that she could act the part of the princess convincingly, and — to be totally honest with herself — now that she had experienced how nice it was to feel the love and admiration of a crowd of people, even though deep down she knew it wasn't really for her.

"I'd be crazy not to do it," she murmured to herself. The French doors were wide open, and from the park she could hear birds singing. She thought about how scared she'd been on her first evening here. Everything had been so foreign and unfamiliar, but now that she had dared to do something out of the ordinary for the first time in her life, and with Mom having actually allowed her to take the plunge, it had paid off, big time! She no longer felt like the old Jenna. After the day's events, she felt just a little bit like Malena. She wondered how much of it would stay with her once she was back home.

But now everything depended on Mom. Mom wouldn't want her to miss the last week of school — even though everybody knew that nothing important ever went on then. They would just play games — "educational" games in some subjects, and silly, time-killing games in others. The English teacher would read something aloud; the music teacher would let them play with the percussion instruments; and everyone — students and teachers alike — would simply be counting down the days.

As for her report card, Bea could take it, in a sealed envelope with the school stamp.

There was really no good reason why Jenna should have to go to school for those five days.

She reached for her cell phone. This time a text message would not be enough; she had to talk to Mom, even if she was in the middle of an etiquette lesson. On a Sunday afternoon! She would tell Mom how much she was enjoying it all, that, not to worry, it wasn't dangerous at all — that it was even *less* dangerous than when she biked from home to school (which, oddly enough, Mom had always let her do).

Jenna keyed in **MOM** and waited. The phone rang and rang and rang. Sunday or not, Mom must have still had clients with her.

"Please don't be angry!" Jenna blurted out as soon as a loud rushing noise at the other end indicated that Mom had accepted the call. "Mom? It's me, Jenna. I know I'm not supposed to disturb you, but I've got to . . ."

Through the rushing sound she heard a voice speaking quickly and emphatically, though she could only make out a few words. "A taxi from the airport," she deciphered, "unfortunately not till about eleven."

So Mom would be occupied for quite a long time.

In which case perhaps she wouldn't miss Jenna all that much, anyway.

"Mom, I want to tell you all about it!" Jenna cried into the phone. In the courtyard, the last rays of the afternoon sun were falling on the cobblestones, making them gleam. "I don't want to come home just yet. Can you hear me? They've asked me to . . ."

Someone said something at the other end, but this time Jenna couldn't even make out any individual words. In between, even the static rushing stopped, as if the connection had been cut completely.

"Mom!" shouted Jenna. "I can't hear you. I'm supposed to do it all again next week. Because it went so well. I'd really, really like to do it."

It was hopeless. The connection was too bad.

"Bye, Mom," cried Jenna. "I'll text you. And please don't be angry. It's really great here."

Then she pressed END.

Mom, she wrote. **Pls pls say yes! Princess & uncle want me 2 stay anoth week. Princess v sad—father died 2 mos ago. I can help her. Having fab time, they think I'm doing xtra well. Pls Mom! Pls?! Luv, Jenna xoxoxo**

Mom always says people must help one another, thought Jenna, trying to ignore her guilty conscience. *She's got to let me stay.*

The answer came at once.

More details, please! Mom

It took Jenna three texts to do so. She hoped that Mom's client wouldn't be too annoyed by the interruption. But who wouldn't be sympathetic once they heard what it was all about?

She went out onto the bedroom's balcony and looked over the courtyard while she waited for the beep. A whole week in this room, in this house, in this park. It might even get boring. But it would be a different boredom from the sort she'd be feeling at home. There, everybody would be leaving on Saturday — even Bea — and there'd be nothing left to do except read, watch TV, and go to the public pool (probably alone), as she did every . . . single . . . summer.

Oh Jenna, wrote Mom (she really had mastered those capital letters now), **in that case I suppose I can't say no. But you must come home in a week's time. Take care of yourself. I miss you. Mom**

Jenna threw her head back and spread her arms out wide. In a moment Mrs. Markas would be coming to ask her if she would stay.

But first she must send a quickie text to her BF, Bea.

"That. Is. Insane!" Bea exclaimed. "Mom, Dad, you've *got* to check this, quick!"

She was sitting on the living-room sofa with one hand full of nuts from the bowl of munchies that her mother always put out on the coffee table on Sunday evenings when they watched whatever movie of the week was on. It was the only show the three of them still watched together and, to be honest, most of the time Bea only watched it to be nice to her parents. But she still liked snuggling up on the sofa with them *sometimes*.

The news was on now.

"What's the matter?" asked her mother, rushing into the living room with a dish towel in her hand. "Good heavens, I thought something terrible had happened! What on earth am I doing standing there alone in the kitchen drying dishes while you're sitting here stuffing your face with nuts?"

Bea didn't bother to answer. "They were just showing the Princess of Scandia's birthday," she said. "You missed it!"

"Scandia, now that's a very peculiar country," said her father, who had also appeared in the doorway, balancing a basket of wet laundry on his hip. Bea had to admit to feeling slightly guilty at that moment, since she was the only member of the family lounging on the sofa eating nuts and doing nothing to help with the housework. But, then again, if she hadn't been, she'd have missed the TV report!

"Listen up, this is major!" Bea insisted. "The princess looked absolutely identical to Jenna — seriously! — except she's blonde. But her face was *identical*."

"That's what you're watching?" said her father in disbelief, and disappeared back into the hallway with his basket. "You'd be better off showing some interest in Scandia's political situation — now that's 'major.' I'm just going to hang up these wet socks before the movie starts. Save me some nuts, please. And see what the forecast is."

Bea rolled her eyes behind his back. "Mom, for real," she said. "The princess was, like, the clone of Jenna. The clone!"

Her mother raised her eyebrows. "I don't know why you're getting so worked up about it," she said. "Everyone looks like someone else. Now perhaps you wouldn't mind helping me with the dishes?"

Bea sank back into the sofa. "Um, I've got to watch the weather forecast for Dad," she said.

But as soon as her mother left the room, she grabbed the phone. She had to tell Jenna about this. Maybe she could catch the eleven o'clock news later and see her blonde double on TV. It was a crazy coincidence.

At about eight o'clock the wind picked up, and by nine it had turned into a gale. The trees in the park bowed their heads, and some branches broke off. Gray clouds scudded across the sky, making it seem as dark as night, and the wind howled like a wolf (not that Jenna had ever heard a wolf howl).

Jenna stood on the balcony overwhelmed with joy. She would have liked to sing a song straight into the eye of this storm. Suddenly it was as if absolutely nothing was impossible! She was Jenna the actress, Malena the princess — she was Jenna in bliss.

And how wonderful it was that at this moment she was *not* on her way home, sitting in the little private plane over the sea, being tossed around by the storm clouds! Everything had worked out perfectly.

Mrs. Markas and Tobias had not even been surprised when she'd told them that Mom had agreed; of course, they didn't know about Mom and her constant worrying.

"That's just what we'd hoped," Tobias said, and immediately sent a message to Bolström. By the evening he would also have given the news to the regent and the princess. Jenna would have liked to talk to her. Perhaps she could have comforted her. They could become friends, like Bea and herself. Though she wasn't sure that Bea really wanted to be her friend anymore, since she hadn't replied to any of the text messages she'd sent. *Perhaps*, thought Jenna — though it hardly seemed possible — *Bea might be jealous*.

It began to rain. The first drops fell, big heavy drops that Jenna could feel splashing one by one on her bare arms.

She stepped back a pace. She could hear the rain hitting the gravel — softly at first, but then ever louder, ever faster. She heard the pebbles grinding together under the weight of the water, and saw the drops jumping up again through the sheer force of the impact, as if they wanted to fly back into the clouds. It was the most powerful, most wonderful downpour she had ever seen. She stayed in the open doorway to watch and listen to it.

And then she heard him.

"Mali!" cried a boy's voice.

Jenna stepped out of the shelter of the doorway and took two paces forward. The rain immediately beat down upon her, and in just a few seconds her hair hung in wet strands. She bent over the balustrade and looked down.

"Hello!" she called softly.

"Mali!" cried the boy. He suddenly emerged from the dense shadows of a rhododendron bush and came and stood below the balcony, his head turned upward, his eyes half closed against the rain, which battered his face. "What happened before on the phone? You suddenly stopped talking."

Recognition cut through Jenna like a bolt of lightning. The regent had been right: The boy from earlier, who had managed to escape the clutches of the guards in the city before accosting them in the car — he was here now, the stalker boy who thought she loved him and he loved her. He had followed her, just as the regent had predicted.

"Why aren't you with Liron?" he called, wiping the rain away from his face with his forearm. "Why . . . ?"

Liron? thought Jenna.

Something was off. If the regent was right, the boy should have been talking about love. He should have been stammering out oaths of devotion, trying to clamber up the balcony to her, trying to embrace her, kiss her. Instead, he was talking about someone else . . .

"Liron?" she whispered. She must call for Tobias, because if the regent was right, the boy could be dangerous.

"So, what happened?" cried the boy. He sounded annoyed — confused and annoyed at the same time. "We waited for you the whole evening! We had the TV on because we thought they were sure to announce that the celebration was off — but nothing! And you didn't come, either, and then this morning you're sitting there in the limo with the Silver Fox as if nothing had happened!"

His words were difficult to make out in the rattle of the rain, but all the same Jenna suddenly knew that he was not crazy. Not crazy, and not in love.

She was almost disappointed.

So why was he here? For a moment she wondered what she should do. She ought to tell Tobias and Mrs. Markas. But she couldn't believe that the boy would do anything to harm her — not now. In fact, it sounded as if he really did know the princess, and might even be friends with her. But if that was the case, why didn't her uncle, the weird regent, know about it?

"Mali?" the boy cried again. "Why don't you come with me? The railings are a joke, and the dogs, well, you know I can handle them."

Jenna was still standing there, half leaning over the balcony while the boy looked up at her, waiting for her answer, when she saw a sudden flash of fear in his eyes. He started, turned, and began to run. He ran like a hare, dodging in and out of the trees as if he was being hunted. And then he was gone.

Once again the courtyard and the park beyond were deserted.

Jenna went back into her room and closed the glass doors. She took off her drenched clothes and turned on the shower — so hot that it was steaming.

She was shivering, and it wasn't just because the rain had soaked her to the skin.

Jonas had not dared to take the bus back into the city. And he didn't want to hitch a ride, either. If she had betrayed him — and of course she had betrayed him! — by now his description would be all over the news: thirteen-year-old boy, North Scandian in appearance.

When it was almost morning, and he was so exhausted from walking in the wind and rain that he couldn't care less whether or not they caught him, a truck drew up beside him.

"Well, now I've seen everything!" the driver declared, leaning out his window. "What's a shrimp like you doing all alone on the road at night, hmm?" Only then did he seem to see the dark hair — though, in the rain, everyone's hair is dark. The driver hesitated for a moment.

"I get it," he mumbled. "No money for the bus fare, hmm? Get in. You can keep me company. Otherwise I'll nod off — the tiredness is always worst toward morning."

Jonas took a deep breath. "Thank you," he muttered. Maybe the driver hadn't had his radio on and so hadn't heard about the search, though now soft music mingled with the noise of the motor.

"It's really no kind of weather to be wandering around in at night," said the driver. "Is everything all right?"

Jonas nodded, and the driver turned up the volume on the radio. A female voice reported on the princess's birthday, then came the weather forecast, the traffic bulletin, and then . . .

". . . twelve-year-old Hugo Haldur," said the announcer, "from a hospital in the north of South Island . . ."

Jonas began to tremble.

"They've been broadcasting that every hour for at least a day now," said the driver. The windshield wipers swept through the water, momentarily clearing the view of the night that stretched ahead. "At first I thought you might be him, but nobody could say you had long blond hair, hmm? Where do you want to go?" He turned down the volume.

Jonas leaned back. "Just to the city," he said in a low voice.

Jenna lay in her four-poster bed and stared at the canopy above her head.

Why hadn't she run to tell them about the boy in the bushes? Why hadn't she asked Tobias and Mrs. Markas if they knew anything about him? And above all, absolutely above all, what had scared the boy so much that he'd run away as if the Devil himself were after him?

Duh! thought Jenna. *Of course! It was ME that frightened him. He suddenly realized that I'm not Malena. Double duh! He suddenly saw that my hair is brown, not blonde, and that my eyes are brown, not blue. And, OK, that I'm too short and too fat to be her, too! But why would that make him so scared?*

She pulled her bedspread up to her chin. *I guess I'd be scared, too, if I was standing on Bea's patio and suddenly Bea wasn't Bea anymore,* she thought. *But who is that boy? Whoever he is, he's definitely not some psycho who thinks I'm in love with him!*

She closed her eyes and turned over on her side. *Something strange is going on,* she thought again. *Something is up for sure.*

She swung her legs out of bed. If she was lucky, Tobias and Mrs. Markas would still be awake. From a hook on the door hung the princess's robe. She took it down and wrapped it around her.

Until she knew who the boy was, she wouldn't be able to sleep, anyway.

PART TWO

13

*J*onas squeezed through the door, which Liron had opened barely a crack.

"It's not her!" he cried, shivering with cold in his wet clothes. "It was all a scam! She looks almost exactly like Mali, but it's not her!"

Liron pulled his son into the apartment and closed the door.

"I know," he said. "Put on some dry clothes, Jonas. I'll make you some hot chocolate."

Jonas stared at him. "You don't know anything!" he cried. "Did you hear me? The princess is not Mali — all this time it wasn't Mali. And it definitely wasn't her this morning at the birthday celebrations."

Liron glanced at his wristwatch. It was now long past midnight. "*Yesterday* morning," he said, and disappeared into the kitchen. "Now go and dry yourself off, Jonas. Otherwise you'll catch cold, and then you'll be no use to anybody."

Jonas leaped behind him and pummeled his back with his fists. "You're such an idiot!" he shouted. "Why won't you listen to what I'm saying? I don't care if I get a cold! If she's not Mali but looks like Mali, then who is she?"

Liron poured some milk into a small pot. "I told you to go and dry yourself."

Jonas sank down on the only kitchen stool. "It was all a big lie," he said flatly. "And now I'm really worried about Mali."

Liron spooned some chocolate powder from a tin, measured it out, and stirred it slowly into the pot. "Jonas, no worries," he said. "Mali is here."

Jenna's bare feet made practically no noise on the marble floor of the corridor. Wasn't it strange that she now felt so at home in this grand house? She turned a corner. Even the darkness didn't frighten her anymore. There was no light in the corridors, and nobody in the house apart from Tobias, Mrs. Markas, and herself. No chef, no servants, and no one to see to the garden. Why should there be? Osterlin hadn't been a royal residence for decades.

Tobias and Mrs. Markas would be in the side wing . . . in the library, at the end of the corridor. If they hadn't gone to bed yet, she would find them there.

Jenna suddenly stopped. Long before she reached the door, she heard voices.

"If I've said no, then it's not just no for one or two months!" cried the regent. His voice sounded agitated.

He must have arrived this evening, thought Jenna. That was a lucky break! Now she could ask him who the boy really was, and if he really did believe all that stuff he'd said about him being crazy. If she was to act the part of Malena, the Little Princess, she must also know who her friends were. And perhaps her enemies.

"Be sensible, Norlin!" said Bolström. Jenna knew it was him even without seeing him. She had almost reached the library now, and the door was slightly open. "The rebels are certainly not going to wait a second longer. Up until now everything's gone well — better than we could ever have imagined, in fact. The child has played her part fabulously well."

Jenna stood still. Although no one could see it, she felt a red glow spreading over her face and neck. Of course, they had all praised her before, but nevertheless it was nice to hear it again when they were talking about it among themselves. She knew she should now knock on the door and go in. Mom would have been shocked if she'd known that her daughter was eavesdropping on someone else's conversation — and a conversation about herself, no less.

"And she'll play it just as fabulously in a week's time, I'm sure of that. So you've achieved everything you set out to achieve. But as long as you have him . . ."

"No!" shouted the regent, and Jenna was astonished to hear the fear that echoed in his voice. "I simply don't want that. Even if he were to lead the rebels . . . even if they got more and more followers . . . no massacre. I'll have no massacre in my country."

Jenna pressed herself tightly against the wall. Gradually the blood ran out of her face, and she felt herself getting light-headed.

"Nobody's talking about a massacre, Your Highness." Mrs. Markas. She was there as well, then. "A massacre is what we want to avoid. Bolström is right: As long as he's living up there in the forest and only has to snap his fingers to let loose the rebels, then every day we have to be on the alert for —"

"Why not simply go for a straightforward solution?" Bolström intervened. "One bullet. He won't even know what hit him. And without him, they won't dare start anything. Good grief, Norlin! As regent it's your duty to protect your country. Do you want a civil war in which far more people would lose their lives? Hundreds, maybe thousands? That's what you would have to answer for, Norlin — those deaths would be on your conscience. *One* life, or *lots of lives*. If you just give me the go-ahead . . ."

"No!" Norlin cried again. His voice was cracking. "No execution. I'm telling you once and for all! We shall find another solution to the problem — if there even *is* a problem. Because there's no evidence he's going to attack us. Nothing's happened, despite the fact that we haven't executed him. He's not that powerful yet. I am the regent, and don't you forget it! And I say no."

"Norlin," said Bolström, "you're too sentimental for your own good."

Jenna turned to leave as quietly as possible. She had heard something she should never have heard. And no one must ever know.

As soon as she reached the wing where her room was located, she began to run. On reaching her door, she yanked it open and flung herself on her bed, then got up again and turned the key in the lock. She left the light burning and slipped under the covers. Her feet were like ice.

During the drive that afternoon Mrs. Markas had said there was nothing to fear from the rebels. And yet she hadn't wanted Jenna to see the crater next to the parliament building or to know anything about any "civil unrest" — Jenna randomly recalled that term from history class. The situation must be more serious than she had been led to believe. Otherwise they wouldn't be insisting that the leader be shot! *Massacre. Civil war.* The words swirled in Jenna's mind.

One life or many, thought Jenna. *Is that how it works? Do people really think like that, do people decide to kill* one *man in order to save* many *lives? Is the regent right, or are Bolström and Mrs. Markas?*

She got up and went to the glass doors. The storm had died down and it was raining, gently and evenly. She didn't want to stay in a house with people who were arguing seriously about whether they should kill someone! This was not a movie, and it was not a book, it was real life. This was really happening! And the fight frightened her.

"Please, no," whispered Jenna. She had wanted to help the princess, and she had wanted to play the part in Bolström's supposed film. But now she wished she'd never come here.

14

"Mali!" cried Jonas, and rushed into the living room.

The TV was on with the sound turned down, and on the sofa in front of it lay Malena. Her blonde hair had fallen over her face, and one arm hung down almost to the carpet, where her cap now sat — a dirty little bundle.

"Mali," Jonas repeated, and knelt before her on the floor.

Malena groaned, then brushed her hair off her face and sat up with a start. "Did you have to wake me?" she mumbled. Whatever else she wanted to say was smothered in a yawn.

"Oh, Mali," said Jonas, staring at the cap. "When I heard the missing persons alert in the car, I knew right away it was you." He laughed. "Hugo . . . who was it?"

"Haldur, I think," said Malena, trying to run her fingers through her matted hair. "That's why I had to ditch the jacket. You can't imagine how cold I was."

Jonas tugged at his wet sweatshirt, which was clinging to his body as if it was glued on. "Wanna bet?" he said.

Malena waved her hand dismissively. "Or how tired I am," she said. "Have you any idea how little sleep I got while I was on the run?"

"Was or wasn't it you today at Osterlin?" asked Jonas. Liron came in with a tray, and put down a mug of steaming hot chocolate for each of them. "Were you there this morning?"

Malena tapped her forehead as if he was mental. "How could it possibly have been me?" she said, picking up the mug. "Ooh! That's hot!"

Jonas sat back on the carpet. "At first glance the girl I saw looked exactly like you," he said. "But it ends up she's got dark hair. And her eyes are brown."

Malena blew on the hot chocolate. "Could it be . . . ?" she said. "Oh, never mind. I'm so glad I'm here now. But we haven't got much time."

"I think you're safe here for the time being, Malena," said Liron. "We all are. Although, of course, as princess you're in danger. You more than any of us."

Malena took a sip from her mug. "I've missed you so much," she whispered.

Then she began to cry.

Everything will be all right in the morning. That's what Mom always used to say, back when Jenna was younger, when she'd had a bad dream and slipped into bed with her. In the day-light, the fears of the night dwindle away. *Don't lie awake at night worrying,* she'd say, *things always look much better in the morning.*

Jenna stretched. It had taken her forever to fall asleep, and the dawn chorus had already started when she had finally felt herself slipping into dreamland. It wasn't always easy to follow Mom's advice. Not when you had overheard a conversation like the one she'd heard that night!

She sat up. Had she really heard the words that kept running through her mind? The sun shone through a crack in the curtains, and tiny particles of dust swirled in its beams. Without even going to the window, Jenna knew that it was a beautiful day. Had she simply imagined it all?

There was a knock at the door. "Hello, Jenna," said Mrs. Markas. "Did you sleep well?" She came in and put a tray down on the table next to the bed, then went to the window and pulled open the curtains. "It's going to be a gorgeous day today! And you can just relax after all the stress of yesterday. There's a pool in the park, if you'd like to go swimming, and I'll have a TV brought to your room. Tobias and I have some things to do this morning, but I'm sure you can find plenty to do on your own."

Jenna nodded. She was not sure how her voice would sound if she spoke.

Tobias and Mrs. Markas had "some things to do." *One bullet. He won't even know what hit him.*

"Thank you," murmured Jenna.

Had it really been Mrs. Markas, in her well-tailored suit, who last night had urged the regent to shoot the rebel leader? Mrs. Markas, who was now smiling at her as if there was no bigger problem in her life than having Jenna made up so well that no one would notice she wasn't the Little Princess?

"You sound tired," said Mrs. Markas anxiously. "Don't you feel well?"

"Oh, I'm fine!" said Jenna, and quickly bent down over the tray so that Mrs. Markas wouldn't see her face. "Strawberry jam — yum!"

Mrs. Markas laughed. "You see," she said, "everything's all right. And I've brought you a few newspapers so you can read how enthusiastic everyone was about you yesterday." She went to the door. "You've got our numbers, Tobias's and mine, if you need us. You don't mind us leaving you here alone for a while, do you?"

Jenna shook her head, and picked up a newspaper. Dominating the front page was a large photo showing her on the balcony, her head leaning on Norlin's shoulder.

"We'll see you at lunchtime, then," said Mrs. Markas, and closed the door behind her.

Tens of thousands waved yesterday as Princess Malena appeared on the balcony for the first time since the death of her father, to acknowledge the cheers of the people on her fourteenth birthday, Jenna read. *Everyone who had witnessed her grief at the funeral ceremony could see for themselves that the princess has evidently recovered since then. She seemed rested, healthy, and even happy. A moving sight presented itself to the cheering crowds on the palace square when for a moment the princess cuddled up close to her uncle, the regent (photo). Because the princess had not appeared in public since the death of her father, there had been rumors in recent weeks about her health and about her relationship with her uncle. All such speculations can now be laid to rest. Even during the drive in the limousine . . .*

Jenna put aside the newspaper.

I'm going to call Mom, she decided. *I don't care if I do disturb her. And if I can't get hold of her, I'll try Bea. I've got to talk to someone!*

"Look!" said Liron, and slammed the newspaper down beside the whole-wheat loaf and bread knife on the scratched Formica kitchen table. "Just as I expected."

Malena and Jonas looked up from their morning coffee.

Malena was first to grab hold of the paper. She stared at the photo. "Just like me," she murmured. "And come next week she'll be standing up there again. Then he'll get what he wants. And I can't stop him."

She rolled a few breadcrumbs around the table with her forefinger.

"Oh no she *won't* be standing up there again," said Jonas grimly. "We've got to stop this fraud before there's a disaster. You don't think Nahira will take this lying down, do you?"

"What about the parliament building? Was it really her?" asked Malena, and for a moment her hand lay motionless by the bread.

"Of course," Liron said. "She's threatened to do it often enough. And after the death of the king, it was only a matter of time."

"It all could have been so different," whispered Malena. "Why did he have to die? No one ever said anything about him having a weak heart."

Liron opened his mouth as if to speak, but then he glanced at Jonas, gently shook his head, and said nothing.

"No matter what," said Jonas, "we have to stop them."

Liron gave a harsh laugh. "Who do you think we are?" he asked.

Malena looked at him. "Well, I'm Malena, Princess of Scandia," she said, and her voice was firm again. "And I'm quite certain that if I appear before my people and say what I think of Norlin's law, and what my father would have thought of it, no one will support it anymore. Everyone will realize that it's only been designed to . . ."

Liron put a finger under her chin. "Go on, then, speak to your people!" he said sardonically. "*Where* are you going to speak to them? Here, from the ghetto projects, where nobody listens to us, anyway? From somewhere in the city? Don't you think the police would grab you before even a dozen people could hear what you had to say? Do you think Norlin would let you get away with it?"

Malena thrust his hand away. "You always treat me like a child!" she exclaimed angrily. "A spoiled little princess who can't understand a thing. Of course I know they would try to stop me. But what about the media? The press? Don't you think they'd listen?"

Liron sank back into his chair. "Ah, Malena," he said. "You've been away at school for two months. What do you think has been going on? Do you think nothing has changed since your father died? Do you think it's the same people behind the cameras and holding the microphones? Writing the headlines? Why do you suppose that all of a sudden everyone is talking about *the district*? About the filth and the vandalism here? About the fact that there are some people who are *advanced* and others who may never get that far?"

"You mean, the journalists have been replaced?" asked Malena.

Liron nodded. "That's always the first change," he said. "Whoever controls what goes into people's heads also controls what happens in the country. Forget TV. Forget the press."

Malena glanced at the newspaper on the table. "You don't think there's anything we can do?" she asked. "We can't stop them passing this law?"

Liron's gaze had followed hers. He looked at the photo on the front page, then he slowly turned toward Malena and Jonas. "Well, now, we might," he murmured. "Let me think about it." He took the knife and rinsed it under the tap. "And you, dear Malena, the first thing *you're* going to do is take a good long shower. And afterward you can get dressed in whatever clothes Jonas can spare. They won't be very royal, but they'll still be better than what you're wearing now. And definitely cleaner."

Malena looked down at her dirty outfit. "So you think we *can* do something after all?" she persisted.

Liron raised his arm and pointed toward the half-open kitchen door. "Out!" he said. "Go on, Your Royal Highness, it's shower time."

No one answered — not the landline nor the cell phone. All she got was ringing.

"Where *are* you, Mom?" Jenna hissed. "I'll have to try Bea."

But there was no response from Bea, either, and when Jenna dialed her mother's number once more, she got the busy signal. She tried Bea again, and the automated recording informed her that the person she was trying to reach was "not available at this time."

"This is going to drive me crazy," moaned Jenna. Her mind went back to the strange boy.

Good thing I didn't ask the regent about him last night, she thought. *Not before I find out more about what's going on.*

She dialed again, but before she had even keyed the last digit, she knew what was coming. "Just when I really need her," Jenna groaned.

A text message simply wouldn't do this time.

Malena sat on the kitchen floor amid a sea of hair. While she had been in the shower, Liron had spread newspapers on the floor.

"Sit down," he'd said. "Now we're really going to make a boy out of you. The cap won't do. And you need to be able to move around freely."

"No!" Malena had cried. She had let her hair grow for as long as she could remember, and she didn't know anyone with hair like hers. Princess's hair.

"Don't you get it? It's too dangerous!" Jonas had said. "And it'll grow back."

When he was done, Malena tentatively rubbed a hand over her head. Liron had cut off a lot, and the short stubble on her scalp felt damp to the touch.

"There you are," said Liron, and held out a mirror. "What do you think? Don't worry, you'll get over the shock."

Out of the mirror a strange boy gazed at her — younger than her, which was weird. He had soft features and big blue eyes, and although he was obviously a South Scandian, he apparently didn't have enough money to get a proper haircut.

"No one will recognize you now," said Jonas. Then he gently caressed Malena's shoulder. "OK, 'bro'?"

Liron crumpled up the newspaper with the hair, and the last strands disappeared into the trash can. "Good," he said. "You're still not safe. But at least you're safer."

15

For a while, Jenna stared at the TV that a smiling Tobias had brought to her room. *One bullet. He won't even know what hit him.* She'd found it difficult to smile back.

There were only three channels. They probably didn't get satellite reception out here in the country. All three channels were Scandian, and all the programs were about Scandia. Only once did Jenna come across a newscast that mentioned America, Europe, the Middle East, and the rest of the outside world. If she'd been at home she would have changed channels immediately, but now she watched it all the way through.

It soon became clear that Scandia was a beautiful place and that all Scandians were happy. They walked tall and beamed at the camera, they always smiled in interviews, and even diseases that affected every other nation in the world seemed to have passed them by.

And yet there was constant talk of trouble, of danger, of fear. Three times they showed the crater next to the parliament building, and grim-faced reporters described the hunt for those responsible. Suspicion, Jenna quickly grasped, pointed to the North Scandians, dark-haired people who lived on North Island or in filthy, run-down slums on the fringes of the capital. When the camera focused on them, they never smiled; they raised their fists threateningly and shouted obscenities.

It was true, then. The danger was even greater than Tobias and Mrs. Markas had admitted. Scandia was gripped by fear of another attack, and perhaps of these dark-haired people in general. And the more shows Jenna watched, the better she understood why. Every northerner who was approached by a friendly reporter with a microphone spoke in an ugly-sounding dialect, and everything they said sounded stupid and badly argued: abuse, complaints, demands. Any one of them seemed capable of violence.

Jenna sighed and changed the channel. A fair-haired singer was standing on the shore of a lake, singing about summer. Maybe she had been wrong about Bolström and Mrs. Markas. Perhaps it really would be best to eliminate the leader, if anyone knew where to find him.

What other solution did the regent have? Right from the start she had found him strange. Maybe he was just a ditherer who didn't want to dirty his hands with an assassination, whereas Bolström and Mrs. Markas understood that sometimes you had to commit a little crime (if you could call murder a little crime) in order to prevent a bigger one. Could that be the situation? It was the sort of question they asked at school — in social studies, or poli-sci, or even in English literature class. The sort of question that sent all the students Googling on their cells under their desks.

The singer on the screen slowly spun around in a kind of slow-motion pirouette and spread his arms wide, while his voice soared on the last note, accompanied by the full orchestra. When the news began after that, Jenna reached for the remote control, but suddenly she saw the palace balcony, the regent, and herself — waving to the citizens and cuddling up to him. Then there was the crowd cheering her — it sounded almost menacing — as they streamed in vast numbers from the palace square out into the streets, while the helicopter containing the camera crew tried to capture a panoramic view from overhead.

Good thing I didn't know it was like that when I was up on the balcony yesterday, thought Jenna. *Good thing I couldn't see how many people wanted to wish "me" a happy birthday. And seriously good thing that yesterday I didn't know anything about the North Scandian rebels — I'd never have been able to hide how frightened I was. Not in that open car, and especially not when that boy suddenly came at us.*

". . . the law," the newscaster was saying. "In order to demonstrate their consent, the regent and his niece will lead the parade next Sunday. In a telephone interview, Princess Malena said that she wholeheartedly endorsed this measure to bring peaceful coexistence with the north and to protect the country against terrorism, so that at last her beloved country could return to the tranquility it deserves."

Jenna clicked off the TV. She hated politics — totally boring. All the same, she was glad that now she understood a bit more about what Mrs. Markas and Bolström were trying to do.

She must try to discuss it with Mom.

❧

"Did you hear that?" cried Malena. She was taller than Jonas, and his pants only reached as far as her ankles. But her waist was much slimmer than his, so Liron had to lend her his belt in order to hold the pants up. "I 'wholeheartedly endorse this measure,' do I? What a big fat lie!"

"Would you express yourself a little more regally, Your Highness?" said Liron. "Of course that was *them*. Incidentally, if we dye your blonde hair black, you'll have no trouble passing for one of those dangerous North Scandian hooligans."

"Never!" Malena protested. "I'd rather pass for a dangerous South Scandian hooligan."

Liron pressed the remote control and the screen went blank. "You wanted to hear my idea," he said.

Jonas patted the seat of the sofa, and Malena sat down next to him.

"We're agreed that we must do all we can to stop this law designed to oppress the North Scandians," said Liron. "I don't think we need to discuss that any further. In recent years, as you'll know, Malena, your father tried more than anyone else to give the north the same rights as the south, after centuries of inequality. It wasn't just a matter of goodwill, either. He realized that a nation living in misery and under oppression will one day rise up, and he knew that wealth and poverty can't go on living peacefully next door to each other."

"Because one day the poor will beat down the doors of the rich," said Jonas. "You always said so."

Liron nodded. "In the old days, during your grandfather's reign, Malena, it was still possible," he said. "We northerners lived in the north and didn't know much about your life here in the south, which seemed a vast distance away. But now we have TV and movies and cell phones and the Internet, and with cars and motorboats and planes the distance between the islands has suddenly shrunk. And of course many of us ended up emigrating to the south to do all the jobs that southerners didn't want to do."

"Yes, I know all that," said Malena. "I'm not ignorant."

Liron held her gaze. "It's essential we remind ourselves of this, especially now," he said. "Now the North Scandians are quite rightly asking for the same rights as the south —"

"OK!" cried Malena. "I know why everything's gone wrong. After all, it was my father who wanted to change the situation."

"And that was the right thing to do," said Liron, "for the south, too. You know as well as I do that the rebels would have attacked years ago if your father hadn't been working toward equal rights for the north. Terrorism no longer seemed necessary, so the rebels didn't get any support."

"No, but they had enough support to carry out the attack on parliament," said Jonas. "And as you said yourself, it was no coincidence that the rebels attacked immediately after the king died."

Liron nodded. "Indeed," he said. "The bombing was intended as a warning to the regent and his cabinet to show what would happen if they chose not to continue what the king had started. Everyone knew there was no support for the king's reforms among the South Scandian ruling classes and the owners of the oil wells and coal mines. And everyone could guess what would happen if he died . . . Sure enough, the regent has lost no time proposing a law that is the exact opposite of what the king wanted."

"And I supposedly 'wholeheartedly endorse it'!" cried Malena. "How can anyone believe that? Why would I want the border closed? Why would I take away all the rights my father gave the North Scandians?"

"In the last couple of months they've kept hammering home to the southerners what a threat we northerners are," said Liron. "Oh, they're cunning! The law has been well thought out. And the attack on parliament truly was a terrible crime. If the explosives had gone off in the right place, and not on the grounds next to the building, hundreds of people would have been killed. *Nothing* can justify such a crime, Malena, not even oppression, poverty — *nothing*. But the attack came at just the right moment for the regent. Because now all southerners are living in fear of all northerners, not just of the rebels. People are trembling in their nice clean homes when they see how we live in our ghettos. You can understand it. They want a south like they had before — neat and tidy, with no fear and no North Scandians."

"Obviously," said Jonas. "If I was a southerner, I'd feel the same way."

"Only it's no longer possible," said Liron. "You can't turn the clock back — ever. The only outcome of this law will be more and more dissatisfied people in the north, increasingly ruthless rebels, and ever-greater danger for all Scandians. Above all else, the new law would be inhuman. You can't leave some people in poverty so that other people can be better off."

"Hear, hear," Malena agreed. "That's exactly what my father used to say."

Liron laughed. "That's why he was so popular in the north," he said. "As you are, too, Malena. Which is precisely why Norlin needs it to look like you're on his side. If *you* supported his law against the north, virtually everyone in the south would believe it's right and proper — especially after what's been reported on TV, day after day, week after week. And what we northerners think doesn't count for anything, anyway."

"Thanks for that recap, but are you going to tell us your idea now?" Jonas asked. "Because if not, I'm going to turn the TV back on."

"I'm going to tell you my idea," said Liron.

"Where *is* she?" Bea exclaimed. "That's what I'd like to know! I'm actually kind of worried."

"However worried you may be, young lady," said her mother, "at your age you should know better than to talk with your mouth full. Although I'll take it as a compliment to my cooking. Of course it would have been even nicer if you'd said, 'Thank you, dearest Mom, that in spite of your tough job, and in spite of the fact that you also do all the housework with a minimum of fuss and a minimum of help from me, your darling daughter, nevertheless you still have time to prepare such wonderful meals.'"

"Wow, Mom, in need of validation much? I'll say it next time — if I can remember all that!" said Bea. "No, but seriously, don't you think something's messed up? Last night, when I called to tell her about her freaky royal blonde doppelgänger, she didn't even answer — her home phone or her cell. And today she wasn't at school. I tried her numbers again — *nada* — so after school I went by her house and guess what? Nobody home!"

"And now you think she must be sick?" her mother asked, dishing out a tiny second helping of pie for herself. Then she dangled the spoon over the pie, let out a sigh, and put it down without digging in. "So desperately ill that she can't answer the phone or open the door? Wouldn't she at least have sent you a text message?"

"*I* sent *her* one!" said Bea. "Again with the no reply!"

Her mother nodded. "Maybe they've gone away?" she suggested. "Summer vacation does start soon."

"No way. They haven't got the money," said Bea. "And if they did, she would have told me — we're BFs! Even if she'd skipped school — *especially* if she'd skipped school — she would have told me. She didn't get permission to be out, either, because I asked all the teachers where she was, and none of them knew."

"All the same, I think that's what it is," said her mother, looking longingly at the pie dish. "Her mother's probably forbidden her to tell you, Bea. You know how strict that woman is."

Bea stared at her plate. "I'll stop by her house again tonight," she murmured. "I just cannot *believe* Jenna wouldn't contact me. We've known each other since, like, preschool. BFFs, Mom! She tells me everything."

Her mother glanced at her, then sank her spoon into the pie. "You never know with people, honey," she said, guiltily raising her spoon to her mouth. "I just hope that you're not going to end up disappointed with your 'BF.'"

The long corridors were empty, and the sunlight falling through the window brought a shine to the bright marble floor.

I've got to ask them, thought Jenna. *At lunch. They've been friendly up to now, so why shouldn't I trust them? And since I've*

seen on TV how dangerous the North Scandians are, I can even
understand Mrs. Markas, sort of, when she says the leader of the
rebels has to be executed. If only Mom would answer the phone!
I wish I could talk to her about it. She can't be missing me that
much if she never wants to talk to me.

She went through the big entrance hall and opened the front door. She had a towel with her, and a bathing suit. A private swimming pool all to herself — Bea would die two times over. Jenna dipped her toe in the water. It was colder than she'd expected.

She looked around. It had been less than smart of her not to change up in her room. Except she would have been too embarrassed to go through that grand mansion wearing nothing but a bathing suit. Then again, she would be even more embarrassed now, changing her clothes here in the garden. There were too many windows looking out onto the park. She had to find a place where no one could see her.

A few hundred feet away she spotted a summerhouse — a round, ornate building with weather vanes on its dome-shaped copper roof, and windows with no glass in them. Perhaps a hundred years ago the princes and princesses had taken their afternoon tea here when the weather was fine.

"That'll do . . ." murmured Jenna.

She was only about fifty feet away from the summerhouse when she heard voices. Whoever was talking in there was making no attempt to keep it quiet.

Jenna's first impulse was to turn around. She had already eavesdropped once, and now she wished she hadn't. But something kept her going.

She crouched down and crept across the lawn until she came to the edge of the gravel path that circled the summerhouse. She couldn't get any closer because the gravel would have crunched under her feet. An aged laurel tree was growing between the lawn and the path; Jenna pressed herself up against its trunk and tried not to make a sound.

"In that case I don't understand why you made us go on searching, Your Highness," said a voice she didn't know. "You stopped the search for the princess when she turned up again — fine. But we've been searching nationwide for this Hugo Haldur, and it's been the exact opposite — you told me on the evening of the birthday to intensify the search."

"My dear Chief of Police" — Jenna recognized the regent's voice — "as I've already explained —"

"*Now*, after DNA analysis of the hair has shown that this so-called Hugo is, in fact, none other than the princess herself," the Chief of Police continued, "only *now* do you tell us —"

"Because we didn't know it ourselves!" shouted the regent. "We told the police: The child has turned up again. It wasn't an abduction, just a foolish prank. She left the school of her own volition because she was afraid of all the pomp and ceremony attached to her birthday, and that's why she disappeared. But then she realized in time what was required of her position and so she came back to the court. You saw for yourself how well she coped with the day. But how were we to know what disguise she'd used to smuggle herself out of the school? In heaven's name, there were more important things to find out."

Jenna caught her breath. The princess had run away from school, so why hadn't anyone told her? Why had they said that the princess had simply been too grief-stricken to parade through the streets that she'd last seen on the day of her father's funeral?

"However, there's another question that needs to be answered," the Chief of Police said sharply. "Who gave the order to search for this . . . Hugo, if in reality there was no such person? If he's a made-up character, no one could possibly have missed him."

"How on earth am I supposed to know that?" cried the regent in an agitated voice that reminded Jenna of something. What was it? "The hospital!" he continued. "It must have been the hospital that asked the police to investigate! Then your officers, yes, *your* officers established that his appearance was similar to that of this other boy, and so . . . it's his parents who must have reported the boy missing."

"May I remind you, Your Highness, that this boy does not exist, and is in actual fact the princess, therefore his parents cannot exist, either," the Chief of Police observed politely.

"Well, what do I know about it?" cried the regent. "Am I supposed to do your job for you? Your people must have filed the missing person's report. Go and ask them."

There was a short pause. "We can't trace the missing person's report," said the Chief of Police. "The police station near the hospital that is supposed to have taken down the details and forwarded them to the Central Office knows nothing about it."

"Then you need to run your business more efficiently!" snapped the regent. "That's disgraceful! You don't even know where the report came from? Is this common practice among the Scandian police? It's shocking! A complete shambles!"

Jenna waited for the response, but there wasn't one. Instead she watched a man dressed in a gray suit slowly make his way across the lawn toward the main building.

She was about to creep away into the bushes on the other side of the lawn, in order to avoid being caught by the regent when he left the summerhouse, but then she heard a familiar sequence of beeps. The regent was making a call.

"Bolström?" he shouted. "Get him before he leaves the grounds! We mustn't let him go back to police headquarters. He mustn't make contact with anyone. I'll explain later. But the man suspects something. He's dangerous."

Jenna doubled over and ran. The bushes were no more than a hundred feet away. She dived behind a thick hydrangea and gasped for breath.

Now she knew what the regent's tone had reminded her of. There was a hint, just a hint, of northern dialect.

The journey had lasted three days and three nights. They had crossed by ship. Jenna's mother had long since guessed where they would eventually land, even though right to the end they had never removed the blindfold.

When she climbed up the short flight of steps to the entrance, she could smell the salt in the air and knew that she had not been mistaken.

As soon as they had closed the door behind her, one of the kidnappers loosened the blindfold. It was just as she'd thought, and for a moment it was almost like meeting an old friend again. Then she saw him on a chair not far from the barred window, both his hands tied, and looking as shocked as her.

"But how can it be you?" gasped Jenna's mother. She had eaten scarcely anything over the last three days, and now the room began to spin. "I thought you were . . ."

"Catch her!" cried the man, and tried to jump up, but his feet were chained to the legs of the chair. Jenna's mother hit the floor hard. The man reached out with his bound hands, as if he wanted to comfort her.

No one had come looking for her.

All day long Jenna had hidden behind the hydrangea, thinking. The glow of the midday sun had softened into the gentler light of the afternoon, and slowly the sky over the horizon turned red. *They'll be searching for me soon,* thought Jenna, *if I don't appear at dinnertime. And they've got dogs. There's no way I can hide.*

She wriggled her shoulders to ease a slight ache. *If I simply go back into the house now, maybe everything will still be OK. If I say I spent a lovely summer's day in the garden and fell asleep in the shade. How would they know I overheard anything? I only have to play my part well enough — harmless little Jenna who knows nothing and suspects nothing. But how long can I keep it up?*

She curled herself into a ball. She was afraid. There were too many strange things, too many things that didn't make sense. Tobias, Mrs. Markas, and the regent had lied to her too much.

They hadn't told her about the danger from the rebels, and they clearly had no qualms about killing the leader! Only the regent was reluctant. And the regent had a North Scandian accent — how did that fit in?

They hadn't told her anything about the princess's escape from school, either, and they had started a hunt for a boy who didn't exist. Why did the regent get so upset when the man in the gray suit pointed out that no one could hope to find a person who didn't exist? And why had he had his own Chief of Police arrested by Bolström?

Jenna shivered and wrapped her arms around her body. After the sun had gone down, it had turned cold.

It could all be innocent, she thought. But she couldn't ask them. Because if she asked the wrong questions, and they thought she suspected something, what would they do to her? *One bullet. He won't even know what hit him. Get him before he leaves the grounds.*

So I can't ask them, asking is dangerous, asking will give me away, Jenna reasoned. *But I can't go on like this, not for a whole week, as if nothing had happened, as if the boy hadn't stood under my balcony in the night, as if Bolström and Mrs. Markas hadn't demanded the death of the rebel leader, as if the regent hadn't had the Chief of Police arrested!*

Something is very wrong, and I'm right in the middle of it.

"Jenna?" Tobias's voice called from the balcony. Jenna ducked deeper into the bushes. Then her cell rang. They weren't stupid. She switched it off before it could ring again and give them a second chance to find out where she was hiding.

"Jenna! We're going to eat."

Did they already suspect something? Could the safest thing be to go back to them, innocent and smiling? Where else could she go?

"Jenna! Where the heck has that girl gone?" shouted Tobias.

I won't be able to act innocent for a whole week, Jenna thought again. *You can't hide fear. So what will they do to me then?*

When she heard the dogs, she knew it was time to make a decision. There were at least three of them, maybe more. They were bound to find her, and she didn't know what they'd been trained to do. Would they just bark, or would they seize her and sink their sharp teeth into her, like the guard dogs you saw in movies?

Jenna curled up again and hid her face in her arms. She was so frightened that she couldn't breathe anymore. The barking drew nearer, she heard the paws on the gravel, heard the excited panting. It could only be seconds till they reached her, and then . . .

A sharp whistle cut through the air. The barking stopped abruptly, as if someone had cut the wires of a loudspeaker, and now the dogs let out shrill yaps of joy. Jenna felt something being thrown over her head, and then a hand pressed down on her mouth.

It was too late.

16

"**Shouldn't you be in bed** by now?" Bea's father asked, looking at his watch. He and Bea's mom had just come back from the movies. He looked at his daughter, who lay snuggled up under a woolen blanket on the sofa, and realized that there was no hope of her being in bed fast asleep when her parents came home ever again. "At least you're watching something educational. Current affairs."

"Shush!" said Bea, gazing at the TV screen. "There was nothing today, though."

"What do you mean, nothing?" her mother asked. She hung up her coat in the hall and flopped into a chair. "That was a good movie we just saw."

"Nothing about Scandia," said Bea. On screen, a woman in a short jacket started pointing at the weather map. Bea turned off the TV. "I was thinking about Jenna."

Her father went to the cupboard and took out a glass. "Bea," he said, "for heaven's sake, don't start imagining things."

Bea watched as he poured himself some soda. "But why is it a peculiar country?" she asked. "The other night you said *Scandia is a very peculiar country*. Meaning what, exactly?"

Her father sat down on the sofa beside her. "If I thought your interest was political," he said, "I'd be happy to tell you all about it. But since I expect you're still chasing after some sort of fantasy . . ."

"Don't be so silly!" said his wife, pouring some soda for herself. "If your daughter's showing an interest, then you shouldn't care why. Make the most of it!"

Bea's father laughed. "OK, then. I'll tell you about Scandia," he said. "Peculiar Scandia, the country of two islands. The origins of their problems go back quite a long way. More than a hundred years, in fact, since the north island was first conquered by Scandia — at the time that was only the name of the south island." He looked at her. "Are you with me so far?"

Bea shook her head. "Not really," she said. All the same, she had a feeling she'd heard something similar somewhere before — probably at school.

Her father sighed.

"What in the world do you learn in history, then?" he asked. "Well, anyway, at that time the people on the south island, the tall, fair-haired people, were much more powerful than the northerners. They had better weapons, machinery, and so on. When they conquered the north, they said they were bringing progress, and the northerners believed them. The new North Scandians probably even admired the South Scandians."

Bea nodded.

"But actually," said her father, "the people from the south were only interested in the north's oil and what they could get out of the mines. And that's how the people in the south grew rich."

"Of course," said Bea.

"'Of course'? 'Of course'? What sort of comment is that?" said her father. "In those days, somehow everybody thought it was perfectly OK for the south to exploit the north. Even the North Scandians. That is, until they got to know more about the south, and some of them were allowed to go to school there. Then the northerners realized that there was no good reason why they should always be poor and the southerners should always be rich, since it was the minerals and the oil from the north that generated all the southerners' wealth."

"You think they'd have figured that out sooner," said Bea, sitting upright.

"Well, yes, I agree, but they didn't realize till they saw the wealth of the south for themselves," said her father. "The South Scandians needed workers for their factories, laborers for their farms, nurses for the sick and old. As more and more North Scandians went to the south to do the manual, dirty, poorly paid work that no rich southerner would think of touching, they saw how wealthy the south was and they started to feel that this wasn't fair."

"And that's why the rebels came," said Bea, "the ones on the news."

Her father nodded. "Exactly," he said. "The king supported equal rights for the North Scandians and the rebels seemed to accept him at his word. But since his death two months ago I think it's all becoming a bit of a mess."

"But what does any of that have to do with Jenna?" asked Bea, slumping back on the sofa. "I still don't get it."

Her father ruffled her hair. "It has nothing to do with Jenna at all, my dear, daft daughter," he said. "Your friend Jenna is sitting somewhere in the Mediterranean in a beachfront hotel laughing her head off when she thinks of the rest of her class still stuck back at school."

"That's what *you* think!" said Bea, and stood up. "But *I* know it's not true!"

Jenna was crying.

She was lying all squashed up in the trunk of a car that was traveling swiftly along smooth roads, rarely slowing down and never stopping. She guessed they were not traveling toward the city, because otherwise there would have been traffic lights and intersections, and the car would have had to stop every now and then.

The noise of the engine droned in her ears, there was a smell of oil or gasoline, and the metal surface she was lying on was hard, although her kidnappers had put a blanket over it. They had blindfolded and gagged her, tied her hands behind her back, and bound her feet with a belt.

The first thing they had done, though, was take away her cell phone.

It all seemed so unreal. They must have suspected something for a long time. Otherwise, why was the regent having her taken away? What had she done wrong?

The ground became bumpy, and the car slowed down. But still she was being thrown around in her narrow prison.

Finally the car stopped.

Doors were opened and slammed shut, and there were voices. Someone opened the trunk.

"Careful!" said a man's voice. It wasn't Tobias or Bolström or Norlin. "If you take her feet . . ."

Hands grasped her under the shoulders and by the legs and lifted her quite gently out of the car. She breathed in the still-mild evening air, which smelled of pine trees. Then she felt the floor of the forest under her back, maybe a cushion of moss covering the ground.

"OK," said the man's voice. "Now I'm going to take off your blindfold."

The knot at the back of her head was untied, and through the tops of gigantic pine trees she saw the sky high above as it slowly took on the leaden tinge of night. She turned her head a little to the side.

"If you promise not to scream," said the man who was obviously in charge, "we'll take the gag out of your mouth, too. There wouldn't be much point in screaming, anyway. We're in the middle of the forest."

Jenna tried to nod in order to show that she'd understood. The man didn't look like the Scandians she'd had to deal with before. He was smaller than them, stockier, with dark hair and skin. Jenna knew where he was from.

"Jonas," said the man authoritatively.

As soon as the boy came out of the shadows of the trees, Jenna recognized him. He bent over her and took off the gag. His eyes were full of hatred.

"Don't think you deserve to be treated so kindly," he said, and raised his foot as if to kick her.

Jenna screamed.

"Jonas!" the man said sharply.

It was the boy from the city; the boy from beneath the balcony. Now everything made sense.

She had fallen into the hands of the rebels.

The regent was furious.

"Have you gone crazy?" he raged. "How could this happen? What do you mean, kidnapped?"

They were standing in Jenna's room.

"You said before, Your Highness, that the fewer the staff here at Osterlin, the less the danger of someone realizing that our princess is not the real princess," said Tobias, bowing slightly. "Mrs. Markas even had to prepare our meals, because you didn't want us to have a cook here."

"And no guards," Mrs. Markas added. "You said the place was secure enough. We've got the alarm system and, more important, the dogs."

"And isn't that the truth?" shouted the regent. "Why didn't the alarm go off? How did they get in and out? They can't have carried her over the gate or the railings."

"Where there are people who install alarm systems, there are people who know how to dismantle alarm systems," said Bolström. "And we don't yet know how they got in. Now, for heaven's sake, calm down, Norlin. The vital thing is to keep a cool head. Not *everything* depends on the princess."

"And the dogs?" cried the regent, as if he hadn't heard Bolström. "The sharpest watchdogs in the whole of Scandia? They're trained to attack anything that moves! So why didn't they attack the kidnappers?"

"We found them wagging their tails near the railings," Tobias said hesitantly.

"Presumably they were thrown some meat to keep them quiet," said Mrs. Markas. "Although . . . well, regardless, they were all in a very good mood."

"Hmm . . ." murmured Bolström.

"Nahira always finds a way!" said the regent, and his face twisted with rage. "She's not just prepared to use force. She's also smart."

Bolström nodded a few times. "Of course, you would know that better than anyone," he said. "It could well be Nahira.

She's the first person one thinks of, you especially, but can we be sure? The disabled alarm and the dogs would make me look in another direction."

The regent stared at him.

"Perhaps it was a mistake to strip your old friend of all his offices and dismiss him," Bolström said gently. "And now, for goodness' sake, don't get yourself all worked up again. What's done is done."

"Liron," the regent muttered. "Of course! Liron . . ."

"We'll have to leave your hands and feet tied," said the man. He helped Jenna up, and supported her so that she could hobble over to a tree where a second boy had spread out the blanket from the trunk. "I think they're loose enough not to cut into your flesh. I'm sorry that we have to treat you, a minor, like this, but you know why it's necessary."

Jenna began to sob.

"Sit down," said the man. "I'll help you. Give her something to drink, Jonas."

The boy brought over a thermos and poured some tea into a mug.

"Personally, I'd rather give you a good beating," he said. His voice was full of anger.

Jenna held the mug between her bound hands, and was surprised by how comforting the warmth was. She took a little sip.

"You needn't be afraid," said the man. He looked into her eyes as if he was searching for something. "We're not going to harm you."

Jenna nodded. She could feel the tears running down her cheeks, and her shoulders shook.

"Please," she whispered, "please . . . it's all a mistake."

"A mistake?" shouted the boy. Jenna was more afraid of him than of anyone else. There was nothing but sheer hatred in his eyes, and if the man hadn't restrained him, he would certainly have hit her by now. "A mistake? Do you think we're idiots?"

Jenna shook her head in desperation. "But I'm not the princess," she said. "I'm not Princess Malena. I'm only a —"

"Traitor!" shouted the boy. "What sort of game do you think you're playing? Do you think we don't know? Why do you think we've dragged you here, you piece of dirt?"

"Please," begged Jenna. If the rebels already knew she was not Malena, why had they kidnapped her?

It was only now that the second boy came slowly toward them. Since spreading out the blanket, he'd been standing motionless by the car. He was taller than the other boy, but looked younger. The most striking thing about him, though, was that, unlike the other two, his short, stubbly hair was as pale as corn.

"No, you are definitely *not* Malena," he said, his light voice full of scorn. "Malena would be ashamed."

Jenna stared at him. She was sure that she had never seen him before. And yet his face looked strangely familiar.

The table in the banquet hall had been set as if for a light lunch. Between the plates, glasses, and cutlery were bread, ham, and cheese still in its wrapping paper, and the four people at the table took turns fishing in jars of olives and gherkins with their fingers. This was no time for table manners.

"It's no use crying over spilt milk," said Bolström. He helped himself to a slice of ham, rolled it up, and stuck it in his mouth. Then he washed it down with a mouthful of wine. "It was a mistake not to guard her properly. We should have taken the risk and assigned her guards. Now it's too late."

Mrs. Markas wiped her fingers on her napkin. "What if she goes public with her story?" she asked.

Bolström nodded. "That, of course, is the biggest danger," he said. "Especially since we don't even know where Malena is. What she and Jenna could get up to . . . especially together . . . I shudder to think."

"And you can say that so calmly?" cried the regent. His fingers were trembling. He was the only one at the table holding a glass of cognac. "Now kindly tell me what we're going to do."

Bolström smiled.

"We must stop Jenna from going public," he said. "Her *or* the princess. And no one apart from our own people must know there's been a kidnapping. The mood in the country has just quieted down. We certainly don't want another round of rumors, particularly now."

Tobias nodded. "But when the law is announced on Sunday, Bolström, it's obvious that people will talk if the princess is missing from the parade. It's not as if the king's . . . propaganda in the last few years hasn't left its mark. The law should go through without any great problems here in the south, but suppose afterward we're forced to . . ." He hesitated for a moment. ". . . actually invade the north? That's beginning to look like a possibility, unfortunately. Will the people support us then? What about all those we've managed to silence since the beginning of your reign, Your Highness? Won't they come crawling out of the woodwork again? We need the princess! Everyone knows she's a friend to the north, and her support is the only thing that's going to stifle criticism of what we're doing."

"At least we hope it will," murmured Bolström.

"Then find her!" screamed the regent. "Find both of them — the real one and the fake!"

"You know that Malena would never march with you in the parade, Norlin," said Bolström. "So it's Jenna we have to get back. But after this experience, will Jenna still want to —"

"She will!" cried the regent. "She will support us, particularly now, after she's been abducted by the rebels. Don't you think she'll hate them?"

Bolström nodded. "If it *is* the rebels who have abducted her," he said. "But if it's Liron . . ." He paused. ". . . then we shall have to think of something else."

17

*A*fter the short break out in the forest, they drove on through the night. Jenna sat in the backseat, still bound hand and foot. Next to her sat the fair-haired boy, and every so often their shoulders touched.

None of them slept much. At one point the driver stopped in order to take a quick nap himself, and Jenna, who had just been lulled to sleep by the droning of the engine, was woken up by the sudden silence.

The night was bright and the stars shone from a cloudless sky. Everything could be seen as clearly as if by day, except that the colors were absorbed by the night, so that trees and bushes stood out in different shades of gray against the anthracite sky.

Forest, thought Jenna, *forest and forest and forest as far as the eye can see.*

Every now and then, even in the deep gloom of the northern night, she had been able to make out the dull sheen of water between the trees. *Forest and forest and forest and lakes.*

Where are they taking me? she wondered. *There's nothing here — no towns, no villages, not even an isolated farm along the road. There's no one to hear me if I scream.*

The boy next to her drew a deep breath in his sleep, and slumped against Jenna's shoulder. With a soft moan, he nestled close, leaned his head on her arm, and went on sleeping.

Jenna stiffened. She was wide awake, and wished the dawn would finally break.

Some time later, maybe an hour, maybe two, the driver stretched, glanced over his shoulder, and then without saying a word, started the engine again. After just a few minutes back on the road, Jenna fell asleep.

She woke up when the car came a little too abruptly to a halt. With a jerk, the blond-haired boy moved his head away from her shoulder and shook himself. Jenna would have liked to rub her eyes, but the bonds made it impossible.

"Everybody out," said the driver, "and stretch your legs."

The two boys got out of the car, and then the driver untied Jenna's hands and feet. "You could try to run away," he said, "but I don't think you'd get very far. We're fast. And there's three of us."

To her surprise, Jenna realized that she was no longer afraid. It was as if fear could wear itself out if it went on long enough, she thought, and she breathed in the cool air of the approaching morning. All she could do was wait.

The car was parked on a little rocky plateau overlooking the water. Below them, mirror-smooth, lay the sea, and on the horizon the sun was just coming up in a red glow, gradually restoring color to the surroundings. The night was over.

"Listen," said the man. The two boys, who were standing with Jenna at the edge of the cliff watching the sunrise, turned to him. Jenna went on looking out over the water. She knew he hadn't been addressing her. All the same, she listened.

"I've agreed to meet the journalist at the ferry port. We've got no choice — we have to trust him. All the same, I shall go on my own first."

"And then?" asked the dark-haired boy.

"When I'm sure that he's come alone, I'll bring him here to you in my car," said the man. "We'll show him both of them, the real princess and the fake. Jenna will tell him her story. When the people hear that they've been deceived, and that the princess at the birthday celebrations was not Malena, do you think they'll believe anything that Norlin tells them?" He sighed. "We can't stop the law from being approved," he said, "but perhaps we can get enough people asking questions to make life difficult for the regent. Then at least he won't dare to attack the north, and the north can take some courage from that. And Nahira can see . . ." He paused.

"That we can achieve something without violence?" asked Jonas.

"That's what I'm hoping," said the man.

"But who's going to publish the story?" asked the blond boy. "After what you told me, will any newspaper touch it? Any radio station? And what makes you so sure we can trust this reporter?"

The man didn't answer at first. Then he spoke softly. "You can't really trust anyone when you're on the run, but I can't see any other way. This reporter has always been on our side so far. And it's a good story. But if I'm not back by evening, hide in the forest. Toward morning, when the fishing boats set sail, Nanuk will come past this bay in his old wooden boat, with no navigation lights — that's been arranged. If you signal him with the flashlight, he'll drop anchor. Then he'll take you to the north. They'll come after you, of course, and if they torture me I don't know if I'd be able to hold out. Hard as I'd try not to, I still might betray you." He looked at the two boys intently. "No one knows what they'll do, how they'll hold up, under torture."

"And then?" the blond one asked. "Then what?"

"Try not to think about it," the man said. "Let's just hope that it doesn't happen."

After the car had disappeared into the forest, the two boys didn't tie Jenna up again. Occasionally they glanced at her and said things in whispers. After a while, they behaved as if she wasn't there.

By now the sun was high in the sky, and it had become warm. Looking out to sea, Jenna noticed a dark streak on the horizon. It must have been North Island.

Suddenly a thought struck her: *How do they know my name?* That evening when he had broken into the grounds at Osterlin, could the boy have overheard conversations about her and found out that way? And who was Nahira?

Toward midday she noticed that the other two were becoming agitated. They looked at their watches and at the position of the sun, and Jonas talked insistently to the blond boy. At one point they came so close to the place where Jenna was lying on the cliff top, trying to catch up on her lost night's sleep, that she could make out some of what they were saying. And also the name of the fair-haired boy. He was called Mali.

With a jolt, Jenna was suddenly wide awake. She remembered that when Jonas had stood below the balcony, he had called out, "Mali!" Now she knew who he meant.

Jenna stared at the fair-haired boy. And at once she realized why he had seemed so familiar to her.

The sun disappeared somewhere behind the forest.

"Here," said Jonas, reluctantly passing Jenna a slice of bread. "Liron wouldn't want us to let you go hungry."

Jenna didn't look at him. She had long since concluded that her three kidnappers thought she was collaborating with the regent in a plot against the north — and against the princess. She had tried a few times to talk to Jonas and Malena, but they had always shouted her down.

She chewed the bread slowly, because she knew it would be all that she'd get. Her stomach rumbled, but she did not feel hungry at all.

When all the bread was gone and the thermos empty — Jonas had obviously filled it with water from a nearby lake — they signaled to her.

Jenna stood up. If he was not back by evening, they were to hide in the forest, that was what the man had said. Liron. What had happened to him?

"Come here!" ordered Jonas. "We're going into the forest now, and don't even think about trying to escape. You know if you tried to run you wouldn't stand a chance. First, we're going to shut your mouth." Before Jenna could defend herself, he had gagged her again. "Now you can't scream for help, even if your people show up here," he said. "So get going!"

My people? thought Jenna. *Who are my people? I wanted to run away from the regent, but they think I'm conspiring with him. I'm afraid of the regent, and I'm afraid of the rebels. I don't have any "people"!*

They found a hiding place just a few hundred feet from the cliffs, in a thick cluster of brambles, though it ended up that they didn't need to hide after all. The night remained quiet. Jonas and Malena took turns keeping watch, but nobody came looking for them. Now and again Jenna nodded off, but it was still dark when Jonas gave her a rough shake awake. She felt as though she hadn't had a wink of sleep.

"Come on, let's go, but keep quiet," he said. It was so dark up there in the north, even on a clear starlit night, but when they left the forest, Jenna saw that the sky was already beginning to lighten on the horizon. "If you think you can give us away," Jonas hissed, "then think again. You won't live to see it."

"Don't talk to her like that," Malena said. But she still gave Jenna an angry look. "Have you got the flashlight?"

They lay down flat on the edge of the cliff, with Jenna between them: They didn't have to tell her what to do. When the first patrol boat passed by, Malena looked at her watch. Jonas seized Jenna by the nape of the neck and pushed her face into the ground, as if worried that she would try to get its attention. But with astonishment Jenna realized she no longer wanted to try. Even in spite of their rough treatment and threats, she was now far less frightened of Jonas and Malena than of Tobias, Mrs. Markas, Bolström, and the regent. And if she did try to scream and leap up and signal to the coast guard, she would end up in their hands again. The coast guard would take her back to Osterlin.

I must be losing it, thought Jenna, *but I'd rather be here with the rebels. Even though they've kidnapped me, tied me up, and gagged me. They did give me some of the little bread they had, and they haven't tortured me. If only I can manage to explain to them that this is all just a big misunderstanding . . .*

"Twelve minutes," whispered Malena. With a friendly chug, as if it wasn't the least bit dangerous, the patrol boat came back from the other direction. "We've got exactly twelve minutes."

The sound faded and Jonas took his hand off Jenna's neck. "It's going to be close," he whispered.

Jenna was the first to see Nanuk's boat. It loomed noiselessly up out of the water, a dusky shadow, its dark sails billowing slightly. Not until it had reached the middle of the bay did Jonas give the signal: a sequence of long and short flashes. Jenna didn't know Morse code, but the man on the cutter seemed to have been waiting for the signal. In the deathly stillness of the dawn she could hear the unnaturally loud sound of the winch as the anchor slid into the water. Then everything was quiet again.

"You first," whispered Jonas. "And not a sound or you'll be in trouble."

Jenna understood why they were both in a hurry. They had to use the interval between patrols, and twelve minutes was not a lot of time for them to clamber down the cliff face. In the gloom, she grabbed at whatever handholds she could find — spurs of rock, roots, the branches of bushes. Once she started to slip and scraped her shin on something sharp, but then she managed to get hold of a branch, and took a deep breath. Above her, Malena let out a cry of pain, and Jonas hurtled past her down into the depths. She heard him land with a thud.

"Jonas!" Malena gave a muffled cry. "Jonas, did you —"

"I'm OK," whispered Jonas, his voice quite close. Then Jenna herself felt the gravelly sand beneath her feet. "No need to panic."

Malena landed last, with a little squeal.

"Start swimming!" commanded Jonas, shoving Jenna in the back.

The water was not nearly as cold as she'd feared. As quietly as possible, she slipped in, and held her breath for a moment. She was afraid to swim with the gag in her mouth, but after the first few strokes she felt calmer. The salt water burned the graze on her shin, but still she swam ahead of Jonas and Malena with powerful strokes, toward the cutter.

What would the two of them have done if I hadn't known how to swim? she wondered. *What would they have done if I'd refused to come with them, or to climb down the cliff? If I were really "in league" with the regent, and if I wanted the coast guards to capture us so that I could be set free, they'd never have had a chance of getting me to the boat without being caught. Not in twelve minutes. No way.*

Malena seemed to be thinking the same thing as she followed Jenna up the rope ladder onto the deck. She gave Jenna a thoughtful look, then pointed to the gag in her mouth. "In a moment," she said. "When we're a bit farther out to sea."

Jenna nodded.

While Jonas was still climbing over the deck rail, the fisherman went to pull up the anchor.

"All aboard?" he asked quietly over his shoulder. "This is where it gets tricky. Hide yourselves under the nets."

Jenna was as quick as Jonas and Malena, and again she saw Malena looking thoughtfully at her. *Maybe now she'll listen to me when all this is over,* thought Jenna. *Maybe now she'll believe me. I don't know what will happen then, but at least I wouldn't be her enemy anymore. And I wouldn't be so alone.*

"Get down!" hissed the fisherman. "They're coming."

Once again the noise of the patrol boat's engine came nearer, and Jenna realized that they hadn't made it in time.

It hadn't been possible, and the fisherman must have known that. How was he going to explain to the coast guard why he had stopped here in the bay and not in the fishing grounds? How had he imagined he could hide his boat, even if the sails were dark red and the hull black? At a distance perhaps the night would have swallowed them up, but now the sun was rising. It had all been for nothing.

She slumped down when the ship's siren hooted. Deafening — three short, three long, three short, again and again. Then the fisherman fired a rocket, which exploded in a red ball high above them. For several seconds, the cutter was bathed in a reddish light, and the fisherman stood at the rail and waved his arms slowly up and down.

Traitor! thought Jenna with a sudden realization, and she looked angrily through the nets as their rescuer continued to wave his arms up and down. Nanuk was going to hand them over to the coast guard. Liron was right — you couldn't trust anybody when you were on the run.

The patrol boat came racing toward them, leaving a bright trail of spray in the dark water. When it was just a few feet away, Jenna could see two uniformed men on board. One of them had a megaphone in his hand.

"Is that you again, Nanuk?" he called. "What is it this time?"

Nanuk cupped his hands in front of his face. "The motor cut out," he shouted. "Same old story. Just this one more time, please, can you tow me across? At least to the harbor?

Otherwise, in this calm, I'll be stuck here till who knows when."

The sound of harsh laughter came through the megaphone. "We told you last time, we're not a free service for broken-down northern fishing boats that should be on the scrap heap. Didn't we warn you to stay at home with your old wreck?"

"Just this once," pleaded Nanuk desperately. The patrol boat had now come alongside the starboard bow, but the two men only scanned the deck of the fishing boat halfheartedly. "What am I supposed to do? I've got to go out to sea. I'm a fisherman. Please, I beg you! How am I going to get home if you don't?"

The coast guards turned their boat away.

"Please!" cried Nanuk. "Don't leave me here. You've always helped me before."

The wooden vessel bobbed up and down in the swelling wake of the patrol boat. Once again the megaphone magnified the guards' braying laughter, and then Jenna heard the click as they switched it off. The patrol disappeared behind a promontory.

"Now we can go," said Nanuk. "All hands on deck! We must get under way before they come back."

"How many times have you done this?" asked Jonas, and Jenna noticed the admiration in his voice.

"Asked them for help?" said Nanuk. The anchor disappeared into its box with a rattle. "Practically every night in the last three or four weeks. Sometimes here, or out there in the sound, sometimes off the coast nearer to home. They've warned me before that I can't use the coast guard as a free towing service. The first few times they came on board and searched my old wreck inch by inch. But not for the last three nights. Of course, it's against all regulations not to check, but the fact is they're sick and tired of me." He laughed softly. "Guards are human, too," he said. "You can just imagine how they're laughing now, thinking about poor old Nanuk, helpless on the calm sea with his broken-down engine. 'In the future he'll stay where he belongs' — that's what they'll be saying." Slowly and almost silently Nanuk maneuvered the cutter out of the bay. "'He won't dare do that again.'"

He switched on the engine and headed north.

"And if they had come on board?" asked Malena. "Then they'd have seen that the engine works after all."

"They would have indeed," said Nanuk, nodding. Jenna was surprised at how fast the old boat plowed through the water.

"And they would have found us," said Malena, standing next to him.

"They would have indeed," said Nanuk.

"And then they would have taken all of us," said Malena.

For a moment Nanuk removed his hands from the wheel and signaled to Malena that she should take over. Then he reached into his shirt pocket and pulled out a cigarette.

"Yes, that wouldn't have been very pleasant," he said.

To their right the sun was rising in the sky.

18

The house lay in isolation. The thick forests that surrounded it rarely played host to hunters, except for a short time in autumn when they came after elk. Otherwise no one disturbed the peace and quiet. The nearest road ended miles away, and the gravel track soon gave way to sand and grass that was nearly impassable when it rained. The coast was so near that you could almost smell the sea. It was an ideal place to set up headquarters, even if it was a long way from the capital.

"What happens next?" asked Lorok, who had been sitting on the rug, impatiently poking the remains of the fire. He was eighteen at most. Sometimes it frightened Nahira to see how young most of her followers were, how eager to embark on adventures, how carelessly willing to risk their lives, how full of hatred.

"We wait," she said.

Meonok, the second boy, who was sitting on the worn-out sofa, stroking the dog, looked up. "We wait, and wait, and wait!" he said. "Is that what we joined your cause for? In five days they'll be passing the law. Then they'll invade."

"You said we'd have to scare them off!" cried Lorok. "Have you forgotten that? What was the point of setting off the bomb near the parliament building? You said that after the king died, the north could expect nothing from the new government, and that the only thing to do now is to show them what they'll get if they refuse to give us our rights."

"And that's what we've done," said Nahira wearily. Once she, too, had found it easy to sit up all night talking, making plans — just like these youngsters now.

"So where has it gotten us?" cried Lorok. "Nowhere! Now they're even taking away what few rights the king had already granted us. And in a few days they'll invade the north, and then —"

"You're right, Lorok," said Nahira. "The attack got us nowhere. On the contrary, it has simply strengthened their argument against the 'dangerous north.'"

"Then we've got to make them *really* afraid of us," said Lorok. "Make them panic! They don't know yet what we're ready to do. They shouldn't feel safe for one minute, one second; they should be scared stiff that a bomb could explode in their cars, their trains, their expensive houses! They need to be so terrified that they'll give in to us just so that they can sleep in peace."

"That is not what will happen," said Nahira. "I've explained this a hundred times. The more they fear us, the more they hate us. And before they give in to us, they'll fight back. For every person killed in their towns, they'll make us pay with a hundred dead in our towns. It's inevitable."

Meonok leaped up. "We're not afraid to die for our homeland and our honor!" he shouted. "Better dead than crushed! Thousands and thousands of North Scandians are ready to become martyrs."

"Calm down, Meonok," said Nahira. "Death is final, you know."

But she knew that they could not understand, they were too young. And there were thousands who thought the same way Lorok and Meonok did. If something wasn't done very soon, there'd be bombs going off all over Scandia.

And I'm the one responsible, thought Nahira. *They still look up to me, these children. It was a mistake to set off the bomb next to parliament. Now they just want more of the same. How could I have forgotten? And once they taste blood, they'll want more. How am I going to keep them under control?* "I'm going to bed," she said.

Sometimes, when she had slept deeply enough, and long enough, she woke up the next morning and knew the answer.

They were on the water for four hours. The boat glided through the waves with its sails puffed out. At some point they passed the fishing grounds, where the fishermen on the other boats signaled to Nanuk before making their way back to their home ports. There, too, Jenna, Malena, and Jonas had to hide under the nets.

"There are traitors in the north as well," was all that Nanuk said.

Once they were ashore, he took them to a run-down shed used for storing nets: a shack of gray wood bleached by wind and salt, standing among similar dilapidated buildings. "No one will think of looking for you here," he said. "But if they should find you, and if they recognize you and ask how you got here, keep quiet as long as you can. You need a story, so that if they torture you, all three of you say the same thing."

"Her, too?" Jonas said, pointing aggressively at Jenna. "Not her, too!"

"Shush!" hissed Malena. "But what should our story be?"

"Tell them you were swimming across from South Island on an inflatable raft," said Nanuk. "Like stupid kids, you thought you could do it, but the raft got a puncture and started to sink. Then you saw a boat from the north, and you shouted for help. A fisherman saw you and swore at you. He swore at you the whole time you were on board, and you told him a bunch of lies."

Malena nodded.

"You were so scared that you didn't get a good look at the boat," Nanuk continued. "All perfectly plausible. You couldn't say for certain who rescued you. And he didn't know who you were."

"You think they'll believe that?" Malena asked.

The fisherman shrugged his shoulders. "We can but try," he said. "Now I've got to disable my engine. If the coast guards pick me up . . ."

"Thank you, Nanuk," said Malena. Jonas also mumbled his thanks, and the fisherman left them.

The shed stank of fish. There were nets hanging on the walls and lying on the floor amid marker buoys, with dried scales stuck everywhere.

"He could have remembered that we need something to eat," Jonas grumbled. "We've already gone a whole day without food."

Malena waved her hand dismissively. Jenna was surprised to see how calm she suddenly seemed. "A chance for you to slim down, Jonas," Malena said. "Drop a couple of pounds." Then she turned to Jenna. "You, too," she added.

Jenna didn't know whether or not to respond. After they had sailed far enough away from South Island, Malena had taken off her gag. When they had reached the fishing grounds, where they kept crossing paths with other boats, Jonas had wanted to put it on her again, but Malena had shaken her head. "She won't scream," she had said. "She could have given us away hours ago if she'd wanted to, Jonas. And I don't know why she didn't. But she won't scream."

At first Jonas had kept a close eye on Jenna in case he had to clap a hand over her mouth, but then he, too, had calmed down. And when they had come ashore, even though he had insisted on tying her hands, he didn't gag her or bind her feet again.

"Now what?" Jonas asked Malena. It seemed almost as if the princess had taken command during the course of their escape. But Malena just shrugged her shoulders.

"We're safe for the time being," she said. "And that's the most important thing."

"And what about Liron?" asked Jonas.

Malena looked down. "He was too trusting," she whispered. "In the end, he was too trusting. He was right, none of the press are willing to take the risk of opposing Norlin. I wouldn't have believed it could happen so quickly."

"What will they do to Liron?" murmured Jonas.

"I do hope they don't hurt him," whispered Malena. "I do hope . . ."

Jenna remembered how Tobias and Mrs. Markas, Bolström and the regent had talked about the rebel leader. *One bullet. He won't even know what hit him.* They weren't squeamish. Jenna didn't imagine they'd spare Liron when they needed to know the whereabouts of the princess. And of her double.

"Well, well, what have we here?" said Bolström. "The conscience of the king, our dark-haired moral guardian! Lovely to see you again after all this time, Liron."

Liron said nothing.

"It probably hasn't been long enough for you, though, eh?" said Bolström. "You could have done without our company for a bit longer, I should think, hmm?"

Norlin cleared his throat. "Liron," he said, "let's settle this business peacefully. I'm sorry we had to bring you here all trussed up. I apologize that my people were obviously rougher than necessary."

Liron looked up.

"Thank goodness that reporter finally realized what he owed to his country. But your attempt to meet up with him leads us to suppose you had something to do with Jenna's disappearance. And also, perhaps, with Malena's."

There was no reaction from Liron.

"You see, Liron," said Bolström, "we couldn't help speculating who could possibly have gotten past the bloodhounds so easily. And there is only one person. Stupid of us not to think of it earlier. Of course, if we had, we never would have dispensed with security guards in the first place."

"It was your son, Liron, wasn't it?" said Norlin. "Jonas is the only one who can get the dogs to obey him. So don't waste our time denying it. You've abducted Jenna, and you wanted to meet the reporter in order to tell him the whole story and to show her to him. You're still hoping to swing public opinion in the south against my new law."

"So?" asked Bolström. "Where are they?"

Liron said nothing.

"Listen, Liron," said Bolström. "We haven't got much time, and we're not prepared to waste even a minute of it. I don't have to remind you that it's in your own best interest to talk."

Liron nodded. "You're threatening me," he said. It was difficult for him to get the words out; his lip had been split. "But you should know me by now, Bolström."

"No, no, Liron, you've got it all wrong," said Norlin. "Of course we're not threatening you. We don't torture people in Scandia. We just hope you'll understand that it's in the interest of the whole nation that —"

Liron smiled. "Oh, Norlin," he said, "you've always confused your own interests with those of the nation. You even got your nations confused."

The regent lashed out, and Liron's head jerked back.

Bolström raised an eyebrow. "How often do I have to tell you, Norlin? You really must learn to control yourself."

All day long, Jonas had been pacing up and down in the shed. His stomach had been rumbling so loudly that Jenna could even hear it when he was over on the other side. She was surprised she didn't feel hungry herself.

A little light came into the shed from a small window above the door. Cobwebs that had trapped decades of dust hung over it like unwashed, ragged curtains. Jenna kept nodding off in the gloom.

She woke up when she felt a tap on her shoulder.

Malena was squatting in front of her, studying her face.

"Thank you for not betraying us," she said. But Jenna could still see uncertainty and even suspicion in her eyes. "You could easily have given us away — several times, in fact."

Since the previous morning, and their escape in the cutter across the sound, when she'd been wondering what her kidnappers were going to do with her, Jenna had stopped wanting to cry. It was as if a glass wall had sprung up between herself and her feelings. She knew she should have been afraid or desperate, but instead she felt . . . strangely indifferent.

Malena's friendly words broke the glass. Now the tears ran down Jenna's cheeks, and suddenly she became aware of how hopeless her situation was. The other two were in danger only from the regent and his people; but even if they escaped and found refuge somewhere, Jenna herself would never feel safe, because the rebels didn't trust her, either.

"What are you bawling about?" asked Jonas angrily. "We haven't touched you, have we? What do you think your people would do to us if they caught us? What do you think they're doing to Liron at this very moment?"

Jenna sobbed.

"She can't do anything about that," said Malena. "In any case, she didn't betray us." And once more there was her uncertain, inquiring gaze.

"Oh, so suddenly you're on her side!" snapped Jonas. "Just because she's your —"

"No," said Malena, "I'm not on 'her side.' But maybe . . ." She looked at Jenna. "Why didn't you scream?" she asked. "Why did you swim with us to the boat and not try to escape? Not even once? We wouldn't have stood a chance."

Jenna sobbed and her shoulders shook. Then she wiped her face with her forearm and took a deep breath.

"I was so scared of them," she whispered. "When you kidnapped me, I was just about to run away myself. Only I didn't know how to get past the dogs."

Jonas let out a jeering laugh. "No one knows how to do that," he said. "Except me, of course. I was with them every day when we lived there. I fed them, talked to them, and played with them. You never know when things like that might be useful, as my father used to say. Liron was on the lookout even then. But it was fun, too — they're good dogs."

So Jonas had lived in Osterlin, that's how he knew Malena. But *why* had Jonas and Liron been living there — two North Scandians, two rebels?

"The dogs would be more likely to attack Bolström," said Malena, "or Norlin, before they'd do anything to Jonas. The dogs love him."

Jenna nodded. She had stopped crying.

"But why were you afraid of the people at Osterlin?" Malena persisted. Jenna could see that she didn't really believe her.

"She's lying!" cried Jonas. "She just wants us to trust her. Why should she suddenly be afraid of her own people? After she's played along with them all this time?"

"I didn't play along with them," said Jenna, and realized that her voice was quite calm now. "I didn't even know what —"

"Yeah, right, you didn't know!" hissed Jonas. "Well, I'd really like to hear how someone can manage to go out in public and pretend to be the Princess of Scandia without knowing she's doing it."

"Of course I knew I was doing it," Jenna replied, glad that she could now feel something like anger again. "Only I didn't know how things were connected. I thought —"

"The southerners play along with tricks like that, sure," said Jonas. "No sweat. They think the new law will be good for them, and they forget everything they once knew. But you! You, you've got North Scandian blood in your veins! Though I suppose you're just a chip off the old block, when it comes right down to it."

Jenna shook her head vehemently. "I keep telling you, it's all a mistake!" she cried. "Of course you're going to think I'm North Scandian because of the way I look. But this is the first time I've been to Scandia in my entire life. It's the first time I've been anywhere!" Her face crumpled. "My mother . . ." She wasn't sure what to say about her mother. But then she thought about her family tree and that long list of names she'd gotten from Imran. How long ago that seemed now! "My father . . ." she began again, ". . . is from Turkey."

"Turkey?" Malena repeated in disbelief.

But now Jonas pounced on Jenna. "Do you think we're stupid?" he raged. "Turkey? Do you really think we're going to believe anything you tell us?"

Malena pulled him away. "If your father is . . . Turkish," she said and, if it were possible, her gaze was now even more searching. "If your father is Turkish, and if you never had anything to do with us and with Scandia before, then how did you get here? And on my birthday, why did you pretend to be me? When you were up on the balcony, why did you even . . . ?"

"It's disgusting!" cried Jonas. "Disgusting!"

Jenna felt the tears rising again. Suddenly she could see how naïve she had been.

"It was all because of the movie," she whispered. "I was supposed to be the lead. But first of all I had to prove —"

"Movie!" Jonas spat. "Now there's a movie, too?" With every word he grew angrier. But before he could hurl himself on Jenna again, Malena stood between them.

"Just let her speak, Jonas!" she said irritably. "We're stuck here, anyway, so why shouldn't she tell us her story? Then we can decide how much we want to believe."

Jonas let out a snort. Above the sheds the seagulls uttered their plaintive cries.

"Well?" said Malena. "What about this movie?"

19

*N*ahira had slept badly. If a problem had no solution, then a solution could hardly present itself to her during the night.

She got out of bed and opened the curtains. In the clearing around the house, where the boys always kept the grass short enough to play football, sat Meonok, Lorok, and a third boy whose name she couldn't remember. They were playing cards. They'd been complaining forever that TV reception was so bad here that they could only watch the news or the weather, and they'd only do that if it was important for an operation.

Other countries have satellite dishes, thought Nahira. *That would probably be the first thing we'd give permission for if we ever gained power: satellite dishes for north and south. The king had wanted to open the country up — he'd wanted Scandians to be free to learn what was going on in the outside world. But now we're light-years away from that again.*

She stuck her head out the window. "I'm making breakfast," she called. "Any of you want coffee?"

"Breakfast!" said Meonok. It sounded as if he was spitting out the word. "All we do is eat and wait. We'll soon be having supper!"

Nahira sighed. "None of you, then?" she said.

"Trumps!" Lorok declared, flashing his hand of cards. "And trumps, and trumps!" The others swore at their loss.

I'm beginning to lose them, thought Nahira. *I must be careful. One morning I'll wake up and they'll be gone, probably to one of the new rebel groups who are impatient, eager to fight — and to die. They've grown up knowing nothing but oppression, but they're not like the previous generation — they also know how unjust it is. I've got to think of something to keep them calm, at least for a while longer. But what will satisfy them that won't cause too much damage?* She put on the kettle for her coffee, and then went and took a shower. She had to take action, soon.

When Jenna finished talking, there was a long silence. Jonas hadn't interrupted her once.

"It sounds way too crazy to be made up," said Malena thoughtfully. "What do you think, Jonas?"

Jonas slapped his stomach, which was rumbling as if it wanted to answer. "It's possible," he mumbled sullenly.

"But I can't help wondering why you didn't suspect anything when they made you put on a wig. Surely there must have been enough blonde girls to play the part. Why did you think they chose you in particular?"

Jenna looked down at the floor. She felt herself turning red. "I guess I believed them when they said I had the best . . . presence," she answered. *Stupid, stupid, stupid!* she thought. It had been so easy for them to flatter her, because she had so much wanted to believe them — that was how vain she'd been. "And then after, when . . . when everything had gone so well, I realized that they must have noticed right away how similar you and I look."

"Yes, and . . . ?" Malena still sounded suspicious.

"I just figured movie people saw things like that," said Jenna. "Talent scouts, casting directors, they'd have an eye for it. And they'd invited so many girls to the audition that there was bound to be one who could easily be made to look like you." Jenna gulped. "But now I know there is no movie. They only staged the whole casting business in order to find a double. But I didn't know that before! Who could imagine such an elaborate . . . hoax?"

Malena gave her another searching look. Then she turned to Jonas.

"We've got to talk," she said.

"I'm afraid we'll get nothing out of him," said Bolström. For hours Norlin had been pacing up and down in the library, waiting. "He says he doesn't know where Malena and Jenna are. We've threatened him, and you know my agents don't hold back. It'll be some time before he looks like he used to."

Norlin groaned.

"There are additional methods, of course," said Bolström. "But I fear they won't help us with Liron."

"In other words, we shan't find the girls before the weekend?" asked Norlin. "Either of them?"

Bolström nodded. "This time I'm afraid you'll have to stand on the balcony by yourself," he said. "We've employed search teams, but the two of them could be anywhere in the country."

"In the north," said Norlin. "That's what you think, too, isn't it?"

Bolström shrugged his shoulders. "The north alone is too big to search, never mind the entire country," he said. "Listen, Norlin, I know you're worried, but we have to do something. Considering the mood of the people, the south is not yet ready for what we're planning — maybe not even for the new law. If we'd had the princess on our side, it would have been all right, but now . . . My agents need to give the situation a . . . let's call it a 'helping hand,' Norlin. They've been asking around, and there are still far too many doubters. Even in the south there'll be resistance to an invasion of the north, that much is certain. So we need more arguments in favor of it. Strong arguments."

"But no deaths!" Norlin cried hysterically. "I don't want to have blood on my hands."

"No deaths," said Bolström soothingly, and he put a reassuring hand on the regent's shoulder. "Just leave it to us."

Malena whispered something to Jonas, and then she sat down next to Jenna on a pile of nets. Jonas was leaning against the wall opposite them.

"So now you understand why they brought you to Scandia," she said.

Jenna nodded. "I was to pretend to be you," she whispered, "so the citizens would believe that the princess and the regent agreed about everything. To help the regent push through his law against the north."

"Something like that," said Malena. "Something like that."

"But why?" asked Jenna. "Why is it important for the princess to agree to the law?"

Malena looked at Jonas. "You tell her the rest of the story," she said. "There's still a long time to go before it's dark enough for us to leave the shed, no matter how loudly our stomachs rumble. Why shouldn't she know everything?"

"Everything?" asked Jonas.

Jenna saw Malena look at Jonas and nod, almost imperceptibly.

"OK," he said, and let himself slide slowly down the wall until he was sitting on the floor. "You know about the rebels? You've heard about the attempt to blow up parliament?"

Jenna nodded.

"OK," Jonas said again. "You know that North and South Scandia are divided by wealth?" Jenna shook her head. "Well," Jonas continued, "the south has all the money, because it owns all the northern mineral mines and oil wells and it relies on cheap labor from the north. Not too fair, right? And so the rebels want change. They've been around for a long time, but at first they were nonviolent. They didn't launch attacks.

They didn't throw bombs and they weren't even armed. At first all they wanted was to negotiate. With the king. About equal rights for the north. To some extent, you see, they still believed that the south was fair and just, which is what the south itself believed and what they'd always been told."

"Their movement kept getting stronger," Malena interjected. "More and more North Scandians joined them. And I presume you know who their leaders were."

Jenna shook her head. "Their leaders?" she asked.

"Two men and a woman," said Jonas. "They'd known one another since they were children, and they'd gone to school together in the south. Liron, Nahira, and Norlin."

Jenna stared at him.

"Norlin?" she repeated. "Who's now passing the law against the north?"

She saw Malena and Jonas exchange a glance.

"Don't you know that Norlin is a North Scandian?" asked Malena. "He just dyed his hair gray. That's why they call him the Silver Fox. Don't you know that he wears blue contact lenses to hide his brown eyes? Haven't you noticed that he's smaller than all his people? Haven't you heard his accent? It keeps on breaking through, even though he practices with one of our best vocal coaches every day."

"I had no idea," murmured Jenna. But everything was beginning to make sense.

"Like I said, they were best friends," Jonas went on. "Each of them would have died for the others — or at least that's what they thought. Norlin and Nahira, anyway. They were engaged."

"Nahira?" asked Jenna. *So that Nahira can see* . . . Liron had said. And Jonas had finished his sentence: . . . *that we can achieve something without the use of terror.*

Jonas nodded.

"But how?" asked Jenna. "How did Norlin become king, while Nahira is . . . on the opposite side?"

"She's leader of the rebels," Jonas answered. "And Norlin is only regent." He now looked as searchingly at her as Malena had done before. "The king was very young then, and he had a twin sister. They loved each other very much. But his sister . . . well, maybe they sent her to the wrong school. Someone must have done something wrong, anyway." He laughed, and Jenna waited.

"She supported the rebels right from the start," said Jonas. "She was a romantic, Liron said, and she admired them — their strength and the fact that they were fighting for a good cause. She wanted her brother, the king, to give in to their demands."

"Your father didn't want that?" asked Jenna.

Malena shook her head. "Not at the time," she said.

"The princess met with the rebels," said Jonas, looking hard at Jenna. "You know the rest."

Jenna shook her head. "No," she said. But she was beginning to have her suspicions.

"She fell in love," said Jonas. "With Norlin. And it turned out that the three soul mates weren't quite so committed after all — especially Norlin and Nahira. Norlin forgot he'd ever been in love with Nahira, and he went and married the king's twin sister."

"That's awful!" Jenna exclaimed.

Jonas and Malena exchanged another look.

"As you can imagine, the king was initially against the marriage, and there was a lot of unrest among the people, with their beloved princess marrying a northerner. But they got used to the idea, and Norlin really was a charming man. He moved to the court, and the king began to think things over, one step at a time."

Jenna nodded.

"Finally, he sent for Liron to come to the court as his adviser on northern affairs," said Jonas. "And the two became friends."

"And that's why the king wanted to pass a law giving rights to the north," said Jenna. "I understand now. But what happened to the princess? The king's sister?"

Malena smiled. "My aunt took her sympathies with the north very seriously," she said. "And that's why she was horrified to see how her husband changed. As soon as he was living at court, Norlin lost all interest in the north and its rights. On the contrary, he spent more and more time with people who were afraid of losing their privileges if the north was given its rights. His hair turned gray, his eyes turned blue, his speech lost its North Scandian accent, and he became more royal than his wife. And then one day she decided to leave him. She realized that he'd only married her because she was the princess — the fast track to the top of the social ladder. She despised him for his ambition, for how he'd turned against his own people. But her brother, the king, wouldn't allow a separation."

"Was he able to stop her?" asked Jenna.

Jonas laughed. "In Scandia, the king has total control, even today," he said. "Why do you think we're so shut off from the rest of the world? The king wouldn't allow a separation because a royal marriage is for life, and moreover the two of them had had a child by then. Norlin was also a very useful prince consort, because he kept the north quiet. If a North Scandian could actually marry the king's sister, the northerners thought, then why did things need to be changed? Couldn't any North Scandian be just as successful, if he was prepared to make the effort? The rebel movement in the north lost its support and went underground. The king couldn't allow his sister to separate from Norlin."

I hate politics, thought Jenna, *and now I know why — because it's always so complicated.*

"And so," said Malena, "she left him. In secret. She left Scandia by night and never came back. The king was heartbroken."

"Not her husband?" asked Jenna.

"He was just afraid he'd be driven out of court," said Malena. "But by then he was far too important to the king. But the king had also begun to turn more and more to Liron for advice. And when his little daughter was born — that's me, by the way — and his wife died, Liron was a great comfort to him in his grief. Jonas and I grew up together, more or less like brother and sister. But all the same, Liron and Jonas have never forgotten who they are."

"I see," murmured Jenna. She looked from Malena to Jonas. "Now let me pick up the story," she said. "I think I know what happened next. Liron was able to convince the king. And so the king wanted to pass a new law in favor of the North Scandians. But shortly before he could get it through, he suddenly died."

Malena turned her face to one side. Jenna thought she saw tears in her eyes.

"I'm so sorry," whispered Jenna. "I didn't think of him as your father."

"Yes, that was bad luck for the north," said Jonas grimly. "But very good luck for the mine owners and the plantation owners and the oil well owners from the south, right? Now everything could remain just as it had always been. Because Norlin, the Silver Fox, was the only member of the family left after the queen and the king had died, and so he took over as regent and as guardian to Malena."

"He's so evil!" said Malena, tears falling down her cheeks.

"And he immediately put an end to the law," Jonas continued. "Instead, his supporters quickly started work on a new one that forbids us northerners to move to the south — unless, that is, the southerners need us — and allows the army of the south to march into the north in order to crush any rebellion. This is the law that is now to be passed as if it's a triumph!"

"And that's why Norlin needs Malena," Jenna concluded. "But because she disappeared, he sent Tobias and Mrs. Markas to find a double. And they set up the whole casting hoax."

"And now you know the whole story," said Jonas. "More or less."

Jenna thought about it. "It worked out well for Norlin that the king died at just the right moment, didn't it?" she said with a questioning look.

Jonas nodded. "Liron was with him the night before," he said. "The king was perfectly fine."

Jenna glanced at the princess. She knew that Malena would be upset by what she was about to say.

"I overheard them saying that they wanted to kill the leader of the rebels before he could stir up trouble," she said quietly. "They've got no qualms about killing people. Not when it suits their needs."

Malena rested her head on her hands and sobbed.

But they haven't told me everything, thought Jenna. *I don't know why I'm so sure, but I know they still haven't told me everything.*

20

*T*hey didn't set out until it was dark.

"Where are we going?" Jenna asked.

Malena shrugged her shoulders. "We need to get something to eat," she said. "And see the news somewhere. I've got to find out what's happening."

"Do you think they'll tell everyone they're searching for us?" asked Jenna.

Malena laughed. "No way!" she said. "Let the world know that I've disappeared? That I'm not behind Norlin and his plans? The regent will find some excuse to explain why I'm not with him at the head of the parade on Sunday. But I'm sure he'll be screaming with rage. Without my support, he'll have to think of something really convincing to persuade the people that we need to have this law against the north, and that we must invade. And I want to know *what* he's come up with."

If you're hungry, you have to eat, thought Jenna as she stood guard in a narrow alley while Jonas levered open a window of an isolated house and cautiously climbed in. *And it's too early in the season to get fruit or vegetables from the fields.* Jenna couldn't remember ever having stolen anything, but now she didn't have even the slightest twinge of conscience.

Jonas jumped back out into the street from the window ledge. He had taken a sheet off one of the beds and filled it with everything edible that he could find: bread, cheese, chorizo sausages, spaghetti (where were they supposed to cook it?), and cans of soup, which they immediately opened with Jonas's knife once they were back in the forest.

"Mmm, delicious, cold pea soup," said Jonas. They passed around the can and took turns drinking it in noisy mouthfuls. "Cold pea soup without a spoon. Like a five-star restaurant."

Jenna had never been to a five-star restaurant, but she could imagine what her mother would say if she could see her daughter now.

"Why are you laughing?" asked Jonas, passing her the can. Jenna took a big mouthful.

"My mother would die of shame," said Jenna, reaching for a sausage. Jonas nodded permission. "She gives lessons in . . . etiquette."

Malena let out a sob.

"I'm sorry, I thought that would make you laugh," said Jenna, shocked. "I thought you'd think it was funny! Most people do."

Malena nodded and tried to smile. "It's all right. I just can't stop thinking about my father. No more for me, thanks," she said as Jonas offered her the soup can again. "You really think," she said hesitantly, and Jenna could see that she was still fighting back the tears, "that Norlin may have . . . that my father's death wasn't . . . ?"

"That's what Liron thinks," said Jonas. "Because he was with him the night before. And your father was as healthy as a horse. It would have been a strange coincidence if the king had died a natural death at precisely that moment."

Malena sobbed again, and Jenna looked for a tissue in the pockets of her jeans. Mom always made sure she had some tissues with her, but just when she really needed them, her pockets were empty.

Jonas stopped eating. "Liron didn't want me to tell you," he murmured. "He thought it would make you even more unhappy. And since Norlin needed you for his plans, Liron didn't think you were in any danger from him. He said there was no point in warning you."

Malena wiped her face with her hand. "I don't know why I'm crying," she said. "It doesn't make him any more dead than he was before."

"That Norlin is repulsive!" said Jenna. "He was so . . . he was so *weird* when I was at Osterlin. I think he's capable of anything."

Jonas paid no attention to her.

"I think it's right that you should know now, Malena," he said. "You should know how evil they are. You can see that once they've realized you'll be of no further use to them, they'll have no scruples about . . . you . . . the three of us."

Jenna stared at him. "Yes," she said. "That's what I think, too." She stopped chewing. "So somehow we've got to . . . we've got to get out of Scandia. Then we can tell the whole story to the media back home, and —"

Jonas laughed. "Genius plan," he said.

Jenna wasn't sure if she should feel offended. "Why not?" she asked. "You can give me back my cell, or we'll go to a telephone booth. I could call my mother and tell her everything, and then she could . . ."

Now Malena stopped crying and looked at her.

"You could call your mother?" Jonas said mockingly.

"Why not?" Jenna asked again. She felt herself getting angry with him. It was obviously the most sensible plan. "Till you took my cell away from me, I'd been sending her text messages all the time, anyway."

"Had you really?" asked Malena. Jenna was relieved that she had calmed down again.

"She wanted to know how I was doing," said Jenna. "I was totally amazed that she even let me go to the audition in the first place! And now she could tell the police what's going on."

"You sent a message to her," Jonas pressed. "And she replied?"

Jenna nodded vigorously. "Of course!" she said. "What's so surprising about that? My mother's kind of . . . protective, and she can freak out over the slightest thing, so I try to keep in touch. And anyway, I thought it was nice —"

"Not possible. There's no network connection to the outside world here," said Jonas. He rummaged in the bedsheet with both hands till he found two more cans. "Lentils? Lima beans?"

"What do you mean, no network connection to the outside world?" asked Jenna. Lentils on top of peas — that certainly wouldn't go down well. Maybe lima beans wouldn't, either. "No connection?"

"There's no transmission," said Jonas. "Lentils, then. Scandia has its own network, but you can't call abroad. And you can't phone in from abroad, either. Mali, pass me my knife."

Jenna stared at Jonas's hands as he tried to break open the can. "But she wrote back to me," she said. "She answered every time."

Darling Jenna, she thought. *I love you.* Mom never said things like that. Mom wasn't like that. And Mom had never written like that, either.

"Someone answered," said Jonas. "But it definitely wasn't your mother."

Enjoy yourself, Jenna! Perhaps I've sometimes been a bit too strict over the last few years.

That wasn't Mom. Mom would never have . . .

"But how could they do that?" cried Jenna. "How did they . . . ?"

"Did they ever have your cell?" asked Malena. She wrinkled up her forehead as she sniffed the lentil soup. "Ugh! Seriously, Jonas, couldn't you have stolen something more appetizing?"

Jenna thought back to the casting call at Roper's Inn, to Tobias and Raphael, and the lists all the girls had written their names on. *You can give any valuables to my colleague here, and he'll give you a receipt. Don't worry, you'll get them back. Schoolbag? Cell phone?*

"Then Mom doesn't even know . . ." gasped Jenna. "Then she must . . . I've been gone since Friday!" She jumped up. "Mom will be going *crazy* with worry!" she cried. "Somehow I've got to . . . to let her know I'm OK!"

Jonas held the can out invitingly. "If you want some, you'd better hurry," he said. "But there's no way you can contact your mother. How could you? You can't get away from here, and that's all there is to it. Believe me, Scandia's borders are impassable."

Jenna had an irresistible urge to run, to kick the tree trunks, anything. "I can't do that to her!" she cried. "You don't understand! My mom always worries so much, anyway, even in the best of times!"

Jonas laughed harshly. "Oh, poor baby, your mommy is worried," he said. "Ask me if I care. Just how important do you think you are? They've murdered Mali's father, they might be torturing *my* father at this very moment, but you're practically having a meltdown because your mommy might be worried." He flung the empty can into the forest.

Jenna hid her face in her hands. Jonas was right. But the fact that he and Malena had it harder than her didn't make things easier. Not for her, and not for her mom.

She suddenly sat up. "But wait, maybe it's a good thing!" she cried. "Back home the police will have been searching for me for days. And if they interview the other girls from school, they'll hear about the audition, and they'll track me down, and then —"

Malena got up and came over. She sat down beside her.

"I don't think so," she said softly. "I don't think they would take any chances, Jenna. In fact, I think your mother may have been . . ."

She stopped.

"They would have made sure she wouldn't send people to look for you," said Jonas. "There's no extradition agreement between the Scandian police and the surrounding countries, but they would have made sure. Trust me."

Jenna felt herself growing nauseous. The forest around her began to spin. It spun faster and faster, then everything went black.

Some time in the late afternoon, Meonok and Lorok took off. Nahira heard the engine start, and she looked out the window just as the station wagon went bumping slowly along the forest track. For a moment she thought of following, but then she didn't even bother to call after them.

If they wanted to leave, she wouldn't be able to stop them. She wondered if they would come back, and what they were planning.

Everything had gone horribly wrong.

"Has she come to?" asked Jonas.

His voice was the first thing Jenna heard. She felt as if she was coming up out of a deep dark tunnel to a place where everything was brighter and louder. When she opened her eyes, Malena's face was hovering just above her.

"Well?" said Malena comfortingly. "Are you back?"

Jenna needed some time to register where she was. The remains of that dizzy feeling were still in her head, but then suddenly she remembered what Malena and Jonas had said.

"I don't feel well," whispered Jenna. Malena wiped the sweat from her forehead with a corner of the bedsheet.

"Oh, come on, the soup's not that bad," she teased. "Look, you have to stop worrying about your mother. It won't help anybody if you dwell on it."

"It's all my fault," groaned Jenna. "If I hadn't been so vain and so proud of myself just because they chose me, if only I'd simply said I didn't want to act in their stupid movie . . ." She sat up. ". . . then they'd have taken another girl. Then nothing would have happened to Mom."

Malena and Jonas exchanged a look. "Yeah, right," said Jonas. "Jenna, forget it."

"It is what it is," said Malena. "And we've got to deal with it. And that means that we've got to start by moving farther inland. Here by the coast is the first place they'll look for us."

They followed the narrow road through the night, and there were no cars in sight — no headlights that loomed, flashed past, and disappeared, just the moon and the stars. Jonas claimed that he could map which way they were going just from the position of the stars. Jenna merely tagged along.

Not until early in the morning did they see the first cars, and immediately they turned off the road onto a sandy track. "We'll sleep away from the road during the day," said Malena. "Then go on again in the evening."

There was grass growing in the middle of the sandy track, and its potholes had not been filled for a long time. Jonas nodded approvingly. "Bet you the house at the end of this track is abandoned," he said. "Rejoice, my lady princesses. Maybe this morning you'll even be able to sleep in an actual bed."

But then they saw the car — an old, rickety Ford. It was parked right beside the house, from one window of which a light was shining.

"Now what?" whispered Jenna.

Jonas shrugged his shoulders. "They've mown the grass," he observed. "There are people living here. But what do they live on? There are no fields around here, no cattle, nothing."

"Let's go back," urged Malena. "It doesn't matter what they do, I don't want anyone to see me."

Jenna gazed at the house. It was small, the wood was painted yellow, and it looked indescribably cozy. Jonas should not have mentioned beds.

"Jenna!" hissed Malena.

At that moment the door opened and a woman stepped into the garden. She waved to them; perhaps she had already seen them from the window.

"Hello!" she called, and came a step nearer. "Can I help you?"

Jenna scarcely saw Jonas; he disappeared the moment he caught sight of the woman. And now something flashed in Malena's eyes — shock, recognition, something that made Malena's voice tremble when she answered.

"We've lost our way," she said, and lowered her head, her eyes on the ground.

The woman smiled wearily. "If you're traveling on foot, you must have set off very early in the morning," she said. "We're pretty far out here. Maybe you'd like something to drink before you go on?"

She reminded Jenna of the witch in the gingerbread house in "Hansel and Gretel." It was a ridiculous thought.

"No, thanks," murmured Malena, and turned to leave. "Sorry we disturbed you. We're off now."

"Malena," said Jenna, and tugged at her sleeve. "Just a quick drink."

In movies there were always streams when you needed them, but ever since they'd eaten the salty soup, they hadn't once been anywhere near fresh water.

Malena looked at her furiously. "You're so stupid!" she hissed.

By now the woman had come close.

"And what are you doing traveling by night?" she asked. She looked roughly the same age as Jenna's mom, but she was small and dark, and seemed totally worn-out.

Malena looked down and fidgeted with her clothes.

"You've run away, haven't you?" said the woman, and lifted Malena's chin with her hand. Malena struck her hand away and leaped back.

The woman smiled. "A boy from the south," she said. "As fair as straw, hiding in the forests of the north. You've run away, my boy, but you needn't be afraid of me."

Jenna saw Malena's shoulders slump. She still wouldn't look directly at the woman.

"You needn't be afraid of me," the woman said again. "I shan't tell anyone. OK? A drink?"

Malena gave in, but she pushed Jenna ahead of her and stayed behind her back.

The low front door led straight into a small room, half kitchen, half living room. There was a television on top of a chest of drawers, but the picture was flickering.

The woman went to the cupboard and took out two glasses. She put them on the table and filled them from a pitcher.

"There you are," she said. "Go on. Our well is famous."

But Malena didn't pick up the glass. She was staring at the TV, on which, barely discernible through the static, was an aerial view, presumably of the capital, taken from a helicopter. With a bound, the woman crossed to the television and turned up the volume.

". . . probably tens of thousands of South Scandian football fans owe their lives solely to the poor quality of North Scandian technology," said the voice of the newscaster. The TV helicopter was circling over a stone oval that was covered with rubble. ". . . only three hours before the playoffs at Scandia Stadium — a game sold out weeks ago — a massive bomb exploded in the stands." The camera showed a close-up of the ruins. "Evidently the timer went off too early, so that only two North Scandian cleaners — the only people in the stadium at the time — were injured. Two hours later, there would have been forty thousand fans gathered here, and judging by the scale of the destruction, the police estimate that without a doubt several thousand of them would have lost their lives."

Jenna leaned on the table. *Nahira,* she thought. The camera showed the roof of the stadium, which had collapsed onto the spectators' seats and shattered into huge blocks of concrete.

"The palace has called an emergency meeting. The regent is speaking of a tragedy for Scandia that once more has only just been averted. There will be a relentless hunt throughout the country for the perpetrators. The immediate suspicion is that the leaders are hiding on North Island, so the crisis committee will be seeking advice as to what means may be used to flush them out and bring them to justice."

Malena took a cautious step backward, and then she signaled to Jenna. "Go!" she whispered.

Jenna glanced at the woman. She was staring at the screen as if hypnotized, and breathing heavily. "The invasion," she murmured. "Now they've got a reason."

"Come on!" Malena hissed again.

It was not polite simply to disappear like that. But the woman was oblivious, anyway. She looked like she was on the verge of collapsing.

Jenna ran after Malena, across the clearing and into the forest.

21

*M*alena didn't look back.

"Mali," whispered Jenna. She didn't dare shout. "Malena, where's Jonas?"

But Malena paid no attention. She ran and ran, pushing the branches aside, jumping over fallen tree trunks, swerving around obstacles. And suddenly Jonas was running alongside them. They ran so far and so fast that Jenna thought her heart would burst, it was beating so violently. Every breath made her throat hurt. Finally, she flung herself on the ground.

For a moment the other two kept on running, but then they realized that Jenna was no longer with them, and they turned back. Maybe they were relieved that she'd given them a reason to stop running themselves.

The three of them sat among some blueberry bushes, speechless and breathless. Jonas was the first to recover.

"Did she recognize you?" he asked.

Malena's shoulders rose and fell with every breath. She shook her head. "You knew right away who she was, didn't you?" she said. "Jonas, she'd turned on the news. There's been an attack on the football stadium."

Jonas looked at her, wide-eyed. "How many dead?" he asked. His voice was almost inaudible, as if he didn't dare speak the dreaded word.

Malena managed a smile. "None — absolutely none," she said. Gradually her breathing became calmer. "The bomb went off too soon."

"At least that's something," said Jonas, and lay on his back in the undergrowth. "But it's still enough to justify an invasion. Now Norlin doesn't need a princess to support his attack on the north. Now even the most tolerant southerner will believe the northerners are dangerous terrorists who have to be stopped and punished. The rebels are so stupid, stupid, stupid. They couldn't have given the regent a better excuse to do what he was going to do anyway."

"No," murmured Malena. "Do you think it was intentional? That the bomb went off too soon? Do you think Nahira just wanted to give them a warning? Do you think —"

"How can Nahira be so stupid?" cried Jonas. "She's handing Norlin the best arguments on a plate. You'd almost think they were in it together."

Malena didn't answer. They lay among the prickly bushes and waited till they could all breathe normally again. Then Jonas propped himself up on his elbows. "So she didn't recognize you?" he asked.

"Nahira?" said Malena. "I don't think so. I hardly looked at her. I stayed behind Jenna as much as I could. She thought I was a South Scandian runaway."

Jenna gazed at her, openmouthed. "Nahira?" she gasped. "That woman was . . . Nahira?"

Malena nodded. "A ridiculous coincidence," she said. "At least Jonas recognized her in time and beat it. But she didn't recognize me. Or you, either."

"The rebel leader?" asked Jenna. "But what's she doing here in the forest when the bomb's going off in the city?"

Jonas laughed scornfully. "She's got her underlings," he said. "She won't dirty her own hands."

Jenna thought back to what she had seen. "But in that case," she murmured, "why was she so shocked when she saw the report? She looked petrified. She didn't even notice that we ran off."

"That's true," said Malena. "She was . . . she looked almost more horrified than we were. Maybe it came as a shock that the bomb had gone off too soon. She'd planned it differently."

"Yes," said Jonas thoughtfully. "That must be it."

The sun was peering over the tops of the pine trees, and gradually its rays began to reach down between the tree trunks to the forest floor. Only then, as the warmth penetrated through to her shoulders, did Jenna realize how cold she had begun to feel after their run.

"Can't we get some sleep?" she asked. "Just a tiny little nap?"

Malena nodded. "It's too dangerous to go on in daylight, anyway," she said. "Especially now, when they'll be combing the whole of the north for the rebels. This place will soon be swarming with soldiers. So let's all take a nap now, while we can."

Jenna closed her eyes and snuggled up between the prickly twigs until she was comfortable. She couldn't understand why she had found the thought of a bed so tempting before. There couldn't be a more wonderful camp than the sun-bathed floor of the forest, there among the blueberry bushes.

Nahira switched off the TV. More and more interviewees had been talking into the reporters' microphones, and she didn't want to go on watching. And anyway, they all said the same thing: The south had been patient with the north for long enough, had offered the northerners rights, had given them the chance to share in the country's progress; but now the north had gone way beyond the limit, and no one in the south could ever feel safe again. It was essential to put the rebels, and the whole of the north, in their place.

"Those stupid boys," muttered Nahira. "Those stupid, reckless boys."

She went to the table and slumped down on one of the chairs. Where did they get the explosives from? The key to the storage unit was still hanging securely on a chain around her neck — that was the first thing she had checked. So they couldn't have got them from there.

And how did they get into the stadium, which would certainly have been well guarded round the clock? They had made plans together, for the stadium as well as for the train station and every other public building in the capital, but Nahira never would have thought they'd be capable of carrying out an almost perfect operation on their own.

"Oh, you stupid boys!" she said again. She was only grateful that there had been no deaths; regardless, this was just the kind of incident the regent needed to justify an invasion. "You stupid, stupid boys!"

She looked around. The two runaways had disappeared — out of the corner of her eye she'd seen them dart off during the news. What was it that had suddenly terrified them?

Nahira reached for the pitcher and poured herself a drink. Her hand was trembling.

Right from the start the fair-haired boy had been excessively timid; he kept hiding behind the northern girl he was traveling with. It was not surprising — Nahira was sure he was a runaway. He had reminded her of someone — the girl did, too, now that she thought about it. But maybe she was just imagining things. Maybe it was simply the shock after that terrible news, and now she was seeing things.

She had to figure out what to do, whether there was still a way to stop Norlin. It was good that she was alone. She needed to think.

"Since when have you been so interested in the news?" asked Bea's mother.

"Since now." Bea turned up the volume on the TV. "They've bombed the stadium in Scandia," she said.

"Don't tell me you're still obsessed with that place," said her mother. She had a ballpoint pen in her hand and was bending over a newspaper. "Another word for *royal* — five letters." She liked crossword puzzles.

"Jenna wasn't at school again today," said Bea. "As for where she might be, everybody is totally clueless. She doesn't reply to text messages. And nobody answers at her house."

"Honey, I already told you, I'm sure they must have just left a little early on vacation," said her mother. "You're starting to get hysterical."

"Regal," Bea replied. "R-E-G-A-L. That's the answer. A five-letter word for *royal*."

"Well?" asked Norlin as Bolström entered the library. "How are people reacting?"

"You shouldn't be drinking cognac in the middle of the day," said Bolström. There was a note of disdain in his voice. "It's a habit you'll find hard to break."

"I didn't ask you for your opinion!" snapped Norlin. He slammed the glass down on the desk so hard that the liquid spilled over the rim and formed a little pool on the polished wood. Norlin took no notice. "What are people saying?"

Bolström sat down in an armchair. "Up to now, it's all very satisfactory," he said. "There's a real climate of fear. All those people who had tickets for the game are imagining how they would have been lying crushed under the ruins. It's all anyone can talk about. And fear clouds judgment."

"What do you mean?" asked Norlin.

"Their fear will turn to hate," said Bolström. "That's how the human mind works, Norlin. So don't you worry. If things go on like this, you won't have to worry about opposition to our invasion of the north. No one is going to sympathize with a nation of terrorists. South Scandians just want justice and peace."

Norlin reached for his bottle of cognac. "And Jenna?" he asked. "Any news of Jenna?"

Bolström took the bottle out of his hand.

"You've got to give an interview," he said.

When Jenna woke up, it was midday. The sun was directly overhead in a sky that was as blue as in a child's painting, and the ground was warm; she felt cozy and comfortable, and ready to sleep again. Next to her she could hear the quiet breathing of Jonas and Malena.

Jenna turned over on her side and tried to slip back into her dream. It had had something to do with Nahira . . . the dream feeling returned, just a tickle . . . Nahira, the woman in the little house in the forest . . . something hadn't been quite right in her dream, and that was why she had woken up.

She nestled a little deeper into the sandy hollow. Nahira's kitchen, the television, the bomb. Nahira was the leader of the rebels. And Bolström laughed and laughed, standing in the library, laughing, a pistol in his hand, pulling the trigger, the little house in the forest . . .

Jenna sat bolt upright. That was it! In an instant she was so wide awake that she knew there was no point trying to sleep again. That was it! As soon as they'd told her about Nahira, she should have realized — of course, Nahira — it couldn't be right . . . and there'd been no guards there, no soldiers, or they'd certainly have seen them, and the soldiers would have seen *them* . . .

"Jonas!" cried Jenna, shaking him by the shoulders. "Malena! Wake up!"

Jonas turned away and grunted angrily in his sleep. Malena stared at her as if she had come from far, far away.

"Malena," said Jenna, without letting go of Jonas's shoulders. "I've got to tell you something."

"What?" asked Malena. She closed her eyes again. Jonas mumbled something in his sleep and tried to push Jenna's hand away as if it was a pesky insect.

"Don't go back to sleep," cried Jenna. "Wake up! Wake up! It's important!"

Malena sighed. "Nightmares?" she asked. But Jenna could see quite clearly that she was now awake. "Can't it wait?"

Jenna shook her head. "Jonas!" she cried desperately.

"Hit him," said Malena, stretching her limbs. "That'll do it. Wow, what gorgeous weather. We could have used a bit more sleep, though."

Jonas gave a jerk when Jenna slapped him lightly on both cheeks with the back of her hand. "No! Hey! Get off me!" he cried. Then he looked around uncertainly. "Argh! I dreamed that someone was hitting me."

"The things people dream," said Malena with a mischievous smile.

Jenna ran out of patience. "Listen, something just occurred to me," she said. She knelt on one knee, and felt a twig sticking into her shin. "And I had to tell you right away. Something's not right."

Jonas yawned. "That's your big revelation? Tell us something we don't know," he said. "Heck yeah, there's something not right — about virtually everything in Scandia. And guess what? There was an attack on the stadium; and some dumb girl just woke me up when I was right in the middle of the nicest dream — and that's *definitely* not right."

"I know, I know, I'm sorry," said Jenna. "But I had a dream, too, and when I woke up . . ." She looked from one to the other and began again. "Look, over the weekend, at Osterlin, I overheard a conversation between Mrs. Markas, Bolström, and Norlin — I told you about it, remember? They were talking about killing the rebel leader?"

Malena nodded. "You did tell us, yes," she said.

"And all the time," Jenna said excitedly, "they were saying they had him under observation."

Jonas looked at her. "Really?" he said. Suddenly he, too, seemed wide awake. "Are you sure about that?"

"You mean there were guards surrounding Nahira's house, and we didn't see them?" asked Malena. "They're watching her all the time? But then they would have seen us as well!"

Jenna shook her head vehemently. "No, no," she said. "If so, they'd have taken us prisoner on the spot. And maybe Nahira, too, after the stadium attack. The point is, I don't think there was anyone there."

"I don't, either," said Jonas. "Nahira definitely wasn't under surveillance."

Malena looked puzzled. "You mean they're observing the wrong hideout?" she asked.

"No!" cried Jenna. She was now so agitated that she kept tugging at the twigs. Tiny green blueberry leaves fluttered to the ground. "They always talked about *him*. *He* won't know what hit *him*, we'll shoot *him* — they were talking about *a man*. Not about Nahira. They weren't talking about the leader of the rebels at all, don't you see? They know the leader of the rebels is a woman."

Malena frowned. "But you said they wanted to kill the leader of the rebels," she insisted. "That was what you heard. You didn't imagine it, did you?"

Jenna pulled at a twig, and the bark scratched her hand. "I thought they were talking about the leader of the rebels. Because they said they wanted to prevent a civil war. That's why I automatically assumed that was who they meant." Between her thumb and forefinger a tiny droplet of blood emerged from the scratch.

"Civil war?" repeated Jonas, looking at Malena.

"And who else could they have meant?" asked Jenna. "But there's no doubt, they were definitely talking about a man."

"And they wanted to kill him so that he couldn't possibly get away," murmured Jonas. "And start a civil war. And only Norlin was against the assassination."

Jenna nodded.

"Mali?" said Jonas. "Mali, are you thinking what I'm thinking?"

Malena didn't answer. Jenna was shocked to see that she was trembling.

"There's only one person I can think of," said Jonas quietly. "Mali? Only one man who could possibly stop them from pushing through their law. Only one person the people would rally around to oppose the Silver Fox, even if that meant a civil war. Mali?"

Malena was now shaking so violently that it frightened Jenna.

"Leave her alone!" she said. "Can't you see she's upset?"

Malena stood up. She took a few deep breaths, and when she spoke, she looked neither at Jenna nor at Jonas.

"He's dead," she said softly. "We know he's dead."

Jonas leaped up and grasped her arm.

"How do we know that, Mali?" he cried. "We saw the coffin, and we were there when it was lowered into the grave. But did you see the body for yourself? Did they let you go and see him one last time, to say good-bye?"

Malena slowly shook her head. She seemed almost to be in a trance. "The doctor said . . ." she whispered. "The doctor didn't want . . ." She began to sob.

"Malena!" cried Jenna, and looked angrily at Jonas.

"He was well — just the evening before, he was perfectly healthy," said Jonas. "Malena, maybe they didn't kill him after all! Maybe . . ."

"Norlin didn't want to," whispered Malena. "Norlin . . ."

"Who on earth are you talking about?" cried Jenna. "Can I be let in on the secret now, please?"

Malena and Jonas looked at each other, and Malena clapped her hands to her face.

Then Jonas turned to Jenna. "We're talking about Malena's father," he said. "We're talking about the King of Scandia."

PART THREE

22

Ever since two runaways had disappeared, Nahira had been sitting waiting at the kitchen table. She couldn't have said what she was waiting for. She only felt that there was nothing she could do. The TV was on with the volume turned down, and the pictures kept repeating themselves. Never before had she felt so helpless.

She leaned her head on her hands. Helpless and utterly weary. Events had taken the worst possible turn.

Nevertheless, the longer she sat there, the more she believed that something was . . . brewing. There was something at the back of her mind, though she had not yet grasped what it was. Something she had seen or heard. Something . . .

She stared at the screen, though by now she could see the images even with her eyes closed. The oval stadium, the ruins. The barricaded streets, roped off with fluttering yellow-and-black tape, the panic-stricken people, gesturing wildly, and then back to the stadium again. The ruins. But that wasn't what was bothering her. No, that was not it.

Her head sank down onto the tabletop, and for a fraction of a second she wondered if she should let sleep take over. But then she sat bolt upright.

Of course! What she had seen had not been on the television screen — it had nothing whatsoever to do with the attack.

The runaways.

"Malena!" whispered Nahira. That was why the boy hadn't wanted to look at her. "The princess . . ."

The stubble-haired boy, the shorn head — there could be only one explanation. Malena was on the run.

"She's running away from Norlin — she's not on his side," murmured Nahira. "Even though on her birthday she . . ."

She stood up. She would make herself a cup of coffee, and maybe something else would come to mind, something quite different from what she had supposed. Something was still missing — she knew that she still hadn't grasped everything.

"The girl!" she said out loud. The kettle was taking forever to boil. She drummed her fingers on the metal between the hot plates, and paced up and down. If she closed her eyes, she could see them both again, and there was no doubt that one of them had been Malena. And the other one? She looked like Malena, too.

The kettle whistled.

Who could look so similar to Malena?

Nahira forgot to make her coffee.

"Jenna," she murmured, and sank down onto the kitchen chair.

Suddenly she knew that all was not yet lost.

"Do you really think it's true?" whispered Malena. She was trembling so much that Jenna wanted to hug her. "But then . . ."

"Then that changes everything!" cried Jonas. "It does, it does! Look, if we've got this right . . ."

"I think we do," said Jenna. "I really think it's true. It all makes sense."

"Then it must be like this," said Jonas. "They wanted the king out of the way before he could change Scandia forever by enacting laws that would result in southerners losing their privileges. But Norlin was against killing him — Jenna says he doesn't seem happy about some of the plans, so perhaps he isn't as callous as Bolström. And that's why they just got rid of the king and *pretended* he was dead. Such kind people!"

"And they've taken him someplace where they can keep him under surveillance round the clock," said Jenna. "But they also know that if he ever got free, it would ruin their plans completely."

"Exactly!" said Jonas. "And that's why Bolström wanted to have him killed. But Norlin was still against it."

Jenna nodded. Malena calmed down.

"Now let's assume," said Jonas, getting louder and increasingly excited, "that the king escaped. What do you think would happen then?"

"You mean if he told everyone what Norlin had done to him?" asked Jenna. "And that the whole funeral was a complete fraud?"

"And that the whole birthday business was a complete fraud, too," said Jonas. "And that Norlin not only kidnapped the king but also deceived the people. Believe me, there'd be such an uprising that Norlin would be forced to abscond abroad as fast as his legs could carry him. Nobody likes to be scammed — and certainly not the people of Scandia."

"And that means . . . ?" said Jenna, looking inquiringly at Jonas.

"That means there's only one thing we can do to save Scandia," said Jonas. "We've got to find the king."

"Yes, we must find your father, Malena," said Jenna.

"Come on, Malena," said Jonas, shaking her by the shoulders. "Where do you think he might be? Where do you think they've taken him? You know Norlin best."

Malena lifted her head. The shaking had stopped, but her eyes were still expressionless.

"I just don't know," she whispered. "I have no idea."

When the station wagon roared into the clearing and screeched to a halt next to the old Ford, Nahira jumped up. The kitchen door flung open, and Lorok, Meonok, and two other men not much older than them stormed in.

"Have you seen the pictures?" cried Meonok. "Have you seen the bombed stadium? Who did it? Who messed the whole thing up? Nahira, were you behind it? Without even telling us?"

Nahira shook her head. The boys looked furious — she had never seen them so angry. She felt relieved, though it dawned on her that the truth was even more dangerous than everything she had feared.

"So it wasn't you," she said. "And how could it have been — there never would have been enough time. But I thought you might have been in contact with our supporters in the south. I was afraid you'd gotten fed up with waiting."

"It wasn't any of them, either!" cried Lorok. "At least none of those we've contacted. And no one has a clue who it might have been."

"Liron?" asked one of the other men. Nahira felt conscious of the fact that once she had known the names of all her supporters. Now there were too many of them.

"Never!" she said. "Liron was always against violence. I'd hoped he'd come to us as soon as Norlin had wheedled himself into power after the king died. But . . ."

Méonok had opened the fridge door to look for something to eat. With an angry expression on his face, he slammed it shut. "You know what I think," he said, looking first at the other three and then challengingly at Nahira. "There's no villain worse than the regent himself."

Nahira nodded thoughtfully. "I think you're right, Meonok," she said. "This bombing is very useful for him — perfect timing. Just like two months ago, when the king died."

The boys looked at her.

"Norlin's preparing to invade the north," she said. "I think we can be certain of that. But there's something we can do."

"We're all ready for action!" cried one of the young men. He didn't yet have enough hair on his chin to shave. "We'll gladly die for our country. For our honor."

Nahira waved her hand dismissively. "No one's asking you to do that," she said. "What you have to do is a little hunting. You need to find his quarry before he does. Because you can be sure that he's out hunting, too."

"Who?" asked Lorok. "Who's looking for who?"

"Just a few hours ago," said Nahira, "I saw Malena. And Jenna. And they were on the run, running away from the regent."

Meonok whistled through his teeth.

I can't tell them that they were both here, thought Nahira, *here in this house, and I never recognized them.* "If we find them first, we'll have a trump card in our hands," she said. "Get as much help as you can. And search this part of the forest carefully. They can't have gone far."

❦

"Why is everything so difficult!" Jonas complained, then swore bitterly under his breath. The sun had gone down behind the trees, but it was still almost as bright as day. "We know he's alive, we know he can save us all — but we don't know where he is, and so there's nothing we can do!"

"And we can't even tell the police," said Jenna. She turned her head. There had been a noise somewhere in the under-growth. "So they can't help us find him."

Jonas laughed caustically. "Definitely not," he said. "They're too busy searching for us."

No one said anything more. They had been thinking and talking all afternoon, but they had failed to come up with an answer. Things were almost worse than before, thought Jenna. To know that there was a way out, to be so close to it — and yet not to be able to reach it.

Then they heard the noise again, nearer this time. "Jonas," said Jenna, "I think I can hear —"

Malena lifted her head, too. "Shhh!" she said, and put her finger to her lips.

In the undergrowth everything was still and silent.

"Girls!" said Jonas. "The sun has hardly gone down, and already you're getting jumpy. What about rabbits, squirrels, and deer? Are they supposed to stop breathing just because we've crawled into their territory?"

Jenna shook her head, relieved.

"Isn't there someplace that Norlin might have mentioned?" Jonas asked for the umpteenth time. "Mali? I don't think they would have put your father in a state prison — that would attract way too much attention. Based on what Jenna told us, he's probably being kept in some perfectly ordinary house, but miles from anywhere. Otherwise, why would they be so scared that he might escape?"

"Yes," murmured Malena.

"Do you think it's more likely to be in the south?" asked Jonas. "Think, Mali! Or in the north? What's your opinion?"

Malena shrugged her shoulders. "Norlin's got so many people working for him," she said softly. "And Scandia is so big. Some forests are so deep that no one's ever found their way through them. He could be —"

She didn't finish her sentence. The men raced into the clearing, all at the same time. Even if they'd been able to scream, it wouldn't have made any difference: There was no one to hear them. Still, the first thing the men did was gag them. There were at least six of them, and they weren't wearing uniforms.

We're goners, thought Jenna, amazed that she was able to think so clearly. *Norlin got us.*

One of the men grasped her shoulders, another her feet. Roughly they put her down on the rusty floor of an old station wagon; next came Malena, and finally Jonas.

If only they hadn't gagged them. Jenna tried to catch Malena's eye. To her astonishment, Malena's expression seemed almost happy.

There was no doubt about it. Malena, the Little Princess of Scandia, was smiling.

23

When the station wagon rattled into the clearing and pulled up outside the little yellow house, Jenna was not surprised. Heavy dark clouds were rolling across the sky, and in the distance she thought she could hear the first rumbles of thunder. Otherwise, all was quiet.

The entire drive, Malena had never stopped smiling. And so Jenna had realized that it was not the regent's men who had captured them; soldiers or police would have been wearing uniforms.

Their kidnappers could only be rebels. The men were taking them back to Nahira.

The rebel leader stood in the open doorway. "Careful!" she cried as the men let go of the tailgate and it crashed down. "I told you to treat them gently. They're not our enemies. And take those gags out."

One of the young men loosened the ropes around Jenna's ankles. "Just wait," he yelled over his shoulder to Nahira. Then he gave Jenna a poke in the ribs. "Get down," he said.

Jenna tried to stretch — she was stiff again. The drive had been short, but she was beginning to feel like she'd done nothing in the last few days but get kidnapped, tied up, and driven around Scandia.

"So, you're back again," said Nahira. "And you, too, Jonas. You, too, this time."

Jenna was surprised to see how totally different Nahira seemed compared to just a few hours ago. Before, she had looked exhausted, almost without hope, but now she seemed younger, full of energy, even happy. "Stupid of me not to have realized right away who my guests were."

She signaled to the three of them to sit down on the sofa. Jonas shook his head defiantly, and one of Nahira's men went to grab him, but Nahira waved him away. "Leave him alone," she said.

The television on top of the chest of drawers was on, though still without any sound. Jenna recognized Bolström, who was talking into a microphone and making expansive gestures.

"The longer they go on talking about the attack on the stadium, the greater they make the danger seem," said a man who had already been sitting in the kitchen when they came in. "I can't stand it anymore. One of them was just saying that it won't be possible to control the rebels without a military invasion of the north. They want to get you, Nahira."

"That's nothing new, Tiloki," said Nahira. "Now if you could just take your eyes off the screen for a moment, the princesses are here."

"Oh, hello," said Tiloki. "I'd never have expected to meet the two of you under these conditions."

Jenna looked at Malena, confused. She was no longer smiling, but she still seemed calm, almost content.

"Well?" she said. "What are you going to do with us?"

Nahira looked at her thoughtfully.

"We don't really know yet, Mali," she said. "My goodness, you've grown since the last time I held you on my knee."

"That's almost ten years ago now," said Malena. "Right around the time you thought it was your duty to return to the north and gather a rebel force around you."

"Yes, that's what I thought then," said Nahira. "And that's what I still think now. You can see what it's come to, Malena. You can see what your uncle is up to. And I know that you don't agree with what he's doing . . ." She closed her eyes and lowered her head. ". . . at least not anymore — even though you looked happy enough waving down from the balcony with him on your birthday — but why else would you be running away from him now? You *are* on the run, all three of you, aren't you?"

Malena nodded. "Why else would I have cut off all my hair?" she said. "And as for my birthday, at the palace and in the open car, that wasn't me, either." She pointed at Jenna. "It was her."

Nahira didn't say anything for a while. "It was Jenna," she murmured at last. "Of course, who else? But if Jenna was obviously so willing to support Norlin, why is she here with you now, and not still helping to deceive the people of Scandia?"

Jenna was shocked to see the anger in Nahira — more than anger, for it was so violent that her voice was quaking. What now blazed at her out of Nahira's eyes was sheer hatred. *How does she know my name?* thought Jenna. *Who told her about me?*

"Jenna had better tell you her story herself," said Malena, and smiled encouragingly at Jenna. "And, Nahira, what she's going to tell you is the truth, so listen carefully. She could have betrayed Jonas and me when we escaped to the north, and several times after that as well. What Jenna says is true, Nahira. Jonas and I both believe her."

"Meonok!" shouted Nahira. "Lorok! Come here. Come and listen to what Jenna has to say."

Jenna looked from one to the other, and took a deep breath. Tiloki stood in front of the oven, and Nahira leaned against the cupboard. Meonok and Lorok remained in the doorway.

On the TV screen, the helicopter circled the ruins of the stadium once more.

". . . and because I was so happy that they'd chosen *me*."

When Jenna had finished her story, there was deathly silence in the kitchen. Toward the end, Jonas and Malena had interrupted her occasionally, and piped in with comments about their escape with Nanuk to the north. Jenna had already realized that both of them were hoping to enlist Nahira's help in searching for the king. She wondered what Nahira would demand in exchange, and she thought of the parliament crater and the devastated stadium.

Tiloki coughed. "So that's how it was," he said, looking thoughtfully toward Nahira. "Well, then . . ."

"Well, then, you can untie us now," said Jonas. "Because we're all on the same side, against the Silver Fox."

Nahira nodded. "Untie them, Meonok."

"However, we're only on the same side because your attack on the stadium didn't succeed," said Malena firmly. "Even if just one person had been killed, Nahira, I'd never work with you on anything. Let's get that clear. We're not going to support you if you launch attacks against people, or put lives in danger. I'm Princess of Scandia, and every single Scandian, whether in the south or the north, is under my protection. I'll never allow you to harm a hair on the head of any one of them."

Lorok sneered and gave a deep bow. "Your Royal Highness," he said, "how, exactly, do you propose to do that?"

But Nahira shook her head at him in annoyance.

"That's how it should be, Malena," she said. "And so far we haven't harmed a hair on any Scandian's head. How could you think that I'd be so stupid and so clumsy as to miss the parliament building if I'd really wanted to hit it?"

"You missed on purpose?" asked Jonas. "That's exactly what Liron said!"

"Liron has known me longer than anyone else," said Nahira. "Apart from Norlin, that is."

Once again, Jenna saw her eyes fill with hatred. *Of course,* she thought. *Of course Nahira hates him. After all, they were once going to be married. And then he married the princess, the king's twin sister, instead.*

"And we had nothing to do with the stadium," said Nahira. "What do you take us for? Hasn't it occurred to you who will benefit from that attack?"

Malena nodded. "Yes, I thought that, too," she said. "Nahira, you've taken us prisoner, but perhaps we'd have come to you of our own accord — I thought about it earlier. We need your help — the help of all your people. If we're quick enough, and if we work together, maybe we can stop my uncle."

"There's nothing I'd rather do," said Nahira. "But how?"

Malena nodded to Jonas, who looked as if he was about to burst.

"The King of Scandia is alive!" he cried. "Jenna overheard Norlin say so."

24

Nahira made coffee and took the steaming pot outside to the clearing. Jonas drank the strong, bitter liquid, but Malena and Jenna shook their heads, and Nahira brought them another pitcher of water instead.

"What it means, then," said Nahira, "is that they're holding him prisoner somewhere. And if we could free the king, there'd be an uprising in the country — and what an uprising it would be! Norlin would have to abandon a lot more than his plans!"

"You mean he'd have to flee Scandia," said Meonok. "What Norlin has done is high treason. And the whole country would back the king if he sent Norlin packing."

"I thought you were all rebels," said Jonas mockingly. "Where has all this sudden enthusiasm for the king come from?"

Lorok made an impatient gesture with his hand. "Then let's set him free," he said, "before they do kill him. They know what a threat he can be to them — that's obvious from the conversation Jenna overheard. And who knows how much longer Norlin can go on protecting him?"

"Yes, great, wonderful, let's set him free!" cried Jonas. "We'd already figured out that much ourselves. We just have to find him first! Scandia's a big place."

"They didn't say where he was being kept?" asked Tiloki. "Did they at least give some indication?"

Jenna shook her head unhappily. "I keep trying to think," she said despairingly. *"Up there in the forest,* they said — I remember that. But there are forests all over Scandia. And whether they meant the north of South Island, or North Island . . ."

"You've got so many supporters, Nahira," Malena urged. "Don't you? If you send them all to look for my father, if you tell them that he's still alive, then maybe someone will remember something he's seen or heard. That's why I wanted to come back to you, anyway. There are only three of us — Jonas, Jenna, and me — but you've got hundreds of followers who will listen to you. If all your people search for him . . ."

"Even if all my people search for him, it'll still be a huge stroke of luck if they find him," said Nahira. "Think, Malena. Are they supposed to search every single house on the islands? And how could they do that without the regent and his people noticing? If Norlin even suspects that we know the king's still alive, and that we're trying to set him free . . . you know yourself that he wouldn't hesitate to have him killed."

"You're giving up?" cried Malena. "Now that we know my father's alive, you're giving up? It wouldn't be exciting enough for you, I guess. No explosions, no bombs, no ruins, nothing that a *real* rebel can enjoy. Is that it, Nahira, is that it?"

Nahira gave her a long look. "You can apologize to me later," she said. "We need another way to find out where they're holding the king. And I know what it is. She has to go back to them."

It took a moment or two for Jenna to realize that Nahira was talking about her. She hadn't mentioned a name, or pointed at her, or even looked in her direction.

"If you really think we can trust her, she must go back to Osterlin."

"But . . ." whispered Jenna.

"She overheard him once, and she can overhear him again," said Nahira, in a tone that brooked no opposition. "She can hunt for clues at night in papers and documents. And if she gets caught, I guess she can say she's sleepwalking — he won't touch her. If she's really smart, she can even try to find out from him directly."

Tiloki laughed cynically.

"Why not?" asked Nahira irritably. "He's a sentimental man. She told us how strangely he behaved when he first saw her. If she goes back to him now, dirty, hungry, and exhausted, and she tells him how she only managed to escape from the rebels by outsmarting them, and how she struggled back to him with no food, no sleep — don't you think even shrewd Mr. Bolström will believe her when she says how much she hates her cruel kidnappers?"

"That won't be enough," said Tiloki. "They won't tell her where they're keeping the king just because of that."

"You're young, Tiloki," said Nahira. "You don't understand people yet." She nodded thoughtfully. "Just imagine how thrilled they'll all be when they've got a princess back, and on Sunday she can step out onto the balcony again with Norlin. She'll be supporting him in full public view. And they're bound to believe Jenna's sincere after she's suffered so much at the hands of the regent's opponents. His enemies are now her enemies." She laughed. "Anyone who's gone through what she's gone through would start asking questions, and if she asks them subtly enough . . ."

Jenna felt panic rising inside her like a wave threatening to engulf her. She didn't want to go back. No way. Not alone. Not now. Not ever. And yet . . .

"I agree that maybe it might be possible to find out," she heard herself saying. Her voice was almost breaking; it sounded strange even to her, croaky and nervous. "There are only a few people at Osterlin, and so maybe at night I could . . ." She hesitated. She didn't feel proud of what she said next, for Malena was certainly no less frightened than she was. But that was the least of her worries now. "Perhaps it would be better if Malena went back instead? She knows her way around better than I do, and she'd certainly be much quicker."

"Nonsense!" said Nahira sharply. "If he's going to tell his secret to anyone at all, he's most likely to confess to you."

Fearfully, Jenna shook her head. "But he'd believe Malena just as easily," she cried. "Malena could also tell him that the rebels captured her and kept her prisoner. That they even cut her hair. She can say you tortured her and so she hates you now — it's no different from me telling them that. She knows her way around Osterlin, she knows everything better than I do, so she would be a much better spy than me!"

Nahira looked at her through narrowed eyes. "So it's true," she murmured. "She doesn't know."

She stood up and walked toward the center of the clearing. Then she stopped, with her back turned to everyone. Above the trees a first flash of lightning ripped open the blue-black sky, and a gust of wind shook the topmost branches.

"Who's going to tell her?" asked Nahira over her shoulder. "Don't you think it's time? Shouldn't she know why she's the right person, indeed the *only* person, to get Norlin's secret out of him? Why he'll have tears in his eyes, tears of joy, when she returns to Osterlin?"

No one moved, and the only sound was the thunder crashing like a mighty drumroll before it faded into a dark rumbling.

"Let's go inside," said Nahira.

Even before they had reached the door, the next flash of lightning lit up the clearing, and the thunder followed it almost immediately. Then the floodgates of the heavens opened and the raindrops smashed down on the leaves in an almost deaf-ening torrent.

Tiloki closed the door behind them.

"Well?" he said.

Jenna stared at him, then at Nahira, and finally at Malena and Jonas. She had figured out long ago that they had not told her everything.

Now she was about to learn the final secret.

"Jenna," said Malena. For a moment it seemed as if she wanted to take her in her arms to protect her against what she now had to tell her. "Nahira is right, you must go to him. You and no one else. He will never do anything to hurt you, Jenna — never. Don't you understand? Norlin is your father."

25

"*N*o," whispered Jenna.

It was as if she was turning hot and cold, as if everything was spinning, as if the kitchen was disappearing behind a veil of mist. There was a rushing in her ears, and her heart pounded to the bursting point. "That's not true!"

That's not true. That can't be true.

That mustn't be true.

Don't let it be true.

It can't be true because it mustn't be true, such a thing mustn't be true, not me, not Jenna, they've got it wrong, definitely, not me.

"I don't want it to be true," whispered Jenna.

To her surprise, it was Jonas who now put an arm around her shoulders.

"It is," he said gently. "Sometimes even the worst things are true."

"He mustn't be my father," whispered Jenna. "He mustn't."

Jonas held her close. "You can't choose your parents," he said. "Believe me, I know."

But Jenna was no longer listening to him. Did none of them understand? Had they all lost their minds?

"He can't be my father!" she cried. "Are you all insane? He married the princess and has always lived in Scandia. And I've never . . ."

Malena knelt down before her. The veils of mist began to clear, the rushing in her ears died away, and only her heart continued its wild beating, as if it wanted to leap out of her chest and fly away from everything.

"It's true," whispered Malena. "Jenna, it's true."

"But — Mom!" cried Jenna. Then she burst into tears.

Mom: tall, blonde, and regal. She knew how people should behave in any kind of situation, how they should move and dress. She knew what cutlery should be placed beside which plate, how to use it, how to greet people, and whom to greet first.

"Mom," whispered Jenna.

Why had she never wondered how Mom knew all those things? She'd just been Mom, a woman without any training or qualifications or family background, someone who'd muddled through from one job to another until at last she'd solved her financial problems by giving courses in social etiquette.

Why had it never struck her that none of this fit — none of it?

"Mom . . ." whispered Jenna, ". . . is the king's sister?"

"His twin sister, yes," said Malena, and offered Jenna her handkerchief. "Here. You're my cousin, so you can have my hanky. Wipe your eyes and blow your nose."

"That's why she would never tell me anything," said Jenna quietly. The kitchen still seemed to be swaying around her. "I had to make up my own family tree for history class. I took the names from Imran."

Malena smiled. "You're Scandian through and through," she said. "The very best kind of Scandian — the kind that the future belongs to, half north and half south."

Jenna blew her nose. The sound was a little jarring — horribly everyday. "Not a foreigner," she murmured. "Norlin."

"Don't be sad," said Malena. "Jonas is right. No one can help who their parents are."

Jenna glanced at Nahira. To her surprise, the hatred had vanished completely from Nahira's face. If Jenna had to describe what she saw there now, it would have been pity.

"She lied to me all those years," whispered Jenna. "Lies, lies, lies. I don't know if I'll ever forgive her."

"But what should she have done?" asked Nahira. "Let you grow up in fear that one day someone from Scandia — the king's men, perhaps, or more likely Norlin's — would come to take you away? She went underground as soon as she left Scandia, got herself forged papers and changed her name, but she must have lived in constant terror that she would be tracked down, that one day they would find her."

"That's why she was always so nervous," murmured Jenna. "That explains it. Oh, poor Mom."

"So, you see, she did the right thing," Jonas agreed. "And now you know. Your mother is the king's sister, the much-loved princess of all the Scandians, and they've grieved for her year after year."

"So does that mean . . . ?" asked Jenna, suddenly sitting bolt upright. "Am I . . . ?"

"Yes you are!" cried Malena. "You're third in line to the throne: I'm first, then comes your mother, and then it's you. Princess Jenna of Scandia, through whom the north and south are united."

"North and south," murmured Jenna. "Of course. Norlin's child."

There was a moment's silence.

"So now you can understand why it's *you* who must go back to him," said Nahira directly. She had kept out of the conversation until then. "He was obviously overjoyed to have you back with him. His long-lost daughter, his Jenna. He almost gave himself away at your first meeting."

"Yes," whispered Jenna. He'd had tears in his eyes, and he'd stammered her name. He loved her, no matter how terrible a man he was, no matter how devious and cruel, how greedy for power; the regent loved her, that much was certain. Norlin, her father. She had always longed to have a father . . .

"For heaven's sake, don't start blubbering again!" said Nahira. "That's the way it is, and you can't change it."

"But I don't want it to be true," whispered Jenna. "I don't want it." The words were almost incomprehensible beneath her sobs. "Make it go away."

Once again it was Jonas who put his arm around her.

"You know that we can't do that, Jenna," he said. "No one can. But I understand how you feel, believe me, I do."

"I can't be the daughter of a . . ." sobbed Jenna. She felt sick. "He's a criminal! I can't be . . . I'm not the daughter of a criminal!"

"Hush, Jenna, it's all right," whispered Jonas. He was the only one talking to her now, the only one comforting her. "The fact that *he's* a criminal doesn't make *you* a criminal. You're still you, and nothing can change that. You're exactly who you were before we told you — the girl who didn't give us away while we were escaping, the girl who wants to save Scandia."

He held her tightly and repeated gently the same sentences over and over, as if they were a magic formula. Slowly Jenna calmed down and her head fell onto his shoulder.

"I'm still me," she whispered. "Yes, it's true."

"Of course it's true," said Malena forcefully. It seemed as if it was only now that she dared speak to Jenna again. "You're still you. And what's more, you're my cousin, and that's . . . not a bad thing! Since I've got no brothers or sisters, I mean."

Jenna looked at her.

"I need time to think about this," Jenna said softly. "It's all got to . . . I've got to get it straight in my head."

Malena smiled. "Oh, definitely, give yourself time," she said. "Another glass of water? After crying all those bucketfuls, you'll need to fill up again, won't you?"

Jenna tried to smile back.

Around her stood Meonok, Lorok, Tiloki, and Nahira. They were all looking at her with a kind of awe, as if she was a newborn child, a miracle — and instead of laughing, she burst into tears once more.

She couldn't change a thing. That was how things were.

26

*J*enna couldn't sleep.

Nahira had even made up beds for the three of them in an empty room; and after the previous sleepless nights, she should have slept like a log.

The storm was over. Through the curtainless window she could see the edge of the forest close by, as impenetrable as a dark wall, while above it, milky white and blue, hung the moon. The stillness was so profound that she could hear it; only occasionally would a bird call out in its sleep. Jenna's pillow was wet with tears.

"Jenna?" whispered Jonas.

Before they had at last gone to bed, they had discussed their plans, and it had taken hours before Nahira was satisfied. The soundless pictures had passed before them on the TV screen — the stadium in ruins, the regent distraught, the Supreme Commander of the Armed Forces gesticulating, the stadium in ruins . . . over and over again.

"Jenna?" whispered Jonas again. "Are you asleep?"

If Jenna had to say how she felt, she wouldn't have been able to find the words. *Despair* was too strong, and yet not strong enough. Everything inside her was numb, as if she would never feel any emotion again — not worry, nor shock, nor fear, and certainly not joy.

"Shut up!" she said.

It was as if the earth had caved in under her feet. There was nothing left for her to stand on; she was in endless free fall. Her whole life had been a lie, and now she had even lost confidence in who she was.

I am not me.

I am still Jenna. But the name is only a label to cover what has been hidden all my life. I am a princess of Scandia, and I have lived a made-up life, and, without knowing it, I have deceived everyone I have ever known.

How ridiculous it was to feel guilty about devising a fake family tree for history.

The only consolation was that she finally knew the answer to the question that had tormented her ever since she had been old enough to ask: "Who's my father?"

It was no longer a secret. Her life was suddenly as clear as crystal, everything had been explained, everything made sense. Except that it was no longer *her* life.

"I want to tell you something," whispered Jonas.

Couldn't he just leave her alone already?

"Haven't you ever wondered about *my* mother? Why I only have Liron . . . though, then again, I guess you don't really know us."

Now he's going to tell me that his mother is dead, thought Jenna. *That she died when he was still a baby. Or that she just died, and he's still grieving. He's going to tell me all his drama — that he's had a hard time, too. So he knows what it's like.*

Like that's *going to comfort me.*

"We lived at court ever since I could remember," whispered Jonas. "You know that now, anyway. And you know that Malena and I grew up together, almost like brother and sister. Her mother was dead, but mine was alive. It wasn't just me she picked up when I fell, and it wasn't just my knee she'd stick the bandage on. She was a mother to both of us. And she was so beautiful. She was the most beautiful woman in the court."

Jonas paused.

Now he's trying to see if I'm awake, thought Jenna, *if I'm listening to him. But he'll keep on talking even if he thinks I'm asleep — I can hear it in his voice. He's talking because he has to talk. I'm just his excuse.*

"She and Liron had the same beliefs, of course — originally," Jonas resumed in a whisper. "She'd been a rebel, just like him. But now she stood on the balcony next to the king, holding Malena's hand and waving to the crowds in the palace square. And she wasn't happy. Liron kept quarreling with the king, trying to convince him that the north and south should have equal rights. But by then she couldn't have cared less about that. She didn't understand why Liron was still so concerned about it, now that he was doing so well and could have done even better."

The words passed over Jenna as if they had no meaning, like quiet music. Soon she would go to sleep. Soon.

"She admired Norlin. 'He's doing the right thing,' she used to say. 'Why do you still bother yourself with these old ideas? We could have a palace of our own if only you'd toe the line. Don't be a fool.'"

Jenna turned over on her side. He could go on talking in his soft, monotonous tone. The first dream images were already waiting behind her eyelids.

"Then one day she left us, went off with a South Scandian courtier. She got a divorce — everything perfectly legal — and married him. Now she's living with him on his estate by the sea, and he owns oil wells, mines, factories. She couldn't care less about the north anymore."

What is he talking about? thought Jenna.

"I know what it's like to be ashamed of your parents," whispered Jonas. "To wonder if maybe one day you might turn out exactly like them. My mother's a traitor, just like your father. So you're not the only one, Jenna. I know just how you feel."

There could be nothing more beautiful than sleep. So warm. So protective. All was well . . .

"Jenna?" whispered Jonas. "Are you listening?"

Then came the first dream.

As dawn broke, the door opened almost silently. There were plenty of dungeons in the castle, down below in the oldest part of the building, where tourists would go shuddering between the thick walls, testing the weight of chains that were heavy enough to prevent even the strongest of prisoners from escaping.

That, of course, was not where they were holding him captive.

"Good morning, Liron," said Norlin.

Throughout the night, the light in the little room they had rigged up as Liron's makeshift cell had been blinking on and off. No matter how tightly he had closed his eyes, even when he had covered his head with his arms, the flashing had continued to pierce his eyelids. On and off. On and off.

"I want to talk to you."

Liron propped himself up on his elbows. There was a TV perched on a bracket high up on the wall. All night long, pictures had been flickering across the screen, and Liron had had to put up with the voices of the reporters, and the interviews. "You don't expect me to get up, do you?" he said. His lips were swollen, and the words came out slowly and awkwardly.

Norlin waved his hand. "Liron!" he said. "Be reasonable. You know we're stronger than you, and if you're going to be stubborn, you'll only make things worse. Not just for yourself. For our people as well."

Liron laughed. He wasn't surprised that laughing hurt, too.

"Tell us where the princesses are," said Norlin. "Tell me where Jenna is. No one else but you could have abducted her — no one except Jonas could have gotten past the dogs. It's useless to deny it. Let me have Jenna back."

"You're overestimating her importance for the success of your plan," said Liron. "Or is this a father's longing? You've achieved what you wanted with your bombing. The mood in the south has finally turned in your favor. People hate the north now because they're afraid of it."

"What makes you think it was *our* bombing?" asked Norlin. Liron could hear the alcohol in his voice. "Everybody knows that Nahira was behind it."

Liron slumped back. "Norlin," he said. "We both know Nahira. That was not her doing. She's not stupid. She knows that something like that would only harm her cause." He laughed again. "You never enjoyed mysteries, did you? The most important question for a detective is always: Who benefits from the crime? Once he knows the answer to that, he knows the identity of the criminal."

"We could have you interrogated again by our *specialists*," said Norlin menacingly.

"Torture?" Liron asked scornfully. "Why aren't you brave enough to say it, since you're brave enough to do it?"

"We don't use torture!" shouted Norlin.

Liron ran his tongue over his split lips, then touched the painful swelling over his cheekbone. "Oh, Norlin," he said. "The ironic thing is that it won't get you anywhere. No matter how much you lie, no matter how many places you bomb and then blame it on the rebels, all you're doing is plunging what used to be a happy country into total misery. You can't possibly believe for one minute that the north is going to swallow your laws and your invasion without a fight? What nation would let itself be treated like that? Believe me, Norlin, if you push on with your plans, you'll find out what it's like to suffer *real* attacks by *real* rebels, and then it won't just be a matter of ruined buildings. You're driving Scandia into civil war, and in the end it's the whole country that's going to suffer."

"So you're not going to talk?" asked Norlin. "To tell us where you've hidden Jenna?"

"Because I don't know," said Liron, turning on one side. "What I don't know I can't say, and no amount of torture can change that."

Norlin slammed the door shut behind him.

27

This time they crossed the sound at night, and the coast guard never came near them. A different fisherman, one of Nahira's followers, took them, hidden below deck, and when they approached the coast of South Island, he switched off his navigation lights. It all went very smoothly.

Two cars were waiting for them when they landed in a remote bay. Nahira accompanied Jenna, along with Tiloki, Lorok, and Meonok. Malena and Jonas were there, too, according to the plan. They waited hours before finally venturing to drive off, but no one seemed to have followed them.

After a few miles, they left the road and drove along a narrow, sandy track. At one point, Tiloki and Lorok had to get out and move some branches that looked as if they had been ripped from the trees in a storm; they came upon similar obstacles a second and third time. No one would ever have suspected that there was a house at the end of this path, but suddenly there it was, in the afternoon sun: rotting wooden boards, gloomy windows, a barn, a stable.

"This is it," said Nahira.

"We'll lose it afterward," said Tiloki. "Do you really want to give it up forever, Nahira? It's one of our best hideouts."

"There's no other way," she said brusquely. "They're sure to test her story. So now try and remember everything, Jenna. Whether they'll believe you or not will depend entirely on how well you can lie. How well you can lie," she said again, hesitantly, "will decide the fate of Scandia."

Jenna nodded, and Lorok blindfolded her. Then he pushed her forward across the unmown grass toward the house.

"Take note of all the sounds," said Nahira. "Take note of the smells, of what you bump into, of what you fall over. You never saw the house we took you to. Your eyes were covered throughout the journey, and we didn't take off the blindfold till you were in the room, and when you escaped, you wouldn't have seen very much of the house, anyway. But we kept you prisoner here for three days, so you must know what you heard, and how it feels to be locked in a room. You have to be able to give them a detailed account." She closed the door behind Jenna, and turned the key in the lock.

The room was small; there was a foldout cot standing against the unplastered wall, and in a corner on the floor there was a bucket. Through the barred window Jenna could see an overgrown clearing, and there were young birch trees everywhere. When she listened carefully, she could hear the splashing of a stream.

The others were talking somewhere in the house. Their voices were muffled by the wooden walls. She couldn't make out what they were saying, but she could distinguish one from another. Four kidnappers — Nahira had drummed that into her — and judging by the voices, one of them was a woman.

Jenna lay down on the cot and pulled the thin blanket over herself. During the nights she would have been freezing. Where was the moon in relation to the window? Surely she wouldn't have to give them such precise details; they wouldn't ask her things like that?

"Nahira!" Jenna called out. "I think I've got it. I know what to say now."

From the depths of the house she could hear the sound of cutlery on china, and someone laughed.

"Nahira!" she cried again. "You can let me out now!"

They must have heard her — the walls were so thin. "Hello, Nahira! I've taken a good look at everything!"

The conversation continued, but then she heard footsteps. They stopped outside the door.

"I hope you're comfy in there," said Nahira. Her voice sounded strangely cold. "I hope you get used to it out here, little Jenna: all alone, in the forest, in the middle of the night, because unfortunately we can't stay any longer. We're just having a little snack, then we'll be going. Starvation is not a nice way to die, and dying of thirst is even worse. Sorry. After a few days, apparently, you lose consciousness, and then it doesn't matter anymore. Good-bye, little Jenna! Good-bye."

"Nahira!" cried Jenna.

The footsteps went away.

"Nahira!" Jenna screamed. She jumped up from the cot and banged her fists on the door. A feeling of nausea rose inside her, and her heart was racing. "Nahira! What are you doing?"

But no one answered. From the next room came a sound like chairs being shoved under a table.

Again Jenna beat on the door with her fists until her hands were burning. "Malena! Jonas!" she screamed. She could not understand what was happening, and she drummed and screamed, and the sweat poured down from her forehead into her eyes. Why were they locking her up? What good would that do them? They could never carry out their plan now.

"Nahira!" cried Jenna. "Malena! Jonas!"

Maybe Nahira was still full of hatred for Norlin, and for Jenna's mother for winning his love. But why weren't Malena and Jonas standing up for her? Could Nahira have locked them up, too, maybe in another room?

"Nahira!" cried Jenna. "Nahira, please! Please, please, please! Nahira!" She was sobbing like a baby.

"Good-bye, little Jenna," said Nahira from outside the door. "Unfortunately we still have a lot to do."

A man's voice laughed.

"Malena," sobbed Jenna, her voice cracking.

"Have a good time, Jenna," said Malena. "Make yourself at home."

"Yes, make yourself nice and cozy," said Jonas. "After all, you do have a bed."

Then an engine started up, followed by another. Jenna heard the cars drive away from the clearing. She threw herself on the bed and buried her face in her arms as waves of panic engulfed her.

Bolström pulled open the door to Norlin's bedroom. The bedside lamp threw out a bright circle of light, but Norlin lay naked on his bed, fast asleep. Opposite the bed was a television set with a huge flickering screen; the sound was off.

"Norlin!" shouted Bolström, and turned the sound up loud enough to wake the dead.

Norlin was startled out of his sleep. He looked at the alarm clock beside his bed.

"Two o'clock in the morning," he said. "Bolström, what in tarnation is going on?"

Bolström tightened the belt of his silk bathrobe and sat down on a chair by the window.

"You'll soon see," he said.

Norlin stared at the screen. Once again there was a helicopter moving across it, with the green light of its night vision device and the clatter of its rotors.

"What is it?" asked Norlin, propping himself up on an elbow. "What happened?"

Bolström gestured with his hand. "They're doing the work for us," he said. "They've attacked the bridge across the southern sound."

The helicopter had almost come down to ground level. The camera panned to the side. A framework of steel and concrete came into view, stretching for a quarter mile across Scandia's deepest gorge, elegantly curved and as delicate as the finest lace — the pride of the country, its center now torn out. Twisted like steel wool, a tangled mass of iron girders reached up out of the ruins; pillars three hundred feet high had broken like matchsticks.

"No!" gasped Norlin. "That wasn't part of the plan, Bolström!"

"It certainly wasn't," said Bolström. The helicopter now dived down toward the bay and flew alongside the bridge, or what was left of it. "And that would certainly not have been my first choice if I'd considered it necessary to stage another bombing. The bridge will cost us a fortune, Norlin. It'll take years to rebuild, and it's a disaster for the Scandian economy. The shortest link between north and south — I can't even begin to describe the consequences." He sighed. "That was why we chose the stadium. The effect on the people was massive, and the damage to the economy minimal."

"So it wasn't us?" asked Norlin. Now he was staring wide-eyed, and all traces of tiredness had disappeared.

"What do you think?" snapped Bolström irritably. He stood up and began to pace back and forth across the room. "We'd have to be crazy to inflict such damage on ourselves. This time it really was the rebels, Norlin, and they're not fooling around. At least they didn't carry out the attack till after midnight, when there wasn't much traffic on the road. We don't yet know how many cars went down. They're still holding back from going full out, but even so, there are bound to have been fatalities. It's serious now, Norlin. The gloves are off. Who knows what their next target is going to be?"

Norlin was breathing heavily. "Then we've got no choice," he murmured. "Everyone can see that, everyone. We've got to crush them. We've got to invade the north. There's no place for people like that in a peaceful Scandia."

Bolström nodded thoughtfully.

"There can't be anyone now who doesn't realize that," he muttered. "Not even the idealists and dreamers. Still, I do wish the price hadn't been so high." He stood next to Norlin's bed. "You've got to get up, Norlin," he said. "We'll fly to the gorge right away, tonight. The regent must be at the scene of the disaster, at once, without delay. You have to give the first interviews. And put the army on red alert. The citizens have to see uniforms everywhere now. That reassures them, and at the same time it makes the scale of the danger clear."

Norlin nodded. "I'm coming," he said. "You can go."

Bolström smiled. "Yes, Your Highness," he said, "but for heaven's sake, put some clothes on." He reached for the bottle on the bedside table. "And you don't mind if I take this with me, do you? At such an early hour, I'm sure you won't be needing it."

With an ironic bow, he pulled the door shut behind him.

Jenna lay on the cot, looking out the window. *Now I really could tell them where the moon is,* she thought. *I can watch it moving along over the tops of the trees. At least that'll be something for me to do.*

At first, she had cried and she had screamed, but she had long since quieted down. She wondered what it would feel like to starve to death. But, then again, she would die of thirst before that. They hadn't even left her any water. It must be terrible to die of thirst.

She burst into tears again. *This can't be happening,* she thought, *it just can't be happening. If I went to sleep now and woke up again, maybe it would all turn out to be a bad dream — everything I've been through since the audition at Roper's Inn a week ago.* Roper's Inn. It seemed a million miles away now.

When she heard the cars arriving in the clearing, she sat up with a start.

"I'm here!" shouted Jenna. It didn't matter who was out there, Norlin, Bolström, anyone, anything was better than lying in this tiny room and dying of thirst. "I'm here. Help! I'm here. It's me, Jenna. Let me out, please, let me out!"

A key turned in the lock, and then the door opened.

"Now you know what it feels like," said Nahira, pulling Jenna out of the room. "Now they'll believe you when you tell them all about it."

Jenna stared at her.

"Nahira only wanted you to get a taste of it for real, Jenna," said Malena, pushing her way past Nahira. "You'd never be able to convince them about how frightened you were if you hadn't experienced it in real life. Bolström is no fool."

"But *you* didn't have to go along with it!" said Jenna. "Not you, or Jonas!"

"Well, we were just being careful," said Nahira. "They didn't want to do it at first. So, did you almost die of panic? That's perfect. Go on, have another good cry, it's all part of it. A tear-stained face will make it all the more convincing."

Jenna wiped her eyes with her sleeve. Maybe it had been necessary to lock her in and make her experience that sense of panic — it probably had been. But she'd also seen an expression of satisfaction in Nahira's eyes. Nahira still didn't know whether she should hate Jenna.

Lorok offered Jenna a glass of water. "Here, you should drink something before you run away," he said. "There's water everywhere in the forest, so there's no need for you to be suffering from thirst when you get there. But you do have to be hungry. There's nothing for you to eat."

Jenna drank greedily. "And where am I going?" she asked.

"Keep following the path till you get to the road, and then turn right," said Nahira. "As soon as a car comes along, wave it down. And later, when the time is right, give us the signal and we'll be there. Good luck, Jenna. Everything depends on you."

Jenna nodded, and Lorok grasped her arm tightly, too tightly, so that later she would be able to show her blue bruises.

"Just a second, Lorok," said Malena. "Don't forget, Jenna," she whispered, "whatever you do from now on, never forget that you are a princess of Scandia."

Jenna gazed at her for a moment, then slapped Lorok's face, tore herself free, and ran. She heard Lorok swear, and then his footsteps pounding the ground behind her. In the dusk it was difficult to avoid tripping and falling among the trees, but the moon shed just enough light to illuminate the path. She hid behind a tree and waited till Lorok had gone past her. Only after a minute or two — which seemed like an eternity — did she cautiously go on, past the fallen branches, as far as the road. And there, once more, she began to run.

Would she have done the same thing if she'd really been escaping? Is that how Lorok would have behaved? As far as her story was concerned, it would have to do.

Behind her the headlights of a car emerged from out of the gloom, and Jenna jumped into the road, waving her arms.

Nahira was waiting in the clearing when Lorok returned.

"Well?" she asked.

Lorok shrugged his shoulders.

"I could have caught her, easily," he said. "Anyone who bothers to think about it would certainly realize that. Only a bad fall could have stopped me, I'm so much faster than her. But they won't think about it much. When baby bunny comes home, his darling little Jenna, so desperate and distraught, they'll believe anything she tells them. Dear oh dear, who could have done such terrible things to her? It's a clever story you've concocted there, Nahira. It could all have happened exactly as she'll tell it."

"Yes, it's a good story, if she tells it well. And she will."

From the house came a cry of rage, and then the hubbub of several raised voices.

"Now what?" Nahira said, worried.

"Nahira!" shouted Tiloki. He came rushing out of the house, panting, with Malena following close behind. "Nahira, come and see this. There's been an attack . . ."

"Another one?" asked Nahira in surprise. "But they've only just—"

"I don't think it was them this time," cried Malena.

Tiloki shut the door behind Nahira. "The bridge over the South Island gorge. That's the last thing they'd choose to destroy. The damage to Scandia's economy will be far too great — isn't that what you've always said? I don't think it was Norlin, Nahira. This time it wasn't him."

In the darkness of the kitchen, the only light came from the flickering images on the screen.

"The horror!" said Nahira.

Now there's nothing I can do to stop it, she thought. *I've lost them.*

She looked at Tiloki despairingly, struggling to voice her thoughts. "For a long time we've posed a threat and been a major force in this struggle, but we've been able to prevent the worst from happening. I knew people were getting desperate, especially after the last few months, but I'd hoped . . . I'd hoped . . ."

What had she hoped? That she'd find a simple solution to the centuries of inequality? That she could keep on her side every boy who'd lost his job, every girl who couldn't even get one to begin with, every mother and father who couldn't find a way to feed their family?

"And now it's going to get worse," she continued in a whisper. "After the new laws are passed, or after the invasion, they'll know who's to blame for their misfortune: Norlin and the south. For every single thing that goes wrong, that will now be the explanation. The hatred will grow, and they won't hesitate to endanger people's lives. This is just the beginning. Once the avalanche has started rolling, once the attacks have begun, nothing can stop it." She fell into silence. *And everything the south does to protect itself will be useless, because they'll be dealing with people who won't hesitate to risk even their own lives. I've tried to prevent it, and I've failed. Who can protect their country against suicide bombers? What threats can Norlin use against people who are ready to make the ultimate sacrifice?*

"Nahira?" asked Tiloki, breaking into her thoughts. "Are you feeling all right?"

Nahira sank down onto a chair.

"Jenna has to succeed," she whispered. "She's got to find out where they're holding the king. Only if we can rescue the king does Scandia stand a chance. Only if the king stops what Norlin has started. But it has to be soon. Good grief, Tiloki, it has to be soon. If it takes too long, there'll be new incidents every day, and the southerners' hatred of the northerners will become so ingrained that even the king himself, back from the dead, won't get any support for his reforms."

Malena looked at Jonas.

"Then let's go," said Meonok. "As soon as Jenna reaches them, they'll want to check her story and find the place where she was held. And they've got to find it abandoned."

Nahira nodded.

"Is everything the way we want it to be when they get here?" she asked.

Meonok nodded.

"Come on, then," said Nahira.

They had discussed every last detail. She was to phone the court at once. Phone the court to get them to come and pick her up. Until then, she must pretend to be a perfectly ordinary North Scandian girl.

"You understand, Jenna?" Nahira had said. "Norlin and Bolström won't want anyone to know that there's someone running around impersonating Malena. So you mustn't let anyone know who you are. Besides, you don't look so much like Malena now, with your dark hair and your brown eyes. Phone Bolström, and they'll come and get you. And that will set the ball rolling."

That was exactly what Jenna did now. Jonas had given her back her cell (it didn't matter if Norlin's people could trace the call — to the contrary, all the better if they could), and Tobias's and Mrs. Markas's numbers were already stored on it. The moment she got into the car, she called them. Although the day was breaking, Jenna was sure that everyone at Osterlin would still be asleep. And indeed, both numbers went straight to voice mail, the automated recordings stating that the persons she was trying to contact were not available.

"No answer?" asked the driver. "Nobody there?"

Jenna shook her head. To her surprise, she realized that she was trembling. Perhaps he would think that she was simply shivering in the cold morning air.

"So where do you want to go?" asked the driver. He glanced sideways at her. "I'm only going as far as the next town, Saarstad."

Where had she heard that name before? "That's where I want to go, too," said Jenna.

He'd certainly believe that — a North Scandian girl working on a farm in the remote north of South Island, hitchhiking to the nearest town because she didn't have enough money for the bus fare. She was grateful that he'd given her a ride without asking too many questions.

During the journey, she tried calling Tobias and Mrs. Markas again, but with the same result.

By the time they drove into the town, the sun was up. On the market square the local bakery was already open, and the wonderful smell of freshly baked bread hung in the air as she got out of the car.

"Good luck, young lady," said the driver. "I hope you'll find someone to give you a ride back. Some tough times ahead for you now. All of you. That bridge business isn't your fault."

"Thank you," whispered Jenna, wondering *What bridge?* as she sat down on a bench near the bakery. She was feeling pretty faint now, she was so famished. But hunger was good. The hungrier she was, the more she would eat when they "rescued" her, and so the more convincing her story would be. Kidnappers allowed their victims to starve.

The market square was filling up with people going to work, bicycles, cars, children with backpacks. But not until nine o'clock did Mrs. Markas finally answer the phone.

"Mrs. Markas speaking," she said. Over the line her voice sounded even harsher than Jenna remembered.

"Hello," whispered Jenna. "It's Jenna. Mrs. Markas, it's me, Jenna."

Jenna was shocked to realize that her voice was trembling. But that was all for the good, too. She'd been kidnapped. She had almost died of fear, hunger, lack of sleep.

There was silence at the other end.

"They kidnapped me, but I escaped. Please come and get me, please, please. Hurry!"

"Jenna?" asked Mrs. Markas. Jenna could hear the disbelief in her voice. "Now this, on top of everything else?"

"Please, Mrs. Markas!" cried Jenna. A passing cyclist turned to look at her. She began to cry. "I escaped. Please, please. I'm scared they'll find me!" Her sobbing became convulsive.

"Where are you?" Mrs. Markas asked. She still sounded suspicious.

"Someplace called Saarstad," sobbed Jenna. "A man gave me a ride when I escaped, but I know they're after me, and if they find me—"

"What did you tell him?" Mrs. Markas asked sharply. "The man in the car?"

Nahira had foreseen this.

"Nothing at all," whispered Jenna. "Just that I wanted to go into town. So he dropped me here. At the market square. I'm sitting on a bench. But I'm so scared!"

"Stay where you are," said Mrs. Markas. "We'll be there in half an hour. We'll come in the helicopter."

Then the line went dead.

Jenna stretched out on the bench. She didn't care what people thought. She was exhausted, and she couldn't go on any longer.

They ended up sending a car, while the helicopter waited in a field outside the town. Tobias leaped out of the driver's seat and took her in his arms.

"Jenna!" he cried. And she wept on his shoulder. People turned around to look at them.

"No public scenes, please," Tobias whispered. "Everything's all right now. You're back with us."

Jenna looked up at him and nodded. *It doesn't matter if I'm all confused and panic-stricken,* she thought, *that's just the shock after the kidnapping. Nothing I do now can possibly give me away.*

Bolström was waiting in the helicopter. He looked as if he hadn't slept a wink all night. He cast a questioning glance at Tobias, who nodded to him.

"What a relief," said Bolström. "Little Jenna is back. And after such an ordeal."

Jenna burst into tears again. "I was so scared," she sobbed. "They . . . they tried . . ." Once more she was too shaken to speak.

"Here, take my handkerchief," said Bolström. "We'll talk about it all later. The regent is waiting."

298

Jenna realized that they couldn't decide whether to trust her. Nahira had warned her that this, too, might happen.

"They were so hideous," she sobbed. "They locked me up, in a tiny room, with bars on the window and nothing but a cot. It was so horrible . . . . I thought I was going to die! They said they'd leave me to starve." She was sobbing so much that she couldn't catch her breath. She could see the tiny room, the moon over the treetops, and she remembered the fear she had felt. "I was so scared. And the woman—"

"Woman?" asked Bolström.

"Nahira," sobbed Jenna. "They called her Nahira. She was . . . I think she was their leader. They all did as she said."

"Nahira," murmured Bolström. Once again he looked closely at her, as if he could read exactly what had happened from her face and her actions. "You've been through an ordeal. Well, we shall see."

He didn't say any more. Jenna wept. Throughout the remainder of the flight, no one said another word.

"Why Nahira?" asked Norlin.

They had taken Jenna to the princess's room at Osterlin — the room she already knew. Mrs. Markas had stayed with her.

"She says that the leader was a woman, a woman named Nahira," said Bolström. "Ask her. I don't know how much we can believe."

"But it was *Liron* who kidnapped her," said Norlin. His face was gray with the shocks of the previous night. "It's only that dreadful son of his who could have kept the dogs quiet. I wouldn't like to think that we'd tortured him without good cause. And just a few hours after Jenna was abducted, Liron was offering a scoop to the newspaper reporter."

"But he didn't tell the reporter what the scoop was, did he?" said Bolström. "Jenna's name was never mentioned, nor was the princess's — just 'a scoop.' People have become very careful, Norlin. We questioned the reporter often enough; you were there yourself."

Norlin nodded. "But it would be a very remarkable coincidence for both of them to try and take her," he said.

"Maybe Liron and Nahira have been working together," said Bolström. "If that's the case, heaven help us all."

"I'd like to see her now," said Norlin. He reached for his bottle of cognac and poured himself a glass. "When all's said and done, she is my daughter."

"Mrs. Markas is with her," said Bolström. "She's pretty exhausted. Don't drink so much, Norlin. It's scarcely morning."

When Norlin entered the room, Jenna was sitting at the table, eating. Her dark hair hung in tangled strands down her back. Her face was pale, and there were deep blue shadows under her eyes.

"She can't stop eating," said Mrs. Markas. "She must not have had any food for days."

Good, thought Jenna, stuffing a piece of cheese into her mouth, followed by a slice of ham. *Good, good, good. The kidnappers wanted me to starve.*

"Jenna," said Norlin. He knelt down in front of her, and the smell of hair lotion and liquor wafted into her nostrils. "Little Jenna." He pulled her to him.

Jenna stiffened. *He's not my father. He mustn't be my father.*

Mrs. Markas came to her aid. "Apparently one of the kidnappers tried to . . . She resisted, and she's covered in bruises. I'm sure you can understand, Your Highness. It's made her a little sensitive."

Jenna relaxed. *Yes, yes, sensitive, that's right,* she thought. She had told Mrs. Markas how she'd managed to get away — precisely as Nahira had drummed it into her: Early in the morning, when all the others were out, the young rebel who had been left behind to guard her had come into her room. He had pulled her out of bed and kissed her. He had torn at her clothes. But in his excitement he had forgotten to close the door behind him. (*We can only hope they'll believe it,* Nahira had said.) Jenna had slapped his face, scratched him, and fought him off, and finally she had managed to get away. He had followed her through the forest, but he tripped and fell, and she'd been able to hide behind a tree. It had still been dark. Then she'd made it to the road and flagged down a ride to the nearest town.

"She looked terrible when we found her, Your Highness," said Mrs. Markas. Jenna realized to her surprise that Mrs. Markas felt sorry for her. "She must have gone without food and sleep for days."

Jenna looked at the table, and grabbed another slice of bread. She took a large bite.

"But what . . . ?" she whispered. "Who . . . ?" Nahira had told her she'd have to ask for an explanation why the rebels had kidnapped her, as anybody in such a situation would. "I don't understand why . . ." She broke into sobs.

"Jenna," whispered Norlin. "What have they done to you?"

Shut up! thought Jenna. *Shut up! Shut up! Shut up! I don't want to listen to you. Go away. You're not my father. Go away.*

"I'm so sorry, Jenna," said Norlin, and slowly rose to his feet. "We had no idea . . ."

Jenna chewed and swallowed, chewed and swallowed. A tear ran down her cheek.

"They'll pay for this!" cried Norlin. "Jenna, you can rest assured they'll get the punishment they deserve. Now you've experienced for yourself how vicious these rebels are, so you'll help us to defeat them, won't you?"

Jenna did not look up, but she nodded. As she raised her cup to her lips, her hand was trembling.

"All right, the first thing we'll do," said Norlin, "is hold a press conference. The makeup artist is here — you understand,

Jenna, that we have to turn you into Malena again. The whole nation must see what you've been through."

Once more he knelt down before her. "And after that you can rest, my dear Jenna," he said softly. "After that you can sleep as long as you want. I shan't let anyone disturb you." His voice was gentle.

He was a tyrant who wanted nothing but power and wealth, and he had kidnapped the king and had had people killed.

He was her father, and she could not stop him from loving her.

"We've mobilized the troops," said Bolström. "Red alert, for the whole country. It's a good thing the girl got away from them, Norlin. I've been thinking about it, and it all makes sense. She says they left her alone in the house with just one guard; all the others had gone — even Nahira. And at exactly that time, the bridge was blown up. That can't be a coincidence, can it?"

"Nahira," murmured Norlin. "We knew right from the start that she was behind the attack on the bridge."

"Fortunately, Jenna has a good idea where she was picked up, and also how she got there," said Bolström. "Thanks to her description, it shouldn't be a problem finding Nahira's hideout."

"It won't be the only one she's got," said Norlin, resting his head on his hand. "She'll have deserted it long ago."

Bolström's cell phone chimed. "Yes, search all the forests in the area," he instructed, "though I doubt you'll find them.

They've probably gone into hiding back up north by now."
He flipped the phone off. "They've found the house, and it's
obvious that someone was being kept prisoner there — all the
evidence points to it," he reported. "They recovered several
long dark hairs on a foldout cot. We'll have them analyzed,
of course, to confirm, but there's no question about it — Jenna
was definitely there."

Norlin didn't respond.

"But I do keep on wondering," Bolström continued, "could
it be a coincidence? Close to Saarstad, of all places?"

"There's no better hiding place than those dense forests
around Saarstad," said Norlin.

"That may be so," mused Bolström. "Well, our people are
there now. Are you ready, Norlin, you and Jenna, to meet the
press?"

Norlin nodded. "Is *she* ready?" he asked. "Has the makeup
artist finished?"

"The makeup artist was rather reluctant this time," said
Bolström. "Of course, we couldn't tell her the same story as
last time — you know, that we wanted to give Princess Malena
a nice surprise. She's become a little suspicious." He sighed.

"So?" asked Norlin. "What did you tell her?"

"That, unfortunately, she's going to have to stay here, much
as we regret the inconvenience," said Bolström. "Here with us
at Osterlin. A short vacation — we can't say exactly how long.
Naturally, she's complaining, saying she needs to get back
to her children, but we can't take any risks. And what to do

with her afterward is something we haven't even begun to think about."

Norlin groaned. "I don't want to bear the guilt," he said. "All these lives, all these people we have to kill."

"Only for the common good, Norlin," said Bolström with a slight bow. "Just keep telling yourself that it's only for the common good. Are you ready? The members of the press are waiting."

Norlin glanced at the mirror above the mantelpiece, but Bolström waved him on.

"The more bleary-eyed you look," he said, "the clearer it will be to the people: *He doesn't spare himself, he's giving his all for us.* And they'll love you for it. This is our chance, Norlin. We've never had a better one."

28

"*Unbelievable. They didn't even* let her shower and change her clothes," said Nahira. "Just put on the blonde wig and the contact lenses. Couldn't they at least have given the girl a few hours' rest, after all she's been through?"

"Shhh!" said Malena. In her hands she turned a black wig with long, smooth hair that shone as only artificial hair can. But that was OK. It would only be seen from a distance and at night.

They had not gone back to the north, of course. At any moment, Jenna might give them the signal that she had uncovered the information, and then they must be ready to strike. The house in which the five of them were now watching the television was situated on a hill not a mile from Osterlin — a large, beautifully kept villa by a lake, in the middle of a park.

"The owner only visits once every few months," Nahira had told Malena and Jonas. "When there are concerts at Osterlin. And he has complete confidence in the caretaker, Arvo, who has worked for him for forty years. He's never had the slightest inkling that we've been here. We're always very careful not to leave any traces behind."

On the screen they could now see Jenna's face in close-up, with Norlin next to her, exhausted and distraught. They were facing countless microphones.

"Scandia has never before experienced a night like this," said Norlin. "Everyone in our beautiful country knows that last night the rebels blew up the bridge linking north to south. Two vehicles plunged down into the abyss. As far as we know, five people died. The ruthlessness of the rebels is becoming more evident by the day, their attacks on our country becoming ever more frequent. Nevertheless, we also have reason to celebrate, because last night we succeeded in liberating my niece, our beloved Princess Malena, from the hands of her North Scandian kidnappers. So as not to jeopardize the rescue mission, we did not inform the country about this abduction. It was Malena's own wish to appear in person before the nation today, in order to reassure every Scandian that our princess has indeed been returned to us safe and sound, and that she will now devote herself body and soul to achieving peace in our land."

"Look at her, she's on the verge of a nervous breakdown," murmured Nahira. "She won't be able to hold on much longer."

A microphone was thrust into Jenna's face. "Tell us about it, Your Highness!" cried a reporter. "What did you experience during your abduction?"

"She won't answer," said Nahira. "They'll have forbidden her to speak, wait and see."

Jenna burst into tears, and Norlin pushed the microphone angrily to one side.

"No questions!" he said. He put his arm around Jenna's shoulders and drew her to him. Nahira wondered if she was the only one to notice that Jenna shuddered. "Heaven knows, the princess has suffered enough. What she needs now is peace and quiet." He caressed Jenna's blonde hair. "The court will issue an official statement later today," he said. "We would ask the people not to be afraid if they now see our troops everywhere throughout the country. They are on hand to protect us all. Because, much as I hate to say it, every Scandian must now accept that Scandia is at war. We are at war against the rebels of the north."

The host in the studio appeared on the screen once more, and he introduced a guest.

"Now they'll have a little discussion," said Nahira. "And someone will be allowed to point out that not all North Scandians are to blame, and that not all North Scandians are rebels, and that every right-thinking southerner is deeply sorry that even those northerners who have always remained faithful to the south will have to suffer, *but* . . . that none of these attacks would have been possible to begin with if the rebels had not had support from broad sections of the ordinary people in the north, which is why all the ordinary people in the north are going to have to suffer now. We don't need to hear all that manipulative spin."

Tiloki turned down the volume.

"What now?" he asked.

"Now, we wait," said Nahira. "Till Jenna gives us the signal. Arvo says the fridge, freezer, and pantry are fully stocked. Anyone in the mood for some roasted duck?"

"Duck," said Jonas. "It's been forever since I had that."

But it really didn't matter to Jonas what he ate. He just had to do something to make the waiting bearable.

❧

Bea pushed open the door of the police station. It had started to rain on the way there, but she had stuck the photograph under her jacket as she biked.

"Calling all cars!" Bea announced, and waited until an aging man in a blue police sweater came out of the back room. "I'd like to report a missing person."

The man raised his eyebrows. "Is that so?" he said. "Well, go ahead, then."

Bea placed the photo on the counter so that Jenna was smiling directly at the police officer. "That's my best friend, Jenna," she said, "and she's been missing since Monday."

"And why aren't her parents looking for her?" asked the policeman.

"Her mother's missing, too," Bea replied.

Then she described what had happened. "And I just saw the news, and there she was again!" cried Bea. "I swear it's her! She looked so . . . so totally freaked out. Maybe they're torturing her. You've got to find out what is going down. You've got to bring her back from Scandia."

The policeman gave a friendly smile. "Now, repeat all that again, nice and slow, so I can write it down," he said. "On Monday your friend Jenna — the girl in this photo — didn't show up at school, and she hasn't been to school since. You can't reach her on her cell. And apparently her mother isn't at home, either. Correct so far?"

Bea nodded.

"At the same time, on the news, you've twice seen a girl who looks remarkably like your dark-haired, brown-eyed friend. Except that the girl on TV is blonde and has blue eyes and also happens to be the Princess of Scandia. Still correct?"

Bea nodded again.

"Today is the start of summer break, and the whole country is going away," said the policeman. "Some people like to travel a few days earlier, to beat the traffic, but the schools frown on that. So what would you say if I suggested that your friend and her mother have both gone off on vacation without telling anyone, and there's absolutely no reason why you should worry yourself about it? Because that's exactly what's happening in thousands of households at this very moment."

"You sound just like my mother," Bea muttered despondently. "But no way it's a coincidence that at this exact moment a supposedly missing princess turns up looking exactly like Jenna."

The policeman picked up the photograph and turned it this

way and that. "Could be, could be," he said in a friendly tone. "My wife would know for sure — she could tell us right away if your friend looks like this princess. I wouldn't know about that! But I'm inclined to think that — even if she does look unusually similar, which is perfectly possible — you're just seeing things because you're so worried about your friend. Which is evidence of a very caring attitude, if I may say so."

Bea gazed at him. "Uh-huh. But you're not going to do anything about it?"

"I couldn't do anything even if I wanted to," said the policeman. "Not under these circumstances. Her mother would have to come and see us."

Bea plucked the photo out of his hands and tucked it away.

"So much for fighting crime!" she said.

Immediately she felt like biting her tongue. Make an enemy of a policeman? Not smart. Sometimes she forgot to wear her bike helmet.

Jenna had slept throughout the entire day. It was important that she be rested and fresh for what she now had to do — Nahira had been insistent about that.

"I'm sure I'll be too scared to sleep," Jenna had said, but Nahira had just laughed.

She spent the time before supper standing by the window. Somewhere out there on the hills must be the house where Nahira, Malena, and Jonas were waiting for her signal. At the end of the bed she felt for the flashlight — no bigger than a ballpoint pen — that she had hidden beneath the mattress the minute she entered the room. Good thing, too, because they searched all her clothes not long after. (*Make sure you stash it at once — that's your only hope,* Nahira had insisted.) Calling or texting was out of the question. They had already demonstrated their control over her cell phone.

The flashlight still lay where she had hidden it. Everything was still according to the plan, she made sure of that.

Jenna was trembling. Once again she sent a text message to her mom's number — it would look suspicious if, under these circumstances, she did not keep on trying to make contact with her mother, Nahira had said. But Jenna did not even bother to read the reply, since she had no idea who actually had written it. They had played a game with her, and now she was playing a game with them.

All across the grounds, guards were on patrol, their guns slung over their shoulders. Nahira had warned her that this would happen after the kidnapping. "But that creates its own problem," she had said. "They can't let the dogs loose if the guards are patrolling. Those beasts would rip the men to pieces."

"They're not beasts!" Jonas had said. He knew how to handle them, and was all set to do so.

When Mrs. Markas came into the room, quietly so as not to wake Jenna if she was still asleep, it was almost a relief. Anything was better than waiting.

"And how are you feeling now?" asked Mrs. Markas. Jenna could still hear the sympathy in her tone. "Did you have a good sleep?"

Jenna nodded. She realized that whenever she tried to speak, the tears were still ready to flow. But whatever! She *had* had a hard time with her kidnappers.

"Well, then, come and have some supper," said Mrs. Markas. "We've brought one of the palace cooks to Osterlin now — the regent insisted. He wants you to regain your strength after going hungry all that time. And it's lovely for us as well, to be able to look forward to delicious food at every meal. Tonight it's sole almondine."

"OK," whispered Jenna.

In the large banquet hall, Norlin, Bolström, and Tobias were already seated at the table. This time it was set as if for a feast: On a sideboard against the wall were steaming platters, plates, and tureens, while an aroma of spices hung in the air.

"Jenna," said Norlin. "You're looking better."

Then he turned back for a moment to Bolström. "That's why I consider it completely unnecessary to move him," he said. "It's sheer coincidence that she—"

Bolström interrupted him. "We can talk about that later," he said, and Jenna thought she saw his eyes flash a warning. "Now then, little Jenna, you really do look as if you've recovered from all your trials and tribulations."

Jenna nodded. "I slept," she murmured.

Bolström gave a signal, and a girl in a white apron, wearing a white cap over her hair, stepped away from the sideboard. She carried a platter to the table and then stood waiting beside Norlin in order to serve him first.

Norlin didn't notice her.

"Poor child," he said, and put his hand on Jenna's arm for a moment. Once again Jenna felt the nausea rising and the tears preparing to fall.

"If you please, Your Highness," whispered the girl. Jenna heard the guttural North Scandian accent and saw that the girl's hand was unsteady.

"We've allowed ourselves the luxury of a cook," said Norlin. "But as for waiters — that seemed to be going a bit too far. To you, too, I imagine, Jenna. So the one's on double duty, serving as well."

"Yes, Your Highness," Jenna murmured in response to the regent.

The cook gazed down at the plate as she served her. Where had Jenna seen her before? She was scarcely older than Jenna herself, and in the glance that she now directed toward her flashed great fear. Even without getting a good look at her face, Jenna suddenly remembered.

That day when she'd stood on the balcony with the regent and waved to the cheering crowd! It seemed an eternity ago. She recalled the walk through the back entrance, through the kitchen door. The cook was Kaira, the kitchen maid fresh from the north who had stumbled in front of her.

"Don't call me *Your Highness*, Jenna," said Norlin. "We've been through so much together — and we shall go through a lot more — and I don't feel it's right for you to go on calling me that. It's so . . . distant. Impersonal. Don't call me *Your Highness*. Call me . . ." He hesitated. "Uncle."

Jenna saw Bolström and Tobias exchange a look.

"Yes, what a nice idea!" cried Tobias. "After all, our regent is the princess's uncle, and you're playing her part. *Uncle* — wonderful." And he nodded to the cook, who had now steadied herself and was serving him last.

Why had they brought this particular girl to Osterlin? Jenna bent over her plate and began to cut up the fish. (Mom had shown her how to do this so many times, even when she was still very young.) Why hadn't they brought the real cook, the big red-haired woman, who had spoken to her so kindly in the palace kitchen?

The fish almost slid off her fork as she answered her own question: The cook would be hard to replace. The kitchen maid was not.

Apart from the regent and his inner circle, none of the people who were here at Osterlin now and saw her as both Jenna and Malena would ever see the light of day again. Prison was the best they could hope for.

Jenna began to cry. Kaira was not important to them. She was just a North Scandian girl, like thousands of others. Doubtful her culinary skills could be exceptional at this early stage of her career! So they could keep her at Osterlin as long as they needed her, and afterward she would be no great loss to anyone.

"Jenna!" Norlin exclaimed, jumping up from his seat. "You're still upset . . . can't you forget what they did to you, my poor girl?"

Jenna shook her head. The tears ran down her face. They wouldn't hesitate to kill the little kitchen-maid as soon as they had no further use for her. "No," she whispered in reply. "They were so cruel."

When she looked up, Bolström gave her a long, searching look.

"I can't eat a thing," she whispered. "I'd like to call my mother, please."

"Of course, dear," Mrs. Markas said.

Then she took her back to her room.

❧

They didn't lock the bedroom door, so they must have felt quite confident that Jenna would not try to get away. But then, why should she, since she had returned to them of her own free will? Of course, this freedom they were allowing her also had to do with the fact that they didn't want her to become suspicious. They had to be careful how they treated her, so that she would continue to play her allotted role convincingly.

She'd dialed Mom's number a few times, just as she would have done had her kidnapping story been true. Of course, there was no answer.

Mrs. Markas had escorted her into the bedroom, to close

the curtains for the night and see her off to bed. "Sleep well, Jenna," she'd said before closing the door behind her. "Tomorrow the world will seem like a much better place."

Just like Mom would say.

Immediately after she left, Jenna slipped out of bed and got dressed again, putting her nightgown back on over her clothes. It was crucial that she be ready to escape at a moment's notice. As she crawled back under the covers, thoughts whirled through her mind at such speed that she could barely make sense of them. So far she had failed on her mission: She'd found out nothing about where they were keeping the king, and the more she thought about it, the more convinced she became that she would learn nothing during the next few hours, either. Bolström would not let her talk to Norlin alone: He'd be concerned — with good reason! — that Norlin's emotions would get the better of him and he'd spill the beans. But even if he did leave them alone together, why should the regent tell her where he was holding the king? Why should he confess to her that the king was still alive, even if she did call him — eww! — *Uncle*?

How, then, had Nahira imagined she would ever find out? By flattering the regent, by showing him how much she admired him, until he revealed all his secrets to her? Double eww! That was absurd. The only thing she could do was keep listening.

Jenna sat up with a jolt. *Listening!* She'd already overheard something, hadn't she? Two sentences kept running through her head — and they had something to do with something she already knew.

All she had to do was put two plus one together; figure out what that something was . . .

That's why I consider it completely unnecessary to move him. It's sheer coincidence that she . . .

Bolström had interrupted the regent as soon as Jenna entered the banquet hall, to keep Norlin from finishing his sentence in front of her.

What might his words have revealed?

. . . *completely unnecessary to move him* . . . Him. The king. Of course! Who else?

And so Bolström must have been urging Norlin to do the opposite before she came into the room. Why, then, did Bolström want the king to be moved from his secret prison?

It had something to do with her.

It's sheer coincidence that she . . .

That she . . . what? Jenna got out of bed again and went to the window. Somewhere out there in the hills Nahira and the others were now sitting at their own window, waiting for her signal. If only she could have asked them!

And then it came to her. All at once, without knowing why, she understood.

That's why I consider it completely unnecessary to move . . . the king from his present hiding place! *It's sheer coincidence that she,* Jenna, was held prisoner in precisely the same area!

Was that what Norlin was about to say? The first part was obviously about the king, it had to be. But he couldn't be a prisoner in the same place that she'd been held by the rebels; Bolström's men would have already searched the house and the surrounding woods. So where else could they have meant? Unless it was the town where she'd been rescued . . .

Saarstad?

Saarstad.

Suddenly she remembered where she had heard that name before. Mom, over dinner the night of Jenna's last birthday, her face slightly flushed: *Not long after that, I met your father. We were head over heels in love, Jenna — madly in love. And one day, when it was my birthday, my eighteenth, we just ran away. We didn't bother with celebrations — we simply went to the seaside, near Saarstad. We sat on the beach, but it was still quite cold at that time of year, and as I had the key* . . .

And then she had stopped, when Jenna had made the mistake of asking about the key — *What key?* — and Mom had pushed aside her glass of wine and ended the birthday meal.

Mom was Princess of Scandia, and she had loved Norlin. The very thought of it made Jenna squeamish. Mom had been with Norlin in Saarstad, and somewhere there on the beach was a house. It *had* to be a house, right? What else would Mom have had a key to?

In Saarstad there was a remote beach house that Norlin knew about, too. It all fit.

Outside, below the window, a guard walked slowly past. Gently, Jenna let the curtain fall.

It all fit, though that still didn't mean she was right. But it was the only clue she had.

Jenna went to the end of the bed and pulled the flashlight out from under the mattress. Before she could give Nahira the signal, she had to be sure: Just a hunch wasn't good enough. She would hunt in the library at Osterlin to see if she could find any records. Any photographs or notes. Anything at all that referred to Saarstad.

❦

They had given the makeup artist a small room under the roof, right next to the little kitchen maid's. The two couldn't talk to each other, though, since the cook seemed to work twenty-four hours a day.

As night fell, the makeup artist was sitting by the window, looking out over the grounds. That morning, Bolström had called her and told her to come to Osterlin. Once again she'd had to make up the dark girl, who'd looked terrible — bleary-eyed and desperate. She'd been foolish enough to ask questions, but probably — almost certainly — it would have made no difference even if she hadn't. Bolström and his crew couldn't afford any risks.

In fact, now that she'd had time to think about it, she was surprised they'd let her go the week before. How stupid she'd been to believe their story about a surprise for the princess! It had been obvious from the start that there was more to it than that. But she hadn't wanted to know the truth. She'd sensed that knowing the truth could be dangerous.

And now it had all been to no avail. Her children were waiting at home — the youngest was still in diapers — and maybe in the meantime someone had notified the police that she was missing. If so, the police would then pretend to be doing all they could. But somehow they supposedly would never find a thing.

Through the trees on the hills opposite Osterlin, she thought she saw an occasional flash of light. Was there a house there? Were people living there, eating their dinner, washing their dishes, drinking a mug of warm milk before they went to bed?

She was surprised at how calm she was. She knew that there was nothing she could do. She was powerless to change her situation. They would come for her whenever it was time for the girl to be turned into Malena — whenever they needed a perfect princess. So where was the real princess now?

But when they didn't need her anymore . . . if one day they had no further use for her . . .

She tried to comfort herself with the thought that that might not be for a very long time. Years, maybe. They would have to kill her. But not yet. Not now.

29

*J*he library was in darkness. Jenna had not switched on her flashlight as she passed through the corridors — by now she knew her way without it. She had tiptoed on stockinged feet — *quiet as a mouse*, she recalled ruefully. All was quiet in the house. Her watch showed that it was a few minutes after midnight.

Through the high glass doors the moon shone coldly into the farthest corners of the room. She could make out the bookcase, and the chair in front of it, where Norlin had been sitting when she first saw him, with Bolström standing behind him as they both waited for her. On the desk lay a folder full of papers.

Almost soundlessly, Jenna bent over it and passed the flashlight's beam over figures, architectural drawings of large buildings and whole rows of houses, a handwritten letter on official stationery. Her fingers trembled as she took out one piece of paper after another to study them. Nothing about the king or where he was being kept prisoner. Why would Norlin leave information like that lying around? Why keep any record at all of what had happened to Malena's father? It was crazy to hope for such a clue.

Nevertheless, she shone the flashlight over the bookcase — nothing there, either, just books, neatly arranged in rows and sections. What, should she take out every volume and leaf through it in the hope that eventually a map with X marking the spot would flutter to the floor? Where else in this room could she search?

She was so wrapped up in her thoughts that for a moment she lost all sense of fear. She let the beam wander around the room like a finger of light, hoping that somehow it might pick out and point to a hiding place or at least a clue. And so it was that her small spotlight fell directly on the face of Bolström when he silently opened the library door.

"And what, exactly, are you doing?" asked Bolström sharply. He didn't sound surprised. His tone frightened Jenna.

In a few swift paces he crossed the room and snatched the flashlight from her hand. "Thought I heard a noise. What are you up to in here, little Jenna, at this time of night?" He twisted the flashlight in his fingers. "And where, may I ask, did you get this?"

Jenna stood, petrified. She should never have let herself get caught!

She looked at Bolström. "I . . ." she mumbled. "I . . ."

"You're not sleepwalking, are you?" asked Bolström. Exactly what Nahira had told her to say. "Well, well. What a surprise."

Jenna could hear the irony in his voice.

"I . . ." she whispered again. "I don't know."

"Well, they say it often happens," said Bolström, and this time she couldn't detect any irony. "It does in the movies, so why not in real life? Young girls sleepwalking when they've experienced something too upsetting for their sensitive little souls." A smile flickered around his lips, but it didn't reach his eyes. "And the flashlight? That, little Jenna, looks very, very suspicious to me."

"I brought it with me," whispered Jenna. "When I ran away. The forest was so dark."

"The forest was so dark," said Bolström, and nodded thoughtfully, almost in slow motion. "Yes, of course. When one is escaping, it is only natural to search the house for a flashlight, even if one runs the risk of being recaptured."

"Yes," whispered Jenna. He didn't believe her. He didn't believe a word.

"But now, little Jenna," said Bolström softly, though his tight grip on her arm did not match the gentleness of his voice, "now you're safe and sound. Now you're back with us, little Jenna. Go back to your bed. Better still, I'll accompany you to your room. Sleepwalkers sometimes fall off roofs — you've heard of such things, too, haven't you?"

It sounded like a threat, but before Jenna could even think about it, Bolström had pushed her firmly out of the library.

Her spy mission had been hopeless right from the start.

When there was a knock on his bedroom door, Norlin thought it was the nervous little cook. He couldn't stand her constant trembling. But instead it was Bolström who strode to his bedside.

"There's no alternative, Norlin," he stated. "We have to silence her. And as quickly as possible. I regret that I fell for her story, too. Because it was all a lie. An ingenious little game. I should have known right away. I had my suspicions, of course. I just didn't act on them soon enough."

"Who?" asked Norlin. "What are you talking about?" Although he already knew.

"I caught her in the library rummaging through your papers," said Bolström. He didn't need to answer Norlin's question. "She had a flashlight, and she certainly didn't get it from us."

"She was desperate," said Norlin. "You saw that for yourself." But he didn't look Bolström in the eye.

Bolström made a dismissive gesture with his hand. "Desperate?" he echoed. "She was panic-stricken. Distraught. But how do we know if she was panicking because of her alleged kidnappers or because of us?"

"You said yourself, it all fits together," said Norlin. His voice was now shrill, and he was crumpling up the bedsheets in his hands.

There was another knock at the door. This time it *was* the little cook. Cautiously, one step after another, as if she were walking on an invisible tightrope, she brought in a tray on which was balanced a bottle of cognac and a glass. Her eyes were dull with fatigue.

"Put it on the bedside table," Norlin said without looking at her. "Then you may go to bed."

The little cook curtsied and backed out toward the door. She almost stumbled over the edge of the carpet.

Bolström watched her go, then pointed to the tray by the bed. "That's going to be the death of you, Norlin," he commented, then continued. "Of course everything made sense — it was meant to. But do you really believe that a girl who breaks free from her prison guard and runs away in blind terror is going to stop to search the house for a flashlight before she leaves?"

"Maybe he had it on him," said Norlin. "All she had to do was grab it."

"And it just happened to be one tiny enough for her to smuggle past us in her clothes so that she could keep it in her room?" said Bolström. "Well, that was some stroke of luck! Like her cell phone — that bothered me, too. How come she's got her cell phone back? All through her supposed abduction, it was switched off, so we couldn't locate her. And now, suddenly, she's got it again and she's up to no good."

Norlin shook his head. "No . . ." he murmured.

"So what was she doing in the library? In the middle of the night? She said she was sleepwalking, but surely you don't believe that, Norlin — if you do, you need your head examined."

With shaking hands, Norlin opened the bottle and poured himself a glass of cognac. "Some for you?" he asked.

Bolström shook his head in annoyance. "All right. She's your daughter," he said. "So I can understand, to a degree, why you're hesitant. But you don't know the first thing about her! You can't tell me you've developed fatherly feelings for her — not for a girl you haven't seen for more than a few hours since her mother ran off. Don't go getting sentimental now, Norlin. In all these years, you've never missed her, and you won't miss her after her next unexpected . . . departure. There's no longer any doubt as to why she came back. Nahira sent her. And who knows how involved Liron is in this business? The girl's a spy. The girl's dangerous. The girl has got to go."

Norlin stared at him, the glass in his hand suspended halfway between tray and mouth. "I won't allow it," he whispered.

"It's not a question of what you will or won't allow, Your Highness," said Bolström with a little bow. "Sometimes I get the impression that you don't fully understand the situation you're in. The girl must go, and so must the king. We don't need them now, anyway. After the attack on the bridge, the people are so incensed that they'll follow you unconditionally, whatever you decide to do against the north, and regardless of their darling Little Princess's opinions. The only question is what we're to tell the people about her tragic fate. The best thing, of course, would be if we could blame the rebels for her death."

"Bolström!" Norlin gasped. "No!" He downed the drink, then poured and drank another. "You can't do that. Not to my own daughter."

"Think about it," said Bolström, and went to the door. "If you're capable of thinking about anything after *that*." He jerked his head in the direction of the bottle.

When he entered the corridor, all was quiet. Then, somewhere in the house, a door slammed.

Kaira was trembling as she put the pot of milk on the stove. Maybe it would work — and it was the only thing she could think of. It *had* to work!

She was horribly afraid.

Once, when she was still very young, her mother had caught her bending over the keyhole to eavesdrop. She had pulled her away from the door by her ear, and it had hurt for the rest of the day. As had her bottom, which had received a solid spanking. Her mother had been of the firm opinion that it was especially important for young North Scandians to be well brought up and to learn how to mind their manners.

"We North Scandians," she had impressed upon her children, "have every opportunity in this country, every opportunity, and soon we shall have even more. Look at the regent — born a North Scandian. Today we can achieve anything, just like a southerner. But we must behave properly, that's the important thing, because good behavior will open any door. If you want to get ahead in Scandia, you have to know how the southerners behave."

She, of course, had never been beyond her tiny community.

And how proud she had been when her daughter had been given a position in the kitchens at court! She had told all the neighbors about it, and all her friends.

"But I'm not even the slightest bit surprised, to be honest," she'd said. "She's a good girl, a smart girl, a hardworking girl, and she knows how to behave — her mother's made sure of that. I've always told my children, all doors are open to us. And Kaira's living proof."

The milk began to foam and rise up the sides of the pot — Kaira hadn't been watching it. She took it off the stove just in time to stop it from spilling over the edge.

What would her mother have said if she'd seen her daughter, her well-brought-up daughter, doubled over, listening in at the keyhole of the regent's bedroom?

Kaira took a mug out of the solid old kitchen cupboard and carefully filled it halfway to the top. She couldn't understand why suddenly the princess had dark hair like her own, and skin almost as dark as a North Scandian's. But she was definitely the princess. Kaira knew her face. She'd seen it in all the newspaper articles her mother read. And, more than that, there was the incident a week ago in the palace kitchen, which still made her feel embarrassed. There was the dark-haired girl who Mr. Bolström just said was the regent's *daughter* — though wasn't the princess the regent's *niece*? — but she was Princess of Scandia. And Kaira would never forget the friendly way she had held out her hand after Kaira had stumbled during her first curtsy, not for the rest of her life.

Cautiously she carried the cup to the door. The milk was hot, and the mug almost burned her fingers. What could she say if she met someone in the corridor? Suppose someone asked her when the princess had ordered the milk? And how the princess had sent the message to her in the kitchen?

She'd think of something. What could be more commonplace than a cook taking a comforting drink late at night to a princess who couldn't sleep? Hadn't Kaira just delivered a nightcap to the regent?

Carefully she climbed the stairs. She listened. The house was as quiet as death.

Jenna lay crying on her bed in the darkness. Bolström's tone had not been unfriendly, in spite of the irony. But what did that mean? Only that he was not yet sure what was to be done with her. Just in case they should need her again, just in case they should decide she must play Malena, the Little Princess, once more, he could not afford to rouse her suspicions.

But she knew he had not believed a word she'd said.

She slipped out of bed and stood at the window. Dark clouds kept rolling across the face of the moon. She strained her eyes to make out the hills in the distance, and now and again she thought she could see a light. So they were waiting over there.

It made no difference — she wouldn't be able to give them a signal, since Bolström had taken her flashlight, though it was more important now than ever. Because Bolström suspected her, she would have no further chance to find out anything.

But that was not the worst problem.

The worst was that they would now have to silence her. Maybe even at this very moment, somewhere in the house, they were actually discussing the best way to do it. She had to get out, tonight, before Bolström and Norlin could do anything to her. But how could she send the rescue signal to Nahira?

Then suddenly she knew how to do it, and for a moment she felt so relieved that she found herself smiling. Bolström had pressed the light switch and pointed to her bed: "Now, beddy-byes for you, my girl," he'd said. "Young ladies need their rest. Don't they say that sleepless nights make ugly sights?" He'd laughed as he'd closed the door behind him.

The guards outside were the only danger if she made her signal with the light switch instead of the flashlight. *Short short short, long long long, short short short.* It was impossible to watch from the window and stand at the switch by the door simultaneously, so it would be difficult to time the signal for the moment when the guards were patrolling the other side of the building, out of range of the flashing light.

She opened the curtain a crack. A guard was just passing below her window, the gravel crunching beneath his feet. He glanced up, and behind the curtain Jenna stood motionless, not daring to breathe. *When he's gone,* she thought, and

waited a few moments. *When he disappears around the corner,*
I'll do it.

She was halfway across the room, heading for the light
switch, her hand already outstretched, when the door flung
open.

Tobias came in and turned on the light. He was carrying
a ladder.

"Jenna, what a bummer," he said.

The very first time she'd seen him, in front of the school,
when he had run after her and Bea, she thought he looked
like a movie star: elegant, cool — cute, even! — and radiantly
friendly.

He was still all that, but now his friendliness sent a shiver
down her spine.

"I'm here to take out your lightbulbs — literally, that is — you
dumb girl. Go ahead, lie on the bed — that's right. What were
you thinking? Why did you try to trick us?"

He placed the ladder under the heavy chandelier and
climbed up. "Oh, and 'BTW,' if you're thinking about getting
up and trying to knock over the ladder, I've got this little toy,"
he said, and pulled something out of his belt.

It was the first time Jenna had ever seen a real gun.

"Hope you're not afraid of the dark!" He laughed.

Jenna blinked back her tears. Even if all was lost, she
wouldn't let him have the satisfaction of seeing her cry.

His job done, Tobias folded the ladder and went to the bedside lamp. "This one, too," he said, and with a single flick of

the wrist removed the bulb from its socket. "Yes, it's going to be a very dark night for you. But comfort yourself with the thought that it won't last long. Though whether what comes next will be much more comforting . . ." He laughed again, and carried the ladder to the door in the darkness. " . . . remains to be seen."

He locked the door behind him as he left.

So it was decided, then. They had made up their minds that they wouldn't need her anymore, and it didn't matter to them what she knew. Though obviously they had no doubt that she already knew everything.

Lying on her bed, Jenna bit the pillow to stop herself from crying. Her only remaining hope was that Norlin might oppose having her killed. Wasn't he her father?

But wasn't she his daughter? Yes. And in spite of that, she hated him. Why should it be any different for him, now that he knew of her betrayal?

Whatever happened, they would hold her prisoner, and then one day even Norlin would stop resisting when Bolström, Tobias, and Mrs. Markas kept whispering in his ear that his daughter was a danger to him as long as she lived. It must be difficult to hide prisoners from the whole country, especially when they were such dangerous prisoners as herself and the king. Too difficult.

All was lost.

30

Without really thinking about it, Jenna had assumed that she would at least have until morning. So it was all the more frightening when, just a few minutes after Tobias had gone, there was a knock on her door.

Jenna put her head in her hands. They'd come to get her. So soon.

She curled up to make herself as small as possible, and buried her face in the pillow, as if that could make her invisible.

"Your Highness, shhh, please!" whispered a terrified voice through the wood of the door. "Please, Your Highness, they mustn't hear us!"

Then there was a soft click as something was placed on the floor. "Please, Your Highness, listen to me!"

Jenna raised her head. "Kaira?" she whispered.

"Oh, you know my name!" whispered the little cook, and Jenna could hear the joy and astonishment in her voice. "You must escape, Your Highness, that's all I wanted to tell you.

I know I shouldn't interfere in royal matters, so please don't think badly of me. But I . . ."

"Yes?" whispered Jenna. As quietly as she could, she got up and crept to the door. She was sure the little cook would hear her heart beating even through the wood.

"I overheard the regent and Mr. Bolström. Oh, I know I shouldn't eavesdrop, so please don't think badly of me," she said again, "but I thought . . ."

Jenna knelt on the floor and laid her ear against the door. "What?" she asked, her voice cracking with fear.

"They're going to kill you, Your Highness. The regent doesn't want to, but I don't think he has any say in the matter, Your Highness. Mr. Bolström says they don't need you anymore — I don't know what that means. The people hate us northerners enough now, anyway, so what should they do with you, Your Highness? It's best to kill you, that's what Mr. Bolström says."

For a moment she was silent, as if she wanted to give Jenna the chance to respond. Then she whispered, "I swore an oath of loyalty to the royal family. Please believe me, I really don't want to do anything to hurt the regent. But if he does agree you should be killed, Your Highness, and you're also a member of the royal family . . ."

Jenna took a deep breath. She couldn't understand why the girl kept calling her "Your Highness" when she had already seen her black hair, her brown eyes, and her olive skin.

"Listen, Kaira," whispered Jenna. She tried to make her voice sound calm. Maybe there was still a way out. "Creep up to your room now, and then keep switching the light on and off. On and off, on and off, do you understand? Then help will come, Kaira. Then everything will be all right."

"If I switch the light on?" whispered the cook. "But why?"

"Not just on, Kaira," whispered Jenna. "On and then off again, on and off again. It's a signal." For a moment she wondered if she should explain to Kaira that the signal was actually three short, three long, three short, but she felt that might be too confusing. And with every passing second, there was an increasing risk that she would be discovered. "Do you understand? Then they'll come and rescue us."

"Oh yes, Your Highness!" whispered Kaira.

Jenna realized that she had just said exactly what Kaira was waiting to hear — because the girl had been taught to expect that royalty would always find a solution.

"Good," said Jenna. "Now go and do what I've told you. As quickly and as quietly as possible, Kaira. And be careful."

She didn't tell her to watch out for the guards down below, patrolling the grounds, because she didn't want to worry the girl even more. All that mattered now was that Kaira give the signal.

"I think it's time," whispered Malena, leaning far out the window. "I think I saw a light flash."

Instantly Nahira was by her side. "That's not a flashlight," she said. "That's a perfectly average overhead light, can't you see? And it's coming from the attic. It's not the signal we agreed on, either." She counted. "On, off, on, off. That's not Jenna — she's too smart to forget our signal."

"But what if she isn't?" asked Malena. She stood up straight and went toward the door. "Or what if she's lost her flashlight?"

"Then why doesn't she at least send an SOS in Morse code?" asked Nahira. "Look for yourself. It could be a trap. Suppose it's Norlin trying to lure us to the house?"

Jonas shook his head. "In that case, why doesn't he use the flashlight and the signal we're waiting for?" he asked. "I think it's a signal from Jenna, too, Nahira. And I think she's in trouble, because otherwise she wouldn't—"

"There," Nahira cut him off. "Now the signals have stopped."

"She's been caught," said Tiloki. "She was supposed to keep on signaling till you answered. So why has she stopped now? She's been caught, Nahira, and that means she's in trouble."

Nahira looked at Malena and then Jonas. "You both agree with Tiloki?" she asked.

Malena and Jonas nodded. "Hurry!" said Jonas. "Please, Nahira."

Meonok and Lorok also nodded.

"The emergency plan, then," said Nahira.

As soon as Kaira had left, Jenna rushed to the bed and ripped off the sheets. She tied them together just as Jonas had shown her, and went to the window. Carefully she drew the curtain to one side. She was just in time to see one of the guards disappear around the corner of the building.

As quietly as she could, she opened the door to the balcony, knotted one end of the sheets to the handle, and went outside. Jonas had been right: If she climbed over the balustrade and used the sheets as a rope ladder, it wouldn't be too high for her to jump. It would only be dangerous if one of the guards came back before she'd made it to her hiding place.

The noise as she dropped onto the gravel was so loud that Jenna was afraid it would wake the whole house. With a few strides she reached the rhododendron bush where she was to hide till it was all over. Jonas had given her an exact description, because that was where he himself had hidden on the night he had first broken into the grounds at Osterlin.

Tiny stones clung to her clothes, and she carefully brushed them off. No scratches — just a little pain in one arm, which wouldn't stop her from running, and that was all that mattered next.

She tried to see whether light signals were coming from the attic, but everything remained in darkness. What if Kaira had not succeeded? What would happen if Nahira didn't come?

Even if the guards didn't spot the knotted sheets, by morning at the latest Mrs. Markas would find out that Jenna had gone. Then they would let out the dogs.

"Do you understand?" Nahira had impressed upon her. "Whether you sneak out freely or have to escape through the window, there's still no way you can get beyond the grounds without our help. They know that, too. They'll let the dogs loose on you, Jenna, and I need hardly tell you what will happen then."

Jenna had shaken her head.

"So under no circumstances are you to leave your room until we've answered your signal and you're sure we're coming," Nahira had said. "Stay where you are. If the dogs get you, it means certain death."

But back then they could not have known what would happen. That Jenna couldn't possibly wait for them to signal to her, no matter how dangerous it was to leave. She huddled up among the branches on the ground.

Then she heard someone yelling. She heard shouts, footsteps on the gravel, and a shrill whistle. All the lights went on in Osterlin.

Jenna pressed herself against the prickly twigs and waited.

Norlin had rushed downstairs as soon as he heard the whistle. It had jerked him out of a shallow, troubled sleep. He felt a roaring in his head. As he ran, he tried to tie the belt of his silken bathrobe, though his fingers would scarcely obey his brain.

The tall shrubs inside the thick iron railings that ran around the entire perimeter of Osterlin's grounds were now lit up by powerful searchlights that cut swaths through the night, swinging their broad beams right and left, into every corner. Guards ran back and forth, flashlights in hand and rifles at the ready.

"The gate is locked!" shouted Bolström. "She must still be on the premises. Release the hounds!"

The dog handler came out of the shadows and quickly made his way toward the kennels.

"Stop!" cried Norlin. The roaring in his head was now almost unbearable. "Stop! Not the dogs! I forbid it!"

The dog handler halted and looked inquiringly from Norlin to Bolström, who seized the regent's arm quite violently.

"Now listen to me, Norlin," he said. "That dirty little cook has just been sending a signal — we caught her red-handed. Who'd have told the stupid creature to do that? It can only have been Jenna. And your enchanting daughter herself has escaped down a pair of knotted sheets. Where do you think she learned that little trick? They trained her!"

Norlin pressed his hands against his temples. "Then she must be found!" he cried. His voice sounded strange even to himself. "If she's still within the perimeters, then she can't get away. The guards must look for her, and Tobias and Mrs. Markas as well. It'll be enough just to capture her — there's no need to kill the girl! If we set the dogs loose, they'll rip her to shreds, Bolström! That's what *they're* trained to do! I forbid it! I forbid it!" His voice was becoming hysterical. Again the dog handler looked uncertainly at Bolström.

"Calm down, Norlin, calm down," said Bolström. "And just think about it: If she has given Nahira and her people a signal, they'll come here to rescue her, and we don't know what will happen then. We don't know their plans, and they could still set a trap for us. We've got to preempt whatever it is, and we've got to do it now."

"I forbid it!" the regent screamed again. Every word roared through his throbbing head, as if it wanted to burst his brain. "I forbid it!" In a single movement, he freed himself from Bolström's grip and turned directly to the dog handler. "If you release the hounds against my orders, that will be high treason. And you know the punishment for high treason." With a swift gesture, he drew the side of his hand across his throat.

The dog handler bowed. His face had turned chalk-white.

"Norlin," said Bolström. "You'll regret this."

"Everybody search!" cried Norlin. "Search the entire estate, search every bush, every nook, every cranny. Within half an hour at most, I want her found, and that's an order."

"You're crazy, Norlin," hissed Bolström. His voice was thick with scorn.

The flashlights threw out their flickering beams, and the guards followed them at a gentle trot, doubled over as they peered under the bushes and shouted across to one another. It wouldn't take much longer.

"Over here!" someone yelled. "Quick, over here!"

He was standing by the hedge that hid the railings, and his flashlight had picked out a piece of torn cloth hanging from one of several broken branches. There was a general rush, and at first no one paid any attention to the shouts that suddenly came from an attic window above. But then everyone stopped and looked up.

"She's outside, you're looking in the wrong place! She's already outside! She's running toward the bridge! She's outside!"

Norlin looked up. Hanging out an attic window, gesticulating wildly, was a woman, and only after a few moments did he recognize her: It was the makeup artist.

The makeup artist had been sitting by the window all night. She'd been thinking about her children, and about the moments with them she would never be able to enjoy: her youngest going to school; her eldest graduating; the three of them growing up, falling in love, having children of their own. Never again would she sing her youngest to sleep, or kiss away the hurt of a tiny scratch, saying, "That will make it all better." Never again would she sit beside the middle child as he chewed on his already half-eaten pencil, frowning in despair over his homework, or cheer him on a Sunday as he played defense for his team, blocking one pass after another. Never again would she ponder with her eldest what color would go best with her eyes, discuss which boy might be a little less stupid than most of the others, or listen with her to her latest favorite song.

To everything and everyone she loved, she had, this night, said a mental good-bye, like a passenger on a sinking ship who, as the hull inevitably turns on its side, realizes in a terrible instant of clarity that the lifeboats are out of reach. She only hoped that someone would look after her children, and although she was not a religious woman, she offered up a little prayer.

She sat perfectly still at the window and looked up at the sky. Now and then the clouds broke to give a glimpse of the Milky Way. As a child, she had thought that the stars were the souls of the dead.

And then, suddenly, she had seen the light from the next room. On, off, on, off, on, off. There was no doubt about it — the little cook was sending a signal. On, off, on, off. Who was it meant for? And why, of all people, the little cook?

On, off, on, off. Should she call out? Should she draw the guards' attention to it? Would they reward her by letting her go, by letting her return to her children, and would everything then be all right again? Or should she instead hope for the little cook to succeed, and for someone to see her signal?

She was still thinking it over when she heard the door to the next room get pulled open. The little cook screamed. Down below on the grounds, someone else had also seen the signals. They hadn't needed her help, anyway.

The makeup artist sat at the window and was astonished to see the entire estate suddenly covered in shifting lights. The guards were running all over the place, their guns drawn, and the regent stood on the steps, swaying around in his silk bathrobe, shouting at Bolström. The whole scene could mean only one thing: The girl who so resembled the princess had managed to escape.

The makeup artist herself now scoured the lawn. From up above she had the perfect view, and as the clouds rolled away from the moon, she could see both the grounds and the road outside it.

On the other side of the railings from where the guards were now examining the hedge, a crouching figure had just emerged. It seemed to wait for a moment, then it ran toward the bridge that spanned a ditch, now overgrown with watercress and reeds. The figure straightened up, and in the moonlight she recognized it at once: the long, dark hair, the young girl's body.

This time the makeup artist didn't need to ponder her decision. She thought of her children and the many years which might still lie ahead of her after all.

"She's outside, you're looking in the wrong place! She's already outside! She's running toward the bridge! She's outside!"

She leaned even farther out the window, and the regent looked up at her. He had recognized her, he had certainly recognized her. Now they would let her go, for what other proof of her loyalty could they require? She would never reveal what she knew. She had even helped them recapture the dark-haired girl.

As if petrified, the dark-haired girl stood looking toward the house, and the makeup artist could clearly see her face.

"It's her, the girl who looks like the princess!"

At the same moment, the guard who had spotted the scrap of cloth was pushing aside the branches of the hedge.

"A section of railing is gone!" he cried.

"You fools!" Bolström swore. "How could you allow this to happen? Set the dogs loose now, at once!"

Norlin made a gesture as if to intervene. Then his arms fell to his sides.

Malena ran.

The most difficult thing, Nahira had said, would be the timing. As soon as the guards discovered the gap in the railings, Malena must let them see her, and must then run like the wind. The gap was too small for them to get through, and so she would have a good start, but once the dogs were loose . . .

But it hadn't been necessary for the guards to see her. From one of the attic windows, someone else had caught sight of her almost as soon as she had come out of the bushes. Malena felt a surge of triumph rising like a hot wave inside her. Now at last she could run, and she ran till the road burned beneath her feet. *Yes, try to catch me, you idiots! Chase me, catch me, come on, I dare you!*

Then she heard the furious barking of the dogs as they leaped out of their kennels into the open air. But Jonas was waiting behind the first bend in the road. She would make it. Before the dogs caught up with her, she would get to Jonas.

When Jenna heard the makeup artist shouting, she knew everything would be all right. True, it was not quite according to plan, but things couldn't have worked out better. Cautiously she peeked out of the bushes, and suddenly the estate was in complete darkness. All she had to do was wait until she heard the dogs go out through the gate.

Then she ran. The clouds had swallowed up the moon again, and the night seemed to her so impenetrable that she could scarcely make out the silhouettes of the trees and bushes, let alone the unevenness of the ground, the molehills, the thistles and nettles that had escaped the mower. She fell, picked herself up, and ran on. She stayed on the grass the whole time — the gravel would have been too noisy — and in the shadow of the bushes, just as Nahira had told her to do.

But the grounds now seemed to be deserted, anyway. She ran around the corner of the building. From the back of the house, the shouts of the guards and the vicious howls of the dogs were muffled.

Jenna felt an immense flood of relief. In just a few seconds she would reach the far railings, where Tiloki would be waiting. And then she would be free.

She raced along the terraces that led down the side of the gardens toward the forested area beyond. In the night, the splashing of a fountain seemed unbearably loud. Just a few more steps. Now right in front of her was the privet hedge behind which lay her route to freedom.

Then suddenly he was standing there in the middle of the path. His silk bathrobe had slipped open under the hastily knotted belt, exposing the buttons of his pajamas, and he was swaying backward and forward, as if he couldn't decide which direction to go.

"My little Jenna," he murmured. "My little girl, what have they done, what have they done to you?"

Jenna froze. Initially she thought he had seen her, but then she realized he was talking to himself. She tried to blend into the shadows and make herself invisible. Why hadn't Norlin gone rushing out of the gate with all the others? Why wasn't he there, where the moving fingers of light were combing the road? She forced herself to hold her breath, and tried to figure out how to get past him.

"The dogs will tear her to pieces," sobbed Norlin, and slapped his forehead with the palms of his hands. "My little girl. My little girl."

And now Jenna understood. Norlin hadn't wanted to be there. He hadn't wanted to witness the dogs catching her. He hadn't wanted to see them ripping his daughter apart.

She saw that there was no way she could get past without him noticing — he was standing directly in her path. If Norlin were to try to catch her, if he merely were to whistle as soon as he saw her, if he were to call for the guards, her escape plan would fail. They mustn't find the other gap in the railings, not yet, not too soon after she slipped through it. For at least a few minutes more, they had to think that the girl they'd chased in vain along the road was Jenna, so that Jenna herself could get away.

But she had no choice. Someone could come up behind her at any moment. If she waited till Norlin went away, it might be too late.

She jumped out from the shadows of the bushes onto the path and ran straight toward him.

"Get out of the way!" she hissed. "Out of the way, Norlin!"

The regent stood still, staring incredulously at her. "Jenna?" He gasped. "My Jenna?"

"Out of the way!" Jenna hissed again, and pushed him. Then she ran toward the hedge just a few steps away. He could have grabbed hold of her. Instead, he simply stood there, watching.

"My Jenna," murmured Norlin from behind her now. "How come my little girl . . . ?"

She heard a quiet whistle and swung around toward the place in the hedge it had come from. Strong hands pulled the bushes apart to create a passageway. Behind it, another doctored railing had been removed from its socket.

"To the jeep!" whispered Tiloki. He ran faster than her, but kept stopping to wait for her to catch up. Lorok had driven the jeep deep into the undergrowth, and now almost silently, lights off, he drove it between the bushes.

Jenna was breathing hard and fast. Not until she climbed into the backseat did she realize that she hadn't heard the dogs for some time now.

And she hadn't heard a sound from Norlin, either. Her father had not called the guards.

Malena knew how fast the dogs were when they were on the chase. She'd been there at Osterlin when they were trained. She tried to breathe evenly. She had a good head start on the hounds, and as soon as she reached Jonas she would be safe.

As planned, he was standing around the first bend in the road, leaning against the thick trunk of an oak tree, and he reached out, grabbed her arm, and pulled her toward him.

"Just keep away from them," he whispered. Only then did he raise his little whistle to his lips and blow. At once the vicious barking of Malena's pursuers turned into an excited yapping, and then they were there: three mastiffs, almost as tall as Jonas. With their ears pricked and their tails wagging joyfully, they frisked around him. He patted their heads, and they uttered little whines of pleasure and licked his hands and face.

"Moro, Sisso, Rojo," whispered Jonas. "Good dogs! Good dogs!"

The tails wagged even more happily, but now it was time to move. Malena could hear the shouts and the footsteps of the guards as they came along the road.

She reached into the bag that Jonas had put down beside the tree, and pulled out the packet. The paper was damp, but in the darkness she couldn't see the bloodstains as she placed the raw meat on the ground. Immediately, the dogs turned their heads, sniffing the air. Their jaws began to slaver.

Malena was already off and running again.

"Sit," Jonas commanded quietly. "Moro, Sisso, Rojo, sit."

The dogs obeyed, though their eyes were still riveted to the packet just a few paces away.

"Stay!" said Jonas. "Good dogs."

Then he, too, began to run. As long as they could still see him, the dogs would stay sitting. And then they would pounce on the meat. The guards wouldn't dare pass them until the handler arrived: He was not the youngest of men, and was taking his time.

"When are we going to meet up with the others?" asked Jenna.

It seemed to her that they had been driving for hours through the gradually brightening dawn, across bumpy fields, between thick bushes, never coming anywhere near an actual road. Lorok drove as confidently as if he were steering the jeep along a broad, smooth-surfaced avenue; he never made a single mistake, never stopped to look for the way, never got a wheel stuck in the mud or in the thorny branches of the hedgerows. It was as if he had been training for years just for this moment.

Jenna began to breathe more steadily, the stress and fear of the night before fading into the past. Gradually her heartbeat returned to normal as well.

"Nahira's taken a different route," said Tiloki from the front passenger seat. "It's another way of confusing the pursuers."

Jenna looked out the window into the early morning light. Maybe the clouds had just freed the moon again, or maybe it was the dawn breaking. Norlin had not summoned the guards. Whether she liked it or not, she owed her escape to her father.

She didn't want to think about it.

They reached a narrow dirt road that they followed for a few miles through the forest, and then Lorok turned off onto an even narrower track. A small car was hidden behind a thick hazel bush, and they changed vehicles, leaving the jeep behind.

"Where are we going?" asked Jenna.

"For a girl who thought she was about to be an actress, don't you ever watch movies?" asked Tiloki. "We've got to make a clean getaway. Someone could easily connect us to the jeep if they saw us near Osterlin. Soon the whole country will be searching for it. Did you find out what you were supposed to find out?"

"I don't know," Jenna muttered. "Maybe."

"Tell Nahira as soon as we see her," said Tiloki. "There's no time to lose."

As they drove, the darkness outside the car windows continued to lift, and things took on their daytime colors — the trees and bushes deep green, the corn a tender pale yellow. Jenna forced herself to think about Nahira and the successful escape. About where the king's prison might be, and how they would rescue him. About what Bea would be thinking back home, since Jenna had not been to school all week. About everything and anything except the fact that Norlin hadn't summoned the guards.

After a while, Tiloki said impatiently, "Lorok, we should have been there long ago."

Lorok steered the car to the left, where a narrow sandy road led into the forest, and a few hundred feet farther on they drove along an overgrown path under drooping branches that brushed the roof of the car with a horrible scratching sound.

"*Now* we're here," said Lorok.

Jenna pushed open the door. In front of her, in a little clearing, were Malena, Jonas, Nahira, and Meonok, leaning against a battered old delivery truck and laughing with relief at the sight of her.

31

Jenna crouched between Jonas and Malena in the open flatbed of the truck as it raced along narrow roads at such a speed that she was afraid it would blow a tire or lose a wheel and go plunging into a tree. She clung to the side till her knuckles showed white through the skin, but Nahira simply laughed.

"Lorok loves roads like these," she said. "No one else can drive like him."

She was sitting opposite Jenna, Malena, and Jonas, next to Tiloki, and she kept pressing the buttons on her cell phone. Jenna had scarcely stepped out of the escape car when she'd grasped her by the shoulders.

"Well?" she'd asked. "Did you find out?"

Jenna would have liked to tell her the whole story: how Bolström had caught her in the library; how they had confiscated her flashlight and removed all the lightbulbs from her bedroom; how the little cook had given the signal for her and most likely been caught; how the makeup artist had betrayed her and, without knowing it, inadvertently helped them with their plan. But there would be time for that later. The vital thing now was to tell Nahira where to search for the king.

When Jenna had reported on the conversation she'd interrupted between Norlin and Bolström, and what she'd recalled afterward — the memories Mom let slip at the birthday dinner — Nahira's face had darkened. She'd hesitated, but only for a moment, and then she'd reached for her cell phone.

"You could be right," she'd said. "And it's better than nothing. Yes, it has to be the Old Navigator's House."

And then she had concentrated solely on the buttons of her cell phone.

"What's the Old Navigator's House?" asked Jenna. Jonas and Malena shrugged their shoulders, but Nahira glanced up for a second.

"It's where they used to meet," she said, and Jenna was shocked to see the anger in her eyes — still, after all these years. "Him and her. While I went on believing . . ." Then she went back to hammering the keypad.

"Who are you sending a message to?" asked Jenna. The truck had turned off onto a track barely broad enough for a donkey, and now it went bumping and swerving down a steep gorge. Every so often they stopped, and Meonok jumped out of the driver's cab to push branches and rocks out of the way. Sometimes Tiloki helped him, and one time they all had to get down and help, too. Jenna was sure that no vehicle had ever driven this way before, and if she had seen the track earlier, she would have thought it was impossible. But Lorok drove with unerring accuracy, as if he sensed every obstacle in advance, knew every bend and every rocky projection.

"I'm sending a message to all our people," said Nahira, "all those who can get to the Old Navigator's House within the next few hours from the north of South Island or the south of North Island. And they'll pass on the message, so it'll go from one to another until all our people know that the king is still alive, and where he's being held. Hundreds, maybe thousands, are just waiting for me to give the signal."

Jenna gazed at her.

"He'll be heavily guarded, even if Norlin and Bolström thought no one would ever find out," said Nahira. "Troops will have been guarding him from the start, and I'm sure Norlin will have sent more by now. They don't know what you've discovered, or what we know ourselves, but your escape will have put them on high alert. They think you were searching for something, but there's no evidence you uncovered anything, and there's probably nothing you could have found, anyway. No, they've got no reason to suspect you know anything about the king, and so they won't move him immediately. They won't want to do anything that might attract attention, in case people notice — that's the most important thing for them at the moment: appearances."

"Are you sure?" asked Malena. "What if they're onto us?"

Nahira shrugged. "In their place, I'd wait," she said. "And watch. And as a precaution, I'd station some more troops around Saarstad — as unobtrusively as possible so that the locals think they're there as protection against the rebels. But we'll be there before the troops. After the rebels blew up the bridge over the South Island gorge . . ." She laughed. "That attack has helped us after all. Norlin's military can only come north along secret paths, and we're much better at that than they are."

Jenna clung to the wooden side panels of the truck, which Lorok was still driving at unbelievable speed down the side of the gorge, and she kept her eyes closed. By now the sun had reached its zenith, and the metal floor of the truck's open bed had become unbearably hot.

"Our people will get to Saarstad before Norlin's troops have even crossed the gorge," said Nahira. "Trust me, the odds are in our favor."

The truck lurched over a boulder and leaned precariously to one side as if it was about to topple over, but it righted itself again. Jonas let out a deep, whistling breath. He looked over the side. "We've reached the bottom," he said.

Then Jenna was brave enough to open her eyes.

They were driving across a narrow riverbed, at a point where there was just a thin trickle of water over the silt and pebbles. After a few feet, Lorok turned toward the upward slope. Jenna groaned. Climbing up would not be one iota safer than going down. Her stomach churned. She lay down on some wooden boards on top of the hot, hard truck bed and closed her eyes. She didn't want to open them again until they were in Saarstad.

32

If anyone had asked Jenna later what she imagined the rescue operation would be like, she would have said, *A lot more exciting than it was*. She had been afraid through all those hours perched on the rough wooden boards of the truck, imagining the regent's troops, rifles, exchanges of gunfire, maybe even hand grenades and other weapons she'd never even heard of. She hadn't visualized anything in detail, just that there'd be a battle, and she'd be in the middle of it.

Early in the afternoon, when they finally reached the outskirts of Saarstad, where cozy little villages, seemingly deserted, dozed idly in the sun, she found the suspense almost unbearable. How could such terrible things happen in such a peaceful setting? Nahira's cell had never stopped chiming, evidence that more and more messages were coming in. Tiloki was also pressing the buttons of his phone incessantly. They had seen the church tower at Saarstad only from a distance, because then they had turned off the road. They had driven around the town until the forest became thinner and Jenna could feel the sea breeze in the air and smell the salt water.

They stopped at an abandoned railroad crossing. Two men were sitting on a bench outside a dilapidated hut, caps pulled low over their eyes, and they scarcely raised their heads as the truck approached. Tired workers smoking a quick cigarette on their break.

"Well?" Nahira shouted at them from above.

One of the men jumped up and swiftly let down the tailgate at the back of the pickup. His weariness seemed to have disappeared in an instant. "Everything's ready," he said.

"Down you get," said Nahira to Jonas, Malena, and Jenna. "This has nothing to do with you three."

"What?" asked Malena. She stayed put, as did Jonas and Jenna.

"Get down and go to the hut," said Nahira. "What's coming next is not for you to see. We're going to storm the Old Navigator's House. It's only about two miles away, and our people are already hidden all around here. Norlin's troops haven't arrived yet, and there are only ten guards at the house. It's possible that everything will go smoothly. But it's also possible that . . ."

"I'm coming with you," said Jonas, looking defiantly at Nahira. "You don't really think I'm staying here, do you?"

"There'll be shooting," said Nahira. "And people are going to get hurt — killed. This is no game, Jonas; you must know that by now. And do you truly think you can be of any help to us in a skirmish? Have you learned how to fight the way my supporters have? You may know how to shoot a gun, but do you know how to hide, how to run for cover, how to deceive the enemy? We can't stage this type of guerrilla combat and look after three children at the same time."

"I'm not a child," said Jonas. "Meonok and Lorok aren't much older than me."

"Nahira!" hissed Tiloki. "Come on!"

"Get down from the truck now," Nahira stated. "And if you don't do it voluntarily, Meonok and Lorok will make you. Go, Jonas. Into the house. We hope it will all be over quickly."

Jenna was the first to jump down, but Malena hesitated. "If what we think is right, Nahira," she said, "then my father is there with his kidnappers. How are you going to make sure you don't hit him when you fire at them? Can't you see we're . . ."

"Malena, get down," Nahira said again. "Didn't you hear me? We've taken care of everything. And there's certainly nothing you can do to help us."

Malena jumped down. Only Jonas continued to refuse.

"Jonas," said Malena. "Nahira's right. We can't be any help to the rebels, and I don't want to do anything to jeopardize my father."

Jonas saw the look in her eyes, then jumped down, too.

Once they were inside the house, he sat tight-lipped in a corner on the dusty floor, not looking up as the noise of the truck faded away outside.

"Jonas," Malena continued. "Don't be like that. We've done all we could, and if it weren't for us, Nahira's followers wouldn't be here now. Jenna got herself into Osterlin, I distracted the guards, and if you hadn't handled the dogs, the plan would have been hopeless from the start. You don't always have to fight with guns, Jonas. There are other ways to support the cause."

"Word," Jonas muttered angrily.

Through the cracked windows they heard a shot in the distance, a cry, and then rapid gunfire. After that, there was nothing but the wind in the trees.

"What now?" whispered Jenna. "What do you think is happening?"

Jonas and Malena didn't answer.

"They've stopped shooting," whispered Jenna. "Is it over?"

"Quiet!" hissed Malena, pressing her ear to the wooden wall. "Wait."

Jenna could see the tension on Malena's face. *And every shot we hear could mean . . .*

Outside, everything was still. Then Jenna thought she heard shouting, and another shot.

"What if they all get captured?" whispered Jenna. "If Norlin's troops are stronger?"

No one was listening to her. The silence was unbearable. Time passed so slowly it seemed as though every clock in the world had stopped.

"It must be over by now," whispered Jenna. She couldn't stand the uncertainty and the helplessness a second longer. "Maybe we should . . ."

At that moment they heard the sound of an engine. It was coming much too quickly toward the hut, and soon Jenna was sure it was the truck.

"Lorok?" whispered Jenna.

With screeching brakes, it came to a halt.

Then the door burst open, and Lorok was standing in the doorway, his eyes wide and wild.

"I'm here to get you!" he cried. "Nahira says you must come. We've got them! We've rescued the king! Come on!"

Jenna felt something giving way inside her. She saw that Malena, too, was swaying uncertainly. You always imagined that victory was something bright and shining . . .

"My father?" whispered Malena.

"Come on!" roared Lorok. His hair was disheveled, and now Jenna saw that there was blood dripping from a wound in his arm. But he didn't seem to be feeling any pain. "Yes! We've won!"

Only when they were sitting on the rough, splintered boards of the truck bed, racing at breakneck speed over the mile or two that led to the Old Navigator's House, did Jenna begin to wonder what would happen next.

By now the sun was coloring the horizon in the warm shades of evening, and the waves slapped against the beach with a soft splish-splash sound, while overhead, without even moving their wings, the gulls circled silently.

The Old Navigator's House lay quite still in the evening light. Jenna saw immediately that it had been neglected for years: The paintwork, once a golden yellow, was flaking off the wooden boards, and what must have formerly been a small but carefully planned garden, protected from the rough sea winds by a stone wall, had now been reclaimed by nature. Only here and there could she see the glow of a few roses, delphiniums, and marigolds, now looking out of place amid the tangled confusion of plants that had grown for centuries on this coast — nettles, goosegrass, and ragged robin that had taken back for themselves what had always belonged to them, while over everything hung the heavy scent of chamomile. A single pine tree grew on the gable side of the house, its top worn thin by countless spring storms and its trunk leaning at such an angle that it seemed to be making a clumsy bow to the house.

On the steps leading to a narrow concrete path, at the side of the house that faced the sea, stood a woman: tall, elegant, and, even in her state of exhaustion, regal.

"Mom?" cried Jenna. She froze, not daring to believe her eyes. "Mom? Is it really you?"

The woman turned and smiled.

"Oh, Mom, Mom!" Jenna ran to her and threw herself into her arms. And then she could no longer hold back the tears.

Her mother pressed her close, as if she would hold her there forever. And Jenna felt tears falling on the back of her neck.

"You're drenching me," she whispered against Mom's shoulder.

Mom's arms held her even tighter. "It doesn't matter," she murmured. "It doesn't matter."

Jenna wept so long and so hard that her whole body ached. She was crying tears of joy and relief that it was all over, but also of regret, because she knew now that nothing in her life would ever be the same as it had been before. Finally she blew her nose and wiped her eyes, and only then did she see the king, her uncle, for the first time.

She wouldn't have known him from his royal garments. His face was gray with exhaustion, his eyes feverish, and he was talking continuously, with wild, unkingly gestures, on a cell phone. She recognized him simply because he looked exactly as Mom would have looked if she had been a man — just as tall, as blond, and as distinguished. She wondered why she had never seen a photograph of him in a newspaper at home. She would have recognized the resemblance immediately.

"What do you mean I can't talk to him?" he was saying. "Yes, of course you must release him. He's Chief of Police."

Jenna remembered the gazebo and the man who had asked so many questions. "I heard Norlin . . ." she started to say, and waited for the king to listen to her.

"Don't disturb him now," whispered Mom. "This whole situation has to be dealt with quickly."

Malena was sitting on the steps just a few paces away from her father, gazing out across the sea. She, too, had wept for a short time in his arms, but now he had other things to attend to. Official matters. Malena's back was straight, and her eyes were already dry.

Seated on the stony ground, with his back against the wall, was a man with his eyes closed, and at that moment another man was putting a bandage on him. The blood was running thick and black-red from a wound in his leg. Jenna looked away. "Help will be here soon," the other man kept saying, but still the wounded man did not open his eyes. He didn't seem to hear. His face looked as white as if all the blood had already flowed out of his body through that gaping wound. Jenna didn't know if he was one of Norlin's men or Nahira's. It didn't matter.

A group of soldiers, their wrists bound, stood expressionless by the house, guarded by Meonok and three other rebels Jenna had never seen before. They held their guns at the ready.

"We won," murmured Jenna. Although she knew it already, she still couldn't feel it.

Jonas came rushing out of the house. He looked happy.

"Everything's OK!" he cried, his voice almost cracking. "Do you want to look inside, where they were kept, before it all starts? It's a crazy prison."

Jenna shook her head.

"What's going to start?" As she asked the question, she heard a quiet hum in the sky.

"The media frenzy," said Jonas, pointing up, where in the distance a black dot was heading toward them from the south, swiftly expanding into the shape of a helicopter. Behind it, coming from the same direction, was another black dot, then another, followed by still more.

"We must keep going," said Jonas with a contented sigh. "Believe me, the battle with the press will be worse than the battle with the enemy."

"As if *you'd* know anything about either," said Malena.

Jenna was relieved to see that she was back to her old self.

"Mom!" cried Bea, her eyes glued to the television screen. She'd been about to turn it off when the news came on, but now she was glad that she'd been too lazy to fish for the remote control, which had fallen to the floor. "Now! Come see for yourself!"

". . . quite extraordinary story," the reporter was saying to the camera. The top button of his shirt was hanging by a long thread, and he looked as if this assignment had caught him by surprise — like he'd had to jump into a car or plane totally unprepared because the producer had sent him off without a minute to spare. Behind him, Bea could see the ocean, though the sun had already gone down, and in front of that a little, weathered, wooden yellow house. People were running everywhere, and a helicopter with a red cross on its fuselage was just taking off. "It appears that for several months the whole of Scandia . . ."

"Mom!" Bea practically screamed. "Move it!"

Her mother came in, wearing her terry-cloth bathrobe and with a towel wrapped around her head. "I was just doing my nails," she said. "What on earth is the matter . . . ?"

Then she stared wide-eyed at the screen.

"Told you!" said Bea triumphantly.

Standing beside a tall, fair-haired man who looked vaguely familiar was Jenna's mother — pale and tired, her clothes all dirty. And next to Jenna's mother, just as dirty, her hair all stringy and matted, stood Jenna.

The strangest thing of all, though, was that she was there in duplicate — there were two girls, one dark-haired and one blonde.

"I . . . don't . . . believe it," murmured Bea's mother.

"I do!" Bea cried. "Told you told you told you!"

"What's all the shouting about?" asked Bea's father, entering the room with the iron in one hand and a shirt in the other. "Has somebody—"

"Hush!" hissed his wife. "Just watch."

" . . . deceived the people," said the tall, fair-haired man. The King of Scandia. "I'm profoundly grateful to those who have rescued me and my sister, who was abducted by the traitors led by my brother-in-law and who has been held prisoner for the last week, just as I have for the last two months. We're now going to return together to the capital. But first it's important that I make one thing perfectly clear . . ."

"Sister?" gasped Bea's mother. "Jenna's mother? Is he saying that all this time that nervous wreck was a princess?"

" . . . stopped," the king was saying. "I want the people of North Island to be able to sleep easily again with my full assurance that in our Scandia, just as I'd planned, soon every citizen will have equal rights. I give my word to every one of you. And indeed it was principally the loyal citizens of North Island who, with the aid of my brave daughter and my niece, brought about the rescue . . ."

"Niece?!" cried Bea, drumming her fists on the coffee table. "OMG, OMG, OMG!"

"That shy little Jenna is a princess?" said her father. "I think I need to sit down."

"Why didn't she tell us?" wondered Bea's mother. She didn't even notice the towel as it slowly slid off her head and fell to the floor.

The announcer back in the studio appeared on the screen. "Washington," he said. "The President of the United States, on his visit to . . ."

Bea pressed the remote control.

"You'd better pinch me," said her mother, and bent down almost in slow motion to pick up the towel. "Or I'd better sit down, too. Better still, both."

"Chill, Mom and Dad," said Bea. "It's not like I didn't already tell you! And here's my next prediction: For sure Jenna will text me tomorrow."

❧

Although she'd never thought about it seriously before, Jenna now realized that she'd always just assumed she knew exactly how kings and princesses lived in their castles. She'd seen it on television, in movies that showed grand banquets in palaces. She figured it was true, and let her imagination run wild. But

Malena's room was totally different from the images on TV.

"What exactly did you think, then?" Malena said indignantly. She had just come from the shower and had a hair dryer in her hand. "That we spend all our time sitting on golden thrones?"

Jenna shook her head.

"Oh, great, dry already!" said Malena, shaking her short blonde stubble. "How many years is it going to take before it's long again? It will drive me to despair!" But she didn't really sound desperate at all.

"Lucky you, being allowed to hang up posters like that," said Jenna, looking enviously at the walls, from which pop stars and celebrities were smiling in all directions. "My mom always banned them. She found them so"— Jenna giggled — "vulgar. Well, this should help her change her mind."

The door opened and in came Jonas. He glanced at Malena, and then threw himself on the bed. "You're starting to look like yourself again," he said.

Malena snorted. "Charming!" she said. "Just waltz right in without knocking. What if I'd been stark naked?"

"That's a risk I'm willing to take," said Jonas. "But whatever, have you heard? They tortured him."

"Your father?" asked Jenna. "How is he?"

Jonas shrugged. "As good as anyone could be after his lips have been split and his eyes beaten black and his entire body covered in bruises. Those savages! If we ever get hold of Norlin, I swear I'll—"

"Jonas!" said Malena.

Jonas glanced at Jenna. "Sorry," he murmured. "But he is a criminal all the same. Even if he is your father."

Jenna looked down at the floor. "Where is he now?" she asked.

"On the lam, of course," answered Jonas. "Along with Bolström and all his cronies. As soon as they heard what had happened, they took off — abroad, I'll bet. The little six-seater jet is gone. We'll never see them again."

The carpet on Malena's floor looked exactly like Bea's, and up by the head of the bed, where Bea always kept a bottle of soda or spring water, there was a big dark stain.

"But all the yes-men," said Jonas, "you know who I mean, Malena — the ones who used to kiss up to the regent with *Your Highness this* and *Your Highness that* — take a wild guess what they're doing now?"

Malena had licked her finger and was now poking a small pimple that was beginning to break the skin on her chin. "Kissing up to my father," she said. "Stupid pimple! What else did you think they'd do? They don't even need to make any changes, all those worms with no brains of their own. Just stay where they've always been: on the side of whoever happens to be in power."

"It's heinous," said Jonas. "Don't even think about watching TV, it'll put you over the edge. The way they're all making statements to the cameras about why they went crawling up Norlin's butt and why they cheered every word he said. Pathetic

losers, all of them. They were deceived, how shocking —
not. Norlin deceived them, big bad Norlin, and now they're
all very upset. How could such a thing happen? By tomorrow
we'll start hearing how they really always suspected something was wrong, and can't their neighbors recall them saying
months ago that they didn't trust that Norlin as far as they
could throw him, and blah blah blah."

"Don't get all worked up, Jonas," said Malena. "That's just
the way it is. That's how people are. And not just Scandians,
either. And for us it's still the best thing, anyway. Now all the
people will be behind my father again."

"Until someone else comes along and seizes power," said
Jonas. "Then they'll be behind *him*. Or her."

But Malena had stopped listening. She was rummaging
very unroyally in a little bag of cosmetics, until finally all its
contents were scattered around the floor in front of the mirror.
"Where is my concealer?" she muttered.

Jenna watched her and said nothing. Malena had her father
back, after believing for two months that he was dead; Jonas's
father was free again and would soon recover from the torture. Tonight celebratory bonfires were being lit all over the
north. The whole of Scandia was celebrating, and for every
Scandian it was a time to rejoice.

Jenna stood up. "I'm going to take off," she said. Of
course, she, too, was safe again, and her mom had been
rescued from the hands of the kidnappers. But there was
still Norlin.

She would never say it to Malena and Jonas, and she was shocked even to admit it to herself, but she wished with all her heart that he would never be caught. She knew he deserved to be punished. But she didn't know how she would feel if he were to stand trial before a court, and every day there were news reports about what he had done, who he had betrayed, who he had tortured.

You are who you are, Jonas had said. *You can't choose your parents. You're still you.*

But Norlin was her father, and she owed her escape to him. He had let her go when the dogs were hunting for her. If he had betrayed her that night, Nahira would never have been able to rescue the king.

"What's the matter?" asked Jonas.

She hoped with all her heart that they wouldn't track him down.

No matter who he is, she thought, *I'm still me.*

In the dining room of the royal residence, there were candles on the table. A young woman in a black dress and white cap was gliding almost silently through the space, serving the diners. And so things in the palace were, after all, just a little bit like Jenna had always imagined them to be.

"But it's amazing that the press came down on our side so promptly," said Liron. It was difficult to understand what he was saying, though the doctor had confirmed that his injuries would soon heal. Instead of eating chicken like the others, he was cautiously dipping his spoon into a bowl of soup. "How did you bring them around? By telling them Norlin had lied about you dying? What if they'd stayed on his side and hadn't come to Saarstad to report on your rescue? Imagine if they'd done the same thing to you as happened to me when I wanted to show them Jenna and the princess together?"

The king waved his hand. "The situation was completely different," he said. "At that time, everyone thought I really was dead, and Norlin was the man in power. So of course they were all afraid to report your revelations. But now I'm back, and if just one newspaper or just one TV station had reported the story, then everyone would have known that Norlin had kidnapped me and had only pretended I was dead so that he could seize power. Naturally they were all clamoring to be among the first to break the news. Better to be on the right side from the start! That's what they're like, my Scandians." He smiled at Jenna. "I haven't yet said a proper thank-you to you," he said. "You were very brave. And it was very hard for you."

Jenna flushed red and looked down at her plate. Next to her, Malena had just picked up a chicken leg and was gnawing at it thoughtfully. Jenna glanced across at her mother to see if she was watching. Then Malena even licked her fingers! Mrs. Sampson and Mr. Fraser, her mother's clients, would have fallen off their chairs.

The doors to the dining room swung open.

"Your Majesty," said a large, red-haired woman in a stained white apron. She was pulling a girl behind her who was resisting and trying to get away. Behind them, two men in gray suits appeared and tried to take them outside again, but the king held up his hand.

"I know, Your Majesty, that it's wrong for me to barge in here like this and so on, and I've never done it before — I'm the cook, you know? Your cook — but today's a special day and I just can't stand it anymore down there in my kitchen without at least telling Your Majesty — all of you, Your Majesty, and you, too, *Your* Highness, and *Your* Highness, and *Your* Highness — how glad I am that it's all going to have a happy ending. How glad all of us are down in the kitchen, Your Majesty. And the whole palace and everyone. But most of all my silly little kitchen maid here wanted to . . ." She pushed the girl forward, and gave her a little nudge in the back. "Go on, Kaira."

"Kaira!" cried Jenna.

The girl looked as if she was about to faint on the spot. Malena fished another chicken leg out of the pool of gravy on her plate.

"The silly creature got herself caught last night making signals with her bedroom light," said the cook. "Signals with her light! Fancy that! Why on earth did she have to do such a thing? Very foolish and all, I don't know, but they were probably quite right to punish her. But they also took away her recipe book, and she hasn't even finished learning yet, so she wanted to ask . . ."

"But of course she'll get it back," said the king. "Your name's Kaira, is it? Come here. You've done the country a great service, and I promise you that it won't go unrecognized."

"You see, Kaira, you silly girl," said the cook. "I told you, now that His Majesty is back . . ."

But now the two men in gray suits stepped forward again, and this time the king did not stop them.

The cook understood. "Oh dear, ever so sorry, Your Majesty, we'll be on our way back to the kitchen." She winked at Malena. "Chocolate fudge cake with meringue," she whispered conspiratorially. "You like that, don't you? For dessert."

Jenna watched them go. In a fairy tale, the king would immediately have said to Kaira, *Of course you'll get your recipe book back, and also its weight in gold,* she thought. *But real kings behave differently from the way you'd expect them to. I must go to the kitchen myself and thank Kaira. She helped save my life, and I'd been worried about what might have happened to her.*

"What's going to happen to the makeup artist?" she asked.

The king gave her a slightly quizzical look, but Malena had now finished nibbling her second chicken leg, and so she was able to give the answer: "We let her go home," she said. "She was unbelievably ashamed at her own treachery. It didn't even console her when I told her how much she'd helped us. *But I didn't know that,* she kept saying. *I really meant to betray her. I'm so ashamed.* But the woman's got three children, Jenna. I expect most people in her situation would have done the same."

Jonas snorted.

"Don't be so self-righteous, my son," said Liron. And he looked longingly at the meat as he stirred his soup.

It was only then that Jenna realized someone was missing.

"Where's Nahira?" she asked. Her mother gave a small start. "Where are the others?" Jenna persisted. "Tiloki? Lorok? Meonok? Where'd they all go?"

The king sighed. "It's complicated," he said. "They disappeared as soon as the press showed up. As soon as it was obvious that Norlin and his people could do no further damage, they took to the forests again. They're rebels, Jenna. Even though they liberated your mother and me, they've been fighting against our country for a long time. They tried to blow up the parliament building."

Jenna's mother placed her hand on her brother's arm.

"They did not!" cried Jonas. "They missed it on purpose!"

"We shall see to it that the rebels go free," said Jenna's mother. "We've already discussed it. And we shall welcome everyone who wants to help build a unified Scandia. Nevertheless, it's going to be a difficult process, especially at the beginning, and in spite of all our celebrations we mustn't forget it. There's still a lot of resentment among the people. The south against the north. The north against the south. Peace doesn't just break out overnight."

For a moment they all were silent. Then Malena leaned back in her chair with a contented sigh and wiped her greasy hands on a brilliant white napkin. "It's OK," she said. "At any rate, it's a lot better than it was."

The doors to the dining room swung open for a second time. Behind a sea of sparklers Jenna could just make out the figure of the cook. Her voice, however, was unmistakable. "Chocolate fudge cake with meringue!" she announced triumphantly. "Chocolate fudge cake for dessert!"

33

*B*ea was kneeling in the driveway next to her bicycle, oiling the spokes of the wheels, when a limousine pulled up at the gate. She knew who it would be even before the doors had opened.

"Jenna!" she cried.

The two girls who got out of the car, ahead of a sort of sullen-looking, dark-haired boy, were wearing identical summer dresses, and on their heads were identical caps sporting the message *Scandia Forever!* But the most striking resemblance between them was their faces.

"Guess who's Jenna," said the first girl. The second came and stood beside her.

Bea looked from one to the other. "*Hello* — you are, of course," she said. "Unbelievable, Jenna, she looks *exactly* like you. Hug!" And she held her arms out to the first girl.

"Unbelievable is right!" cried the second, and pulled the cap off her head. Long dark hair fell down over her shoulders. "So that's how well you know your BFF?"

"OMG, how totally embarrassing!" squealed Bea, and flung her arms around Jenna's neck. "But you *do* look almost identical. Group hug?"

"Oh, I'm just here so I can finally give you the short version of my family tree," said Jenna. "Meet my cousin, Malena."

Bea laughed. "You have *got* to stay for dinner — all of you!" she said. "Spaghetti and meatballs?"

The sullen boy nodded quite enthusiastically, and two inconspicuous men in gray suits and with bored expressions positioned themselves at the garden gate.